The Devil's Chair

A Novel of Lake Superior

Alexander Binning

Bayeux Arts Inc.
119 Stratton Crescent S.W.
Calgary, Alberta, Canada T3H 1T7

National Library of Canada Cataloguing in Publication

Binning, Alexander, 1944-
  The Devil's Chair/Alexander Binning.

  ISBN 1-896209-88-2
  1. Title.

PS8553.I659D48 2003
C813'.6   C2003-905331-8

Printed in Canada

The publisher gratefully acknowledges the generous support of
the Canada Council for the Arts, the Alberta Foundation for the
Arts, and the Government of Canada through the Book
Publishing Industry Development Program.

Cover:
Thunder Cape - Lake Superior
H. Keith Bowey
Egg Tempera. 12" X 18"
From the private collection of Graham A. MacDonald
Calgary, Alberta

Back Cover:
Indian Girl cleaning fish, Hudson Bay Region
Archives of Ontario. Acc. 6440. S 11689

Kipling Dam, Matagami River, 1966
Author's photo

In Grateful Remembrance

Wayland Drew

"a northern star-thrower"

Acknowledgements

The author gratefully acknowledges permission from the University of California Press for use of a brief portion of Rainer Maria Rilke's *Duino Elegies*, C.F. MacIntyre, translator, (Berkeley, 1961); the author also acknowledges citation from the following works: Alexander Henry, *Travels and Adventures* (1809), (Edmonton: Hurtig, 1971); Mary E. Boyle, *In Search of Our Ancestors* (London: George G. Harrap and Company, 1927); Alanson Skinner, 'Bear Customs of the Cree and Other Algonkin Indians of Northern Ontario' *Ontario Historical Society, Papers and Records*, 12 (1914); Frank Myers, comp. 'The Bear-walk *Inland Seas*, 9 (1953).

For if a man extols his own faith and disparages another because of devotion to his own and because he wants to glorify it, he seriously injures his own.

Asoka
Rock Edict XII
(Third Century, B.C.)

Well, a bearwalker is a very bad person. That is the Devil's work what he is doing.

Testimony of James Nahwaikezhik.
Gore Bay, Manitoulin Island, October, 1945

The Devil's Chair

Contents

1

The Mashkisibi

i

Angus Ashabish raised a dark hand to shade his eyes and looked out towards the distant Adriatic Sea, just faintly visible beyond the Dalmatian shoreline. It was mid-May, 1945 and the lands north of Trieste had only recently been liberated from the Nazi yoke. Here, high on the edges of the Julian Alps, Angus was finding, for the first time in months, some time to do nothing: to just stop, breathe, look, listen, remember. The local birds had easily survived the years of conflict. Like black and white boomerangs, Alpine Swifts soared high out of the local mountain crags as though nothing ever had been amiss. The sea shone warm and blue in the distance, a much lighter blue than Ontario's Lake Superior. But like Lake Superior, the Adriatic could do wondrous things with the light, as it was doing now; and like Superior, it had an unmistakable smell which Angus had first picked up miles before ever standing on its shore. Angus's thoughts were now back in Northern Ontario, in those ancient settlements he collectively called home, but which, in many cases, were little more than a scar in the wilderness or a memory along a roadside. The most permanent of these was at the mouth of the Mashkisibi River, just where it eased its dark way into the northeastern edge of that great and unforgiving inland sea. He had grown up there amidst the rocks and the trees and the tombstones of ancient fur traders, mainly Scots and French, some of whose blood ran in his own veins, mixed with generations of the Ojibwa, the Cree, and who knows who else. The shadow of a Swift darted across his eyes, ending the reverie.

Angus turned and looked back inland towards the Alps. The river he could see running down from these mountains had strength and it reminded him of the powerful Mashkisibi, spilling it way down from the inland Shield country into Superior. This river was not as large, but it too seemed to emerge from some obscure, hidden terrain of trees and rock which few ever visited. My mind is so tired, he thought. I need to go home and lose myself for awhile in that country and try and put this hideous business behind me.

Privately, Angus regretted that he was still here in the war zone. It was only by a curious personal circumstance. Because he was perceived to be used to rough country conditons, he had been asked by his Lieutenant to accompany some of the New Zealanders into the territory between Trieste and Tarvisio. This was a critical area of conflict where, only a few weeks ago, there had been a concerted attempt by the allied forces to liberate the area before the Balkan Partisans arrived. In fact, the Slavs arrived in Trieste a day before the allies. Nevertheless, there was good will and a desire to accommodate displayed by both sides. Angus was then *volunteered* to became part of a good-will exchange with the boisterous Partisans. A few of Tito's men had offered to take anybody interested up to see some of the places where the resistance fighters had holed up in the mountains, and Angus was urged to raise his hand. A trek into the mountain wilderness would, to be sure, be a welcome change from the past months of military discipline. Angus got on well with the rough and ready Slavs, some of whom quickly recognized him as a man of the land, although most of the Partisans did not claim to know much about North American Indians.

The morning had been sunny and warm, but now a wind was building up. A good-natured Croatian walked over towards Angus and said firmly: "You take. Is vorm. You need." Angus took the great coat from him and thanked him. He was not sure that he would need such a coat, and looked at the soldier with slight puzzlement.

"You are sure I will need this?" asked Angus.

"Yah - is coming now, vot ve call za Bura - zat is za vind you are feeling, yah? It comes down from za mountains, strong like herd of running horses. It can knock you over like bullet sometimes."

"Does that happen often?" Angus asked.

"When is very vorm over Adriatic Sea - the cold vind rushes down from za mountains through the *Hrusica* - vot English call maybe, *za Pear Tree Pass*? - through za iron gates of Postojna. You like drink now? Haff some *Sljivovica*. Is our national drink. Yah?"

Angus put on the coat. The men built up the fire in a shelter of trees and then started to pass around to their mixed-bag of guests, gourds of wine, more of the fiery plum brandy, bread and cheese. The New Zealanders warmed to the occasion and much gesturing and gesticulation and trading of souvenirs took place. Toasts were constant, the Slavs always repeating with a smile:

"Ziveli! - Long Live!"

The wind picked up and in an hour the temperature had dropped by ten degrees. Angus pulled up the collar of his coat and drew it more tightly around his body and walked a short distance into an exposed and open space that afforded a good view down the pass. He knew of such a wind as this. It was rare, but sometimes it came down the Mashkisibi and carried everything before it far out over Lake Superior. Usually it came during a late and warm Indian summer. Angus stood still, closed his eyes and braced his feet for a moment against the mounting force of the Bura - taking the measure of it. He then walked back over to the shelter of the fire and proposed a toast to the Slavs, many of whom were now stretched out on the ground, some of them fighting much-needed sleep.

ii

The *Mashkibisi* - the *Bad River* in old Ojibwa parlance - rises far to the northeast of that sheltered spot on the Lake Superior coast where it finally empties with a rush into the cove guarding the small village where Angus had been born. On an ancient glacial beach terrace, slightly above and behind the houses, a small cemetery sleeps in a grove of pine and spruce. The stones and wooden crosses mark many generations of Voyageurs and fur traders, their local Indian companions and wives, those at least who, by one route or another, had come to embrace the faith. A short distance away there was also the traditional Indian burial ground with its miniature grave houses surrounded by small picket fences. In the first grave yard there could be found headstones of more recent vintage. These were set over fishermen, loggers, miners, railway labourers, mothers, daughters and sons, and the inevitable young, snatched early by eternity while still in the cradle. And in one corner, marked off by a low fence, there was the monument of honour, for those who had fought in four wars.

Some fifty miles inland from the mouth of the Mashkisibi, back in the rolling green and grey patches of the Shield country, resided a descendent of those whom the eighteenth century fur traders had called the *gens de terre* - the *people of the land*. This was Jonas Beardy, friend of Angus Ashabish. Jonas was a modern representative of those old Cree nomads who had resided just to the north of the Ojibwa, for he was still a hunter and gatherer. With his daughter Joanna - The Little Sturgeon - he made his living

16

not just along the banks of the river, but throughout the entire breadth of the watershed. He knew the tributaries of the Mashkisibi intimately.

Among their own people, most of whom were now living on reserves or in the towns, Joanna was known as a good and daring swimmer, always being the first to breach the Mashkisibi in spring after break-up, when the river was still cold and full of spite. Her father was in his forties. Joanna's mother, Suzette Papatie, (the second wife of Jonas Beardy), had died three years earlier of tuberculosis. After the passing of his first wife, Naomi, Jonas had taken Joanna to live with relatives in the country southwest of Lake Mistassini in central Quebec. There, among those known as *the people of the stone fence*, he had met Suzette, and two years later they were married in a bush wedding. While Little Sturgeon had been born of the first wife, she had been devoted to the second, for she had come of age under her care; and Suzette had imparted to her much of what a young girl of the Mistassini should know. Joanna was proud when Jonas and Suzette were married according to the formal *nibawiwin* ceremony, an act which signified more than a temporary liaison. If the people in the town of Mashkisibi had ever known Jonas's real name, most had long forgotten it in favour of the more familiar Farmer Jones. Some of the young knew Little Sturgeon by her proper name, Joanna, but in her absence they were more likely to refer to her as *Farmer Jones's Daughter*.

When Joanna was twelve, a swimming tournament was held at the local public high school in Mashkisibi Town. Her friends at the Catholic elementary school for girls where she attended, told her to enter and so she did, winning easily against an older group of competitors. The coach at the podium suddenly found himself searching for a name, and after some fumbling at the microphone, he announced the winner as *Little Sturgeon Jones* an appellation which brought down the house. Little Sturgeon laughed as well, but as the girls tracked out to the shower room, she asked her friend: "Why did they laugh? Did I do something funny?"

"No Joanna - not at all - they just don't know what to call you anymore. You have too many names. Let's go over to my aunt's bakery. We'll celebrate." The two girls, one as blonde as the other was brown, then sprinted along the school road toward the main street of Mashkisibi.

Jonas Beardy was not often seen in town. His appearance was unmistakable however, for his long, lean frame was always covered in blue denim rather than the customary tanned hide or the red and black checked fabric jackets of the loggers. Not only was he *called* Farmer Jones but he also *looked* the part. He was more frequently seen in Mashkisibi in summer than in winter.

While his daughter was young, Jonas Beardy had continued to live off the land as was the old custom. Even during his lifetime there had been many changes in the back country and in the way people of the bush did things. Jonas was a master of adjustment and adaptability, demonstrated by his infrequent visits to Mashkisibi to obtain essentials. With the coming of railways and miners and lumberjacks to the Mashkisibi country, a different pattern of forest fires had developed from the Indian point of view, one sufficient to replace the need for the old slash and burn methods practised by the ancients when they wished to foster what they called "good rabbit lands". After the war, Jonas had developed his own distinct seasonal migratory mode of existence. He determined that if one kept an accurate record of where the fires had been, then one would know where to go in a given year, for a plentiful supply of rabbits. In winter, Farmer Jones kept frozen rabbits piled high, like cord wood, in a shed at his bush camp. He would sometimes come in to Mashkisibi and sell the meat and fur to the town folk or to selected shopkeepers. When he did so, he would always stop in at Ardo Kulduhn's Lebanese Restaurant to have some strong oriental coffee, to talk with him about the wisdom of the Koran, and to leave him a personal supply of rabbit meat.

There was another crop which Jonas had learned to cultivate, and it was undoubtedly the source of his nickname. This crop was also based on a hunting and gathering strategy, a crop fertilized by work crews in the timber industry or in hydro work camps. Farmer Jones was a specialist in the harvesting of this crop, and he usually managed to take off at least two a year: one in late spring and another in the fall. A curious sight awaited the occasional visitor to the Beardy camp. Always the guest would find there a great pyramid covered in canvas. The size of this pyramid varied in size, depending on the time of year. At first glance, it appeared that some latter-day, prehistoric mound-builder had been at work in the middle of the boreal forest. The building blocks were architecturally unique, for they consisted of six, twelve, and twenty-four packs of empty beer bottles.

Farmer Jones knew all of the rivers and streams of the region, how they were connected, which were full and which ran dry. Once a year he would go to Mashkisibi or down to the Sault and obtain from the forest company managers, or from the government foresters, charts of where there would be bush work going on over the next year. On a large tanned moose-hide stretched out on his cabin wall, he then etched a fine cartographic approximation of his territory and on this he identified, by coloured quills and beads, the locations of the camps for that year. His practice was to build small rafts which he then cached at certain points near these camps, usually on the closest feeder streams or near the main river. With these he would float the accumulated empties, which he gathered at the camps, out to the Mashkisibi where he would then transfer them to a large raft. Then he would float it to his camp, to his main "beer-stack" as he called it, not far from the Mashkisibi. Twice a year Jonas took his entire crop to town on a barge rented from the local band council. He would usually clear about $3,000 a shipment.

In earlier years he had sometimes worked other river systems and taken bottles into other towns, but since 1968 he worked only into Mashkisibi so that Joanna might get to know the people there. When she was eight, he had put her into the school run by the Catholics, for he trusted them. He wanted her to become comfortable with "white ways" in order to employ those ways to her advantage, as he had done. He would tell her frequently that "there are many worlds" and that it was "best to be able to move in at least two worlds at once." It was a view he shared with Angus Ashabish. He had made arrangements with Angus that Joanna could live with Minnie Maywins, Angus's widowed sister, and hence Joanna and Kakayosha Maywins, became like sisters.

It was always a signal day in Mashkisibi when Jonas Beardy was reported to be on the river with his cargo. It was usually shortly after the passing of spring break-up that the long, narrow barge would come sliding down the river to the top of the first of the hydro head-ponds which blocked further approach to the town, still a good ten miles away. His procedure was to pull into what was known locally as Farmer Jones's Landing and unload onto the shore. Normally, somebody would have spotted Jonas Beardy well in advance and the news would spread quickly. A truck from the Council might already be waiting, but if not it would be there soon. Local tribesman came to help with the work and within a few days there would be a grand party at the Fireweed Hall. Farmer Jones always did his banking first, for he knew the weaknesses of his brothers. He liked to think that he set them a good example of business before pleasure. This was a point of view derived from the white man's world, one which he did not entirely despise. There was now a well-funded trust account set up for Little Sturgeon to use for education or some other purpose. It was well known that he had also set up a relief account for the reserve and had picked up many food and legal bills for band members, and that he never asked to be repaid.

"Put it into the trust account," he would say to anybody who offered to repay him. It was late spring and Jonas had come to Mashkisibi to pick up Joanna at school year end and to transact some business with the local forester at Black Pebble Lake, some twenty miles south of the town.

iii

That same spring, Angus Ashabish, Kakayosha Maywins, now twenty-one, and the Little Sturgeon, now fifteen, decided to go and meet Farmer Jones at the landing. Angus was always keen to talk with Jonas Beardy about the state of the back country and about the old Cree ways. It had been arranged that Jonas would, as usual, come back to the Fireweed Reserve for the evening meal and stay over as long as he wished. Tonight, they would eat moose, whitefish, wildrice, vegetables from Minnie's garden, and fresh berries. The following Monday, Jonas would do his banking, and during the week there would be a social at the Fireweed Hall.

Angus and Kakayosha and Joanna arrived at the landing around ten o'clock on a Saturday morning. It was cool and Kakayosha started a small blaze in the fire circle on a small flat above the river. This was the favoured gathering location for those who came and waited at Farmer Jones's Landing. It commanded a fine view up the Mashkisibi to third bend. Angus lifted a cooler out of the rear of his 1958 Ford pickup and brought it up to the flat. The Little Sturgeon was already in her swim suit and down at river's edge, deciding which route she would plot across the cold waters.

"She's amazing!" Kaka said to her uncle.

"We have eggs, fish and makings for bannock," he said. "I could make it up, but I know you do it better."

"I had a good teacher didn't I?" said Kakayosha, and

she winked at her Uncle.

"The very best," Angus said. "But you should know that I have had long practise in getting the women to work for me, making my breakfast."

"Come on! I know how reclusive you are! If there were all these women floating in and out of your tent, don't you think I would know about it?"

"Well - perhaps you are right. Your Aunt Maggie and I were close."

Kakayosha walked over to Angus and looked up at him for a long moment as she took the cooler from him. She put it down and then put a hand on his shoulder and leaned up and kissed him. "I wish I had been old enough to remember her better Uncle."

Angus had several nieces, but he had become godfather to Kakayosha - *A Bird in Everlasting Flight* - after the death of her own father when she was nine years old. Angus was very fond of his sister Minnie, and wanted to make things easier for her. He knew about loss himself.

"So, I have a new bannock recipe," said Kakayosha. "Shall I try it out on you? Of course I shall. You can make the tea." Kakayosha picked up the cooler and walked it over to the fire and started rummaging around in the contents. She looked down to the river and could see Joanna twenty yards out into the river.

"Now tell me," Angus said, "what did you make of those birch bark scrolls I gave you to look at last month?"

"Really strange stuff, uncle. But beautiful. Where did you get them again?"

"From an old lady over at La Pointe. She knew my father, and he told me to get to know her. So I started to work the fishery over there many years ago, after the war. She was very wise and she told me things about those scrolls, which, by the way, she had received from an old one herself. I will perhaps tell you what she told me sometime if you are interested. Which is to say, if you make good bannock."

"I always make good bannock."

"Then it only remains to know if you are interested."

"Will it be good for me to know these things uncle?"

"Knowledge is two-headed. It can be useful and inwardly satisfying, but it can also consume you." Kakayosha did not reply but continued working on her food preparations. Angus sat down on a log and looked up the river and then out towards Little Sturgeon.

"The scrolls are beautifully made aren't they. Do you know how they were made?"

"You get the inner bark of the birch in spring. The rolls take the incisions well when new and fresh like that. Then you keep them in a good place and every so often you apply a bit of oil to them to keep them supple and moist. I like to use fish oil. But bear grease is also good." Angus walked down to the shore and kept his eyes fixed on the swimmer making strong and steady progess across the river.

Ten minutes later, Kakayosha walked down to Angus with some fresh bannock.

"This is good, niece. Very good. With any luck, Jonas will not arrive until late and we can just sit here and eat and do nothing."

"Speak for yourself Uncle. I promised mom I would gather some roots and chokecherries for her."

"I won't stop you niece. I love to watch you work. But now tell me first, how is your knowledge of roots?"

"Getting pretty good. I take the kids out from school as often as I can into the bush. More fun for me and them."

"That's good. The best thing to do with a school room is empty it."

Kakayosha moved off along the edge of the forest where chokecherries grew and Angus lay down and half closed his eyes. But his eyes were fixed on Joanna on the far side of the Mashkisibi. He then closed them, knowing how strong she was, and knowing that Kakayosha was also watching her from the edge of the forest. When Angus slept he usually dreamed. And when he woke up he usually thought about his dreams. On this occasion he did not dream. He merely revived to the gentle prodding of a moccasin and Kaka's excited announcement that she could see Jonas's raft coming around third bend.

"I can see him at the rear. He has a bright red shirt on."

"Are you sure it's him. He always wears blue."

"Yes, yes. It's him."

Kakayosha bounded down the slope to the primitive wharf and walked out to the end, waving her hand at Joanna who was now half way back across the river. Angus ambled down slowly and sat down upon a large rock near the wharf. He and Kaka stared up the river as the barge made its steady way toward them. The sound of a less-than-well-tuned engine eventually added itself to the murmur of the river, as though the Mashkisibi was gargling. Unmistakable backfiring from a different direction added another layer to this river music. A pick-up truck rolled into the parking lot. Kaka's cousin, Dugah Beshue, along with some of his cronies, were all stuffed into a rusting contraption which had *Pictographia* written on the sides, surrounded by stylized musical notes which looked as though they had been painted in red ochre on a rock face. Kakayosha turned around and waved at them and started to walk over towards the rambunctious crowd of would-be musicians piling out of the cab.

"Hey you savages," she yelled, "didn't anybody tell you all these bottles coming in here are empty, not full? What are you guys doing here?"

"Heard you been studyin' medicine with our crazy uncle there, Kaka. Thought we would see if you any good yet," said Dugah Beshue. "See if you can fill them bottles up again."

"I don't perform yet. Specially for guys who just make self-interested requests. Heck, you could all go to the Bear Pit and watch somebody turn empty glasses into full." The young men all laughed.

"So, since we here anyway, we might as well help Farmer Jones unload I guess," said Misconometos, known also as *The Red Insect*.

Jonas Beardy was now steering the barge into the landing and Little Sturgeon had swum along side and climbed up the tire ladder onto the boat. Jonas gave her a great hug and a warm blanket. After the craft was secured and general greetings conveyed, Angus and Jonas sat down by the fire and ate while the young men and women started the work of unloading bottles.

That night, after dinner at Minnie Maywins's house, Joanna told Jonas Beardy that she wanted to work at Black Pebble Lake, for the park, rather than go back into the bush as previously planned. Kakayosha would be working there, as well as some of her other friends. Jonas had been looking forward to having his daughter with him in the bush again, but he quickly relented. His daughter was growing up. She had done well in her first year of high school. She needed to have her growing time with people her own age. There would now be two items of business to take care of at Black Pebble Lake.

2

Black Pebble Lake

i

For over an hour the screech of a lathe had alternated with the periodic hum of passing cars and trucks. In keeping with his work, Victor Simpson was adept at the fabrication of flint tools and arrow heads, and could often be found puttering around in the evening trying to simulate some obscure type of ancient utensil, tool or weapon. Making boomerangs had become his main contribution to the resolution of weekend boredom at Black Pebble Lake Park headquarters. Victor's large glasses and scholarly ways had caused Wolfie Wisdom, a perennial seasonal employee, to bestow upon him the nickname *Rims*. Victor was a practical and artistic man, and these qualities were recognized by many who lived in the compound. Whenever the kitchen staff ever needed anything fixed or improvised, they could usually count on Victor to do the job.

The lathe had fallen silent for several minutes. The door of the department workshop finally opened from within and Victor emerged into the early afternoon sunlight, his hands full of labour. He walked across the green towards the steps of the dining hall accompanied by a rising series of cheers emanating from the randomly scattered bodies reposing on the lawn in front of the building. Kirsti Kallela, Olivia Wilson and Joanna Beardy were seated on the steps and they began a rhythmic clapping in order to get the crowd motivated.

With just a touch of ritual Victor Simpson passed out his latest batch of plywood imitations to all who asked for one, keeping one for himself tucked up under his arm. Victor then broke into a trot that escalated in speed. He exercised a smooth and powerful side-arm delivery, ending with a sharp flick of the wrist, which sent the boomerang soaring into a high curving arc over the staff house. For upward of ten seconds its V-shaped silhouette cut a dark swath against the July blue canopy and then it swept down and in to almost the precise point from where Victor had released. He caught up with it and plucked it out of the air. His gait had changed only slightly, lending an air of grace to the entire performance.

The test flight completed, the others knew that they might now follow suit. Within seconds the air was filled with a flock of wooden birds whose lack of intrinsic calls were compensated for by a steady series of earthbound "ooohs" and "ahhhs." Joanna Beardy, who was one of the first to start throwing, looked at Kirsti and said: "This is such a gas. My dad would love this."

It was a grand entertainment, this sending into space what Victor Simpson called his flock of fake homing pigeons. Those who banished and then courted the wooden birds grandstanded to the others who were satisfied to just sit and watch. There were always newcomers anxious to try their hand at the old Aboriginal art, and the spectacle was known to last from noon until supper hour.

Burl Manion stood leaning on the railing of the Dining Hall porch. He was content to just be a watcher on this Sunday. He had been up early and taken a long hike along the coast, seeking relief from the work of the last three evenings - evenings spent over his typewriter. It was not in his job description, but his collaboration with the archaeologists over the last year had moved him to start working on a manuscript dealing with the history of Mashkisibi country. The archaeologists were interested in his knowledge of wildlife more than history, particularly with respect to his capacity to identify old animal bones and fragments. Such specimens were much valued when they showed up in their excavations. Victor Simpson and his colleagues were always anxious to drag Burl into their make-shift, booze-filled lab near Tawab's Cove and consult him on what they called *faunal analysis*. He was a willing captive however, and he admired them as savvy bush workers. Such bone analysis was a welcome change from his normal routines, inspecting moose entrails or confiscated pelts.

The weekend before he had tried his hand at boomerang throwing. Images of a far away continent had subsequently played about the edges of his thoughts, breaking in unannounced when he was concentrating on quite different matters. More than once he had found himself pondering the strange device and how such a tool might have come to be. At the library in Mashkisibi he learned that the boomerang was not used exclusively by the Aborigines of Australia. Felix Smith, foreman of the work crew at Black Pebble, and a good hunter, was interested when Burl told him that a non-returning boomerang was used by the Hopi Indians of Arizona for taking jackrabbits. Students of the weapon had noticed that even contemporary Australian Aboriginals did not really understand the principle of their ancient invention, and that only after test-throwing a new one could they be sure that it would function properly.

Watching the frolic before him and the happy use of the device as a toy drove home anew the idea that possession of such a complex device by a conservative people was odd. Was the boomerang the perfect metaphor for an island people far removed from outer influence? Everything sent out from that great island continent was destined to come back, washed up on some near or distant beach. Could it be that, in some remote age, the boomerang had been viewed by the "Head Men" as a dubious achievement? Perhaps those who had first stumbled upon it, and then crafted it, might have been later admonished. When it missed its target, it could come hurtling back upon the sender and do him harm. Perhaps this early adventure into innovative technology had left a bad taste in the Aboriginal mouth, giving birth to a belief that all such tampering could only be detrimental to the tribal good. If so, then that early taboo, born of the fear of some potential tribal nemesis, had certainly been potent. As the centuries unfolded and modernity caught up with them, even in the *outback*, the image of the unprogressive Aboriginal of Australia had gradually become a stereotype, familiar around the globe. Not many people were prepared to identify the Aboriginal's implacable cultural conservatism with a positive state of equilibrium. Burl sensed the presence of a person standing behind him on the steps. He turned and saw Felix Smith.

"Felix," he said, "do you suppose the old Aborigines in Australia ever hung around the beach, tossing these things around just for the hell-uv-it?"

Joanna Beardy and Kirsti Kallela came running over to the Dining Hall and plopped down on the steps just below where Burl and Felix were talking. The sweat was pouring off both of them. Burl handed them the towel he was sitting on. After catching her breath, Kirsti leapt up again and ran into the dining hall to get some lemonade. She came back with a tray of glasses and the conversation flowed about the amazing nature of boomerangs. Before they had finished their drinks, Burl pointed to some new players arriving on the scene. A small train of children was being led across the green to the spot where Victor had dumped some boomerangs. They were guided by a young woman in light tan moccasins, cut-off denim shorts and a loose fitting blouse of bright blue. Her hair was black and fell to the middle of her back, held halfway down by a brightly coloured beaded clasp. She gathered the children on the grass in a circle and gave out a boomerang to each one. She waved to Victor who then came over and had a few words with her. He nodded, as if in agreement, and then proceeded to give a quick lesson to the children on how to throw the boomerang.

"Who is that then?" Burl asked.

"That's Kakayosha Maywins," said Joanna Beardy. "She's my sorta-sister from Mashkisibi. She lives with her mother there. Her mother and uncle are friends of my dad, and I live with them when I'm going to school. She dresses really bush-trendy don't you think? I'd love to look like her."

"Everybody I talk to thinks you look just fine as you are Joanna," said Burl.

"That's exactly right," Kirsti added.

"Is she a teacher or something Joanna?" asked Burl.

"Yeah. She teaches at the Fireweed Reserve School. Mr. Anderson hired her to run a programme for young people at the park over the summer. Then she got me on to work in the kitchen and help the bull-cooks. She's great with kids, really." Joanna fell silent and worked on her lemonade. Across the green, Kakayosha Maywins was trying to keep the children in check while the first one took instruction from Victor. From their positions seated on the grass the youngsters watched keenly as Victor ran the first in a short circle and then guided his hand in the release. One at a time, Kakayosha sent them up for a practice throw and after the last one had thrown, she turned them all loose. In short order, the sky was filled with a new flock of wooden birds.

"She's good isn't she," said Kirsti. "She kept them all together until they knew what they were doing.

"She probably gets that from her Uncle Angus," Joanna said, and paused. "She's really into kids." Refreshed from the lemonade, Joanna Beardy ran over to the pile of boomerangs, picked up two and ran back over to the steps. Olivia Wilson was sitting alone at the top of the stairs, away from the others.

"Olivia! Come on down and try it out. I have two here," Joanna yelled up to her. Olivia answered only by a slight shake of the head. Kirsti Kallela turned around and looked up at Olivia.

"Come on Olivia. It's a piece of cake," said Kirsti. "Show us your stuff." Olivia got up nervously and worked her way down the steps to where Joanna was waiting for her.

"Here, take this one," said Joanna. "It's real simple." Olivia took the boomerang and looked at it, and then ran her hand slowly along its smooth length. The two girls moved off towards the centre of the green. "You've just finished senior school haven't you?" Joanna asked Olivia. She did not wait for an answer. "I'm just going into ten next year."

"You're a good swimmer aren't you," Olivia said with a half smile on her face. "I've seen you in the pool."

"I get lots of practice in the rivers when I'm out with my dad. It helps. Here - hold it like this - by the very tip - but with a good firm grip." Joanna pranced off and sent her boomerang into the blue with remarkable force. After she had plucked it out of the air again, Olivia looked at her and said:

"Where do you get so much power?"

"You don't need too much power. It's all in the wrist. Go on - try it."

Olivia ran in a narrow circle but held back at the last moment. Joanna ran up to her. "Run in a larger arc. Let's run together, and when I say let go, we both let go."

Kirsti and Burl were watching from the steps as Joanna put Olivia through her paces.

"My that girl is self-conscious," Kirsti whispered to Burl. "She has real talent though. I think it will be good for her to be out here this summer. Her parents keep a real tight reign on her."

"You know them? Who are they?"

"The Wilsons. Real fundamentalists. People of very few

words. They live on the edge of Mashkisibi. He runs an auto repair shop. Not very friendly people. Before they would let her come out here, he insisted on meeting me as the employer and then grilled me a lot on the sleeping arrangements out here."

"You're from Thunder Bay aren't you? How do you know them?"

"I was actually born in Mashkisibi and went to grade school there. That's how I remember the Wilsons. My folks wanted me to go to school in the Bay, and so we all moved over there when I was in grade eight. My Dad got a job in the mill over there. My folks are both gone now. Died in a car accident."

"I'm real sorry to hear that. Some time ago?"

"Three years. Seems like yesterday." Kirsti looked out to the green, her face a mask. Neither spoke. Burl took the empty glass from her hand.

"Can I get you another?"

"Thanks." Burl disappeared up the steps and into the kitchen and returned with two full glasses. They watched the proceedings in silence for a moment, and then Burl said:

"So then, did you tell Mr. Wilson what a brothel we run out here?"

The clang of the Sunday evening supper bell brought the afternoon games to a halt. It announced that the evening meal would be served in fifteen minutes. The boomerang crowd filtered off the green and towards the bunkhouses to clean up. The chatter at the long wooden tables was lively and engaging among the young who, three times a day, had to mix with the older veterans of the bush. The ethic of the lumber camp was still strong with many of the latter, and even the best youthful efforts to engage them in what many had been raised to understand as polite *table talk*, were often met with indifference or sometimes churlishness. Even the most charming and tactful, male or female, could not open up Boisant Bollard to mealtime conversation. In his chopped manner, he would mutter: "Table is for eat - *manger*."

Boisant Bollard was a fixture at Black Pebble Lake. His mind was not there however. It was back in the Abitibi forests of the 1930s where he had been trained to the saw and axe and where he had worked for over thirty years. For Boisant it was something akin to a moral imperative that one entered the dining room, sat down, ate and kept one's mouth shut. Boisant was usually the first seated at what he considered to be *his* personal chair. The cooks always warned new arrivals that nobody dare occupy it. Boisant Bollard was usually the first to leave. After supper a mix of the staff house residents usually adjourned to the basement for ping-pong, music, and conversation, and if these activities went too far into the night, Boisant Bollard could be heard the next morning complaining to the cooks: "Too much par-tee! Too much par-tee!" They would give Boisant a cookie and coffee, but say nothing.

His appeals were limited in effect for the times had, in fact, changed. The cooks were no longer the authoritarian figures of the camp of Boisant's youth. He had out-lived or out-stayed his comrades. There were few French-speakers around Black Pebble Lake or Mashkisibi anymore, although that had not always been the case. Certain mature women around Mashkisibi were ever anxious to mother old Boisant; but even if a woman spoke French it was no guarantee of getting any closer to him or of drawing him into community social life. The other veterans of the bush might have known something of his past, his people, his place of birth, but if they did, they were not saying, at least not to the young. Ollie Finch, the truck driver, was fond of saying: "a man's privacy in the bush is his own."

"We're going to play cards, Boisant. Want to play?"

"Time for sleep - time for sleep," he would reply.

"Well - if you change your mind..."

"*Oui, merci - bonsoir.*"

34

Victor Simpson and Burl Manion frequently took their evening meal together in the dining hall on Sunday. The former usually slept in the bunkhouse with his crew south of Tawab's Cove, but on weekends he would often come to Black Pebble or Mashkisibi. When the dining hall started to empty they would stay behind and help Will and June Bender clean up the kitchen and have a second cup of coffee. Victor was in an upbeat mood after the afternoon's exercise and a steak dinner.

"Finally got all the paper work done on Project Rising Water, Burl. That's a relief. I think it will go over okay with the higher-ups. Next year we should be able to do a helluva lot more. All kinds of local support for it around Mashkisibi and the Fireweed Reserve. Also at Lakehead and at the ROM."

"Good title for the project," said Burl. "It has a kind apocalyptic and public safety ring to it. Hard to resist in political terms."

"It helps that the Assistant Deputy Minister used to be an archaeologist as well," Victor countered. "We had to get a winner at that level one day."

"So when do you figure you can start?"

"With any luck, this fall. That would be ideal when the leaves and bugs are down. Then next fiscal we will really go at it. Going to try and plug into a lot of community employment funds so I can hire locals. Angus Ashabish at Fireweed is very keen and is putting in a word with the Elders. I told him there would be some jobs for a few people on the reserve if they're interested. Have you been up to Mashkisibi No. 1 lately?"

"Yeah - the work on the dam is going along pretty fast and the other two are pretty well finished, although the water is still running about normal. They want to fill up the headpond of No.1 first and the ones further back second and third. Guess that makes sense from a gravity point of view."

"Right. So the idea is we will probably concentrate on

the lands behind No. 1 first and the others in years two and three. Just hope they go for the extended budget line. Hope you will be around to get involved in it a bit. We could use you."

"Wouldn't miss it."

"By the way Burl, have you ever met Angus Ashabish?"

"No. Just Kaka."

"I'm going to meet him at Tawab's Cove one of these evenings. Perhaps you would be interested. He's a remarkable source and a remarkable man."

"Super idea. I would like that. If he's as sharp as his niece, he's probably pretty special."

"*Very unique* is how I would put it," said Victor. "He knows a lot about the country around those dams and so I'm going to go out with him as often as he likes. He's fond of saying 'anything that takes us back' is good."

ii

Following supper hour that night, Burl Manion went out to putter along the shoreline of Black Pebble Lake, which was more like a large pond than a lake. He followed the path around to the far shore and found a rock to perch on, one that gave a good view across to the bunkhouse. In the centre of the lake a pair of loons dove with regularity below the still, glass-like surface. Burl could recall the loons on the southern lakes in the cottage country of Haliburton, but that was at least twenty years ago when he was still in grade school. These retiring creatures had pushed ever further north over the last two decades. Despite the close proximity of the busy highway, this pair still stubbornly nested on Black Pebble.

"So you are probably my midnight callers," Burl said to the loons. Two nights before, he had been jolted awake by the first scream around 11:30. It was a mad, forlorn cry and at first he had thought of wolves. That is how long I have been away, he thought, and he allowed a faint smile to cross his face. Then it had come again, chilling and insane, like glass breaking voluntarily in an old deserted house. A third time it came, bolting him upright and fully awake in his bed. With some discomfort, even now, he thought of how those calls brought forth feelings which had long reposed dormant. That midnight episode had been akin to being fully awake in the middle of a dream. Something resembling mystery had clawed its way up from below the layers of secular ooze long settled upon his urbanized mind. This momentary encounter in the night with a long forgotten, elusive *something*, had been as fleeting as the call of the loon itself. It emerged, Lazarus-like, from his memory, and then vanished before he could endow the shadow with a face, or even a form. He remembered the cold sweat washing over him, similar to that provoked by fear or loss or sudden illness, and how, with a shiver, he had slid back down into his bed to bundle himself against this philosophical chill. Yet he had remained strangely anxious to hear that ghostly sound one more time. It did not return. Eventually he had drifted off into a restless sleep, but one bedeviled by a persisting mood of foreboding. He could not recall when he awoke, but when he did he was weary, as if he had not slept at all.

Burl slowly got to his feet so as not to startle the loons and started to walk back to the bunkhouse. How odd it was, he thought, that two such small and retiring creatures could so thoroughly unhinge the mind of a man.

He shuffled off along the back loop which would take him back to the compound via the far side of the lake. There were some fine new boardwalk sidings which pushed one further out into the pond, ending in secluded little viewing blinds. He went up the third of these sidings, and when he reached the end he found Kakayosha and Olivia curled up on the benches, watching the loons, closer in at this angle. He scuffed his feet slightly in order to announce his presence and not scare off the loons. Kakayosha looked back at him

37

and put her finger to her mouth and pointed out towards the floating pair. Burl held back from the blind and just watched. Kakayosha and Olivia were trading a pair of binoculars back and forth. Kakayosha beckoned Burl to join them. Stealthily, on tip-toes, he slid in. They whispered in hushed tones and watched the birds move off slowly towards the centre of Black Pebble Lake.

"This is incredible" said Kakayosha a little more loudly. "We've been watching them for about half an hour."

"I don't know if I have met you properly, Miss. I'm Burl Manion."

"I'm Olivia Wilson." She looked down almost immediately and then turned her head out towards the pond again.

"She's a fantastic talent Burl. You should see her drawing."

"Oh yes - I see now. You are the one Kirsti Kalella hired lately, is that right? She told me how good you are."

"Thank you. I really just draw what I see. Don't have any real training or anything."

"I'm sure we'll keep you busy this summer. I have some things of my own I could throw at you if you start to run short. And I'm sure Kaka can always use you with the children as well."

"Anytime," said Kakayosha. "Kid's love to draw - but they can always use some help."

"I'm not very good with people" said Olivia, "but I'll try if you need me."

"I've been watching those loons from the other side," Burl said, "but I think you guys found the perfect spot over here. Anyway, I'll leave you in peace again. I'm going to head back."

When Burl arrived at the trail head he walked across the compound green towards the Headquarters building. The late evening hours were the best for writing. He could listen to his classical albums, safe in the knowledge that he would not usually be disturbed. His office was an exercise in eccentricity and comfort, too much so perhaps, for it had become a favoured place for his co-workers to drop in during the day for all kinds of mindless chit-chat. Attempting concentrated work of any kind during office hours was quite hopeless unless one closed the door. "Then people think you are mad at them" he had complained to Kirsti Kallela, the new wildlife biologist on staff, who had similar problems, but of a somewhat different origin. She had the blond and statuesque good looks of her Finnish compatriots, and quickly became the target of every male in the office. Burl's office was garnished with potted plants, fabric wall-hangings, a well-framed Morriseau print and a variety of prehistoric artifacts nicely mounted in glass cases. Solid cedar shelves made from two by four lengths, rose from floor to ceiling. They covered two walls and were filled with books and reports. There were also diverse animal parts mounted on the walls and by the door, on a pedestal made from an old mining pipe, there was a stuffed raven seated upon a bust of Rachmaninoff. Kirsti Kallela knew a lot about ravens, and so this little arrangement had become an early talking point. "A very intelligent bird" she had said, "sitting on a very intelligent composer." She was amused when Burl had explained to her the historical connection between Rachmaninoff and Edgar Allen Poe and how a Russian version of one his poems had inspired the master to write a large choral symphony.

"I must listen to *The Bells* sometime then," she replied. Burl offered to loan her his recording of the work, and she accepted. She had then told him that she played the violin - "very badly." Over the subsequent few weeks, he took some inner satisfaction knowing that, nondescript as he was, she seemed to enjoy his company more than that of the other men who came calling.

The office building, as Burl approached, was dark except for a light shining out of a basement window. Passing by the window, he could faintly hear the sound of music. He let himself in quietly by the main door and padded over to his office, flipped on the light and put on his moccasins. He then went down the hallway to the door which led to the basement. There was no mistaking it. It was not a radio. Somebody was playing the violin and there was no doubt about who it was. Burl quietly eased the door open a notch, letting the sound rise clear and pure from below. He froze and listened. The melody was familiar. Yes, he thought, it was the *Meditation* from *Thäis* - no doubt a favourite with aspiring violinists.

Burl eased the door shut and walked gingerly back to his office. He sat down at his desk and turned to the loose-leaf manuscript which sat in one of his in-baskets. "This is perfect," he whispered to himself, "music to edit by."

The work did not proceed with any concentration. He gave himself over to the music. Half an hour later he looked at the raven for a moment and then slowly folded up the manuscript and put it back in the in-basket. Very quietly, he rose and let himself out of the building. Back in his room, he stretched out on the bed and looked at the ceiling, his hands behind his head. He got up and went over to a shelf on which there were a number of manuscript boxes piled one on top of the other, and pulled out the one at the bottom. He looked at it but did not open it, then placed it on his small desk. He lay down again and switched on the radio. It produced only the news and a variety of popular and country and western stations. He got up again and walked over to his desk and put his hands on the lid of the manuscript box and gently removed it. The top sheet seemed to wink at him saying: "You see, you were right to quit. There is the proof again, right over in the office basement. You should have no regrets. Music is for the *talented*." The familiar handwriting on the script now greeted him, bringing back memories of all those evenings and weekends during his teen years put in attempting to dance with the gods. The old feelings of ecstasy which accompany the boldest acts of creation briefly rose in his blood, causing a momentary rush. Burl picked up the cover page. *Symphony No. 1. "Memorial" Op. 6, by Burl Manion.* He lifted out the rest of the score and turned through it, page by page. He had not looked at it for years. All the toil, all the sweat, all the crudities of style and all the botched harmonies. The Cover Page winked at him again: "Not to worry. You see, too many gifts have to coalesce fortuitously in one mind in order to compose. You only had the music, not the other gifts. Nice try, but don't feel bad about it. Even the great composers had their doubts. Why should a rank amateur like you feel bad about it?" Burl placed the score back in the box and slipped it into the drawer and closed it. The music moved stillborn from the pages into his inner ear. Music that only he could or ever would hear.

Burl reached over and switched the bedside light off and slid down into the warmth of the flannel sheets. In the darkness the music and the woman's face burned into his mind and then quickly into his body. "My god, she really is good." He caressed himself as he had done so many times. He would wait for her as he had waited for all the others, the ones who never arrived.

The next day, Burl walked down to Kirsti's office just at coffee time and knocked gently on the side door frame. Kirsti spun about in her swivel chair.

"Hi! Come on in. Have a chair."

"Its too nice to stay inside on a day like this for coffee. Want to stroll outside?"

"Sure. Good idea. I've been working on a really useless set of stats for head office. Need to get away from it."

Burl walked over to the window and pointed over to the Black Pebble Lake trail head. "I walked that last evening. Shall we go down to the first viewing blind? Maybe the loons will still be around."

"Let's do it," Kirsti said.

On the trail, Burl made his confession to being an audio-voyeur the evening before.

"Hope you don't mind. I work in the office in the evenings quite often, but I became totally absorbed in your playing. You really have it, you know that don't you?"

"Why thank you. I'm not quite so sure about that, but I hope you don't mind if I practise there in the evenings."

"What's to mind? You should charge me for the privilege."

"Oh, that's nice of you to say that. Its good to know there's someone here who really appreciates classical music so much. I'm not really sure how far I can go with it. But I was encouraged early. All those Finlander relatives you know. Going on about Sibelius and about making our own entertainment in the bush and so on. My people are really *quite crazy* you know."

"Myself, I think Sibelius should be made our National composer here. Fabulous stuff. I heard his fifth played in Toronto once. Blew me away. He's just as much about Canada as Finland."

Burl and Kirsti reached the first viewing platform at the end of one of the siding boardwalks. They leaned on the railing overlooking the water and did not speak. June's mid-morning sun hit the lake from an angle, turning the surface into a spectacle of dancing diamonds. On the far shore the two predictable black silhouettes moved steadily through the opaque radiance.

"Ah yes," said Burl. "There they are. Do you see them? The same ones that were here last night probably."

"Such a beautiful bird," said Kirsti. They watched the even progress of the mated pair moving along the intense shimmering horizon. One of them suddenly disappeared beneath the surface.

"So how did you end up inspecting entrails then?" Kirsti asked.

"It was a compromise."

"Between?"

"Between the sacred and the profane. A move away from divinity."

"Divinity? - Really?"

"Yes - of a sort."

"Where were you studying then?"

"At the feet of the masters."

"Which faith?"

"The church of musical composition. Kind of Catholic I suppose. So many true saints - and many people would say Bach was the Pope. Although the Lutherans wouldn't say that of course."

"You're kidding me. You were studying composition?"

"Only after a fashion. Mostly self-taught, although I did some formal study of harmony. Unfortunately, I didn't have what it takes. I'm okay with it though. Not uptight - not bitter." Kirsti looked straight into Burl's eyes hard and long until he finally looked away.

"Did you finish some things?" Kirsti asked.

"Nothing that should ever see the light of day. Now I just listen"

"I'm glad you're smiling when you say that," Kirsti said, moving her eyes back in line with Burl's.

"Its true. I was certainly smiling last night, listening to you. Anyway - so - one needs to make a living, and I thought - by becoming a wildlife technician I could find an excuse to be in the outdoors, the places where so many musicians like to find their inspiration. Or so we are told. Northern Ontario is not exactly the Vienna Woods of course. I can't imagine Beethoven or Schubert getting much done here if they had to wander through the bush plagued by mosquitos and blackflies. Autumn and winter would be the time for composing I think. Do you suppose Sibelius had a well-screened porch?"

"I'm sure he did." Kirsti looked at Burl, trying to suppress laughter, but it pushed through and she quickly turned and looked out over the lake and leaned her arms on the railing. She saw the loon that had dived come up over by the far edge of the pond.

3

Tawab's Cove

i

A speck moved slowly down the sunpath which, in the low light, defined a shimmering crimson-gold highway across *Kitchi-Gami*. From a position on top of a flat outcrop some fifty feet above the little harbour, Burl Manion and Victor Simpson sat watching as Angus Ashabish, fisherman, slowly came in out of the infinity of Lake Superior. On reaching the outer limits of Tawab's Cove he cut the engine and covered the last few hundred yards by rowing.

"This is his usual way in calm waters," Victor said. "It's almost like some kind of ritual prayer offered at the close of day." The two men watched quietly as Angus worked the oars with a smooth regularity, hinting neither at an anxiety to be in on the shore nor at a reluctance to leave the lake. Man and boat moved over the surface without sound or the creation of foam.

"Looks like he's been working the northern part of his fishing grounds today," Victor added. Burl and Victor started walking down the short road to the pier.

"Was talkin' with Jonas Beardy down here once, just about this time of the evening too, now that I think about it. In fact, it was Jonas who first introduced me to Angus a couple of summers ago. He told me that around Mashkisibi Angus is known as a 'man of *mashkiki*.' - among his own people, that is."

"*Mashkiki*? "

"Yeah - Ojibwa for *medicine*, or *power* perhaps. Jonas said that even though it doesn't show often, Angus has a vain streak in him. Because he's a man of power and respected, he apparently takes some pleasure in encroaching upon those rocks out there - 'in order to test his own strength against that of the evil one' Jonas said." Angus Ashasbish was now just a few hundred yards or so from the dock.

"You see that patch of fireweed down in the flats, just in on the shore from where Angus's boat is? That's where the old village used to be. Angus told me a bit about it."

"How long ago was it abandoned?"

"I think maybe around 1919 or 1920. Aftermath of the great flu epidemic. Most of the survivors moved south to the so-called *new settlement* or else up to Mashkisibi."

"Yeah - that epidemic of 1918 was a bugger, no matter where you lived," Burl said. He raised his hand over his eyes to get a little better view of the old village site. "I've been pulling together some information on that new settlement. Most of the locals who think about it at all think it's just a normal piece of reserve land - you know - one of those more or less isolated chunks of land given out under the 1850 treaties. But there's a lot of quiet talk that those people are all there now as squatters - which is pretty hard to comprehend."

"Squatters? How so?"

"Well - near as I can tell - the new settlement was supposed to be attached to the old Saulteur lands at the Sault. That land was given over to them because of the way the canals were buggering up the fishery. But strange events one night seem to have left the lands of the new settlement alienated to outside interests. Nobody was using the land there in those days, and so nobody noticed - at least nobody who was going to say anything. There are no documents - only long memories." Burl put his backpack down and took the binoculars from Victor and fixed them on Angus who was now crossing the mouth of a small stream which emptied into Tawab's Cove just north of the pier. Another hundred yards would bring him to the boat ramp where his rather battered dodge half-ton truck was parked.

"I filed for reference what Jonas told me that evening." Victor said. "After I got to know Angus a little better he once confided to me that he *did* challenge the rocks now and then, but usually with a light heart. He said that he knew there were a lot of white people, like me for instance, who were interested in Indian beliefs and legends, and in ideas which he himself took with a grain of salt, just as many people do the fuzzier aspects of their own religion. 'Belief gets harder and harder,' he said to me." Burl gave the binoculars back to Victor and picked up his back-pack.

On the last stretch of path down to the pier, Victor dropped a few more details. He told Burl that Angus had been born further south, perhaps on the American side, and had blood connections with the ancient *Saulteur* - "the people of the rapids" - the folk of old *Bawating* - the best fishermen of them all. This honourable connection with those who used to work the great whitefishery prior to the building of the canals - the canals which eventually destroyed it - had been important in setting the pattern of his life. Unlike the legendary hunter of the east shore, after whom *Tawab*'s Cove had been named, Angus understood fish better than he understood game. He preferred to follow the whitefish - the *Atikameg* - the "caribou of the waters" - more than moose and deer in the bush. Victor had also learned from Angus something of what it was to work on Lake Superior since the end of the last war. This was a formative time for Angus, who in 1945 was still a young man. The years of the sucker had been difficult, especially for the trout, but he had managed to survive easily enough.

47

He knew those areas of the shoreline where the destructive suckers did not go and where good fish were still to be found. He had done a little more logging and trapping in those years, but now the fish were coming back along with the new artificial strain, *the splake*. There were things to learn about this new fish, he had told Victor. "God did not make it." It would be necessary to learn to follow it, to talk to it, to grasp its favourite jokes, and to console it when removing the hook.

A tourist was not likely to pick up on these nuances, and was more likely to see only a run-of-the-mill fisherman, perhaps a *sportsman* like himself. A more thoughtful stranger, lingering at the dock, might discern other things. He could not fail to notice that Angus Ashabish's catch was considerable and varied, well-sorted, and that he must therefore be a man long used to extracting his living from the lake.

The boat slid onto the shore just below the ramp. In appearance, Angus was unremarkable. His skin was dark and leathery befitting a man who had spent so many hours in the sun, confronting the elements. His hands were calloused from rough work but strong and able. His eyes, blacker than pitch, lit up slightly during conversation. And when Victor greeted him, and introduced him to Burl, little tributaries of laughter played across his face as he smiled and extended his hand. The three men indulged in some end-of-day small talk, Angus giving a brief account of the day's fishing trip and confirming that he had worked north. On his run home he told them he had cut in close to pass the sacred rocks of *Nanibojou*, not failing to throw some tobacco into the water, but giving the rocks only a narrow berth. Most of the people in this quarter referred to this shoal as *the Devil's Chair*. It was not always so named, but the European version was not far off the mark. Victor and Burl helped him unload his catch into his truck and then Angus took six large whitefish out of a pail, wrapped them in newspaper and handed the package to Victor. "Take these back to Black Pebble and see what June can do with them," he said.

"I believe your niece is working with us this summer Angus," said Burl. "We're all enjoying having her around the place. She lights it up, even in rainy weather."

Angus looked firmly and steadily into Burl's eyes and then his face slowly broke into a relaxed grin. "I am glad that you understand that Burl. That is a nice way for you to put it. She is very special. I am glad she's working at the park. The park is a good thing. I hope she will learn even more about plants while she is there."

ii

Over the summer and fall, Burl got into the habit of going to sit on the rocks above Tawab's Cove at sunset in order to watch the world and the lake wind down together. He did not always see or greet Angus, preferring to leave him to go about his business. From time to time however, he went down to the wharf and they would talk at some length about things of mutual interest, and in doing so, the two men defined some personal middle ground, a place somewhere between intimacy and acquaintanceship. With the passing of the months, Burl came to understand that even among those who had a closer tie or kinship with Angus Ashabish, there were few who claimed any genuine understanding of the layers of civilization which made up the geology of his mind. The people who met him in only casual circumstances usually fell victim to the normal round of expectations suspended in the outlook of the modern tourist: *here, surely, is an uncomplicated Native fisherman!* Such men as this were presumed to be provincial in outlook, retaining a certain rusticity along with, perhaps, vestiges of an esoteric knowledge which lingered on in behaviour. These traits, according to such conventional observation, were merely the remains of a continuing connection with land and water.

Soon enough, Burl understood that there was nothing provincial or restricted about the past experiences of Angus Ashabish. He learned how he had seen Paris during the Second World War and about his experiences of the killing fields. He therefore had a good understanding of what European civilization was capable of, if he had not already understood. Angus had been wounded. A German bullet made from Polish scrap iron had pierced his left shoulder. On Remembrance Day, in the Legion Hall in Mashkisibi, he would proudly show off the scar to the German and Canadian veterans, and then show them the bullet which he still kept in a small hide pouch. Upon his return to civilian life, he had taken up employment in a respectable number of jobs, including farming in Alberta. Having tried his hand at prairie agriculture, he returned to his hearth in the Shield country. In common with farmers, he liked the land, and preferred to make his living from it. With all of these things behind him, Angus was better rounded than many of his contemporaries, regardless of background. On one occasion, Burl made that precise observation to him, but such facts were of little consequence to Angus. He told Burl that he had tried to achieve an understanding of the way in which old tribal ideas lingered in his mind and how they tempered his views of the modern world. He did not see himself living a private interior life, steeped in some archaic *Algonkian* way, a way which had in fact vanished. Nor did he recognize himself as a member of some by-passed minority, doomed to forever react against a larger civilization - a civilization reputed to be powerful and to which all must submit, as the ancient Jews to the Romans. Whatever *Western Civilization* was, he recognized himself as part of it. He saw it as his fate to be a part of this mosaic of timeless heritages and cultural memories, and it was his people's fate as well. "True" he said, his "personal visions" were held together by sinews of Algonkianism. "My past, like yours" he would say, is woven into a larger fabric. He called it the "dream of civilization." But whatever this

50

civilization was, it was not just *Algonkian* or *Western*: it merely existed. "Like a fish, civilization has a soft underbelly of weakness." Angus likened his ability to survive in the world as something similar to his ability to catch fish for a living.

Conversations such as these became more frequent at the old pier at Tawab's cove. Burl, in turn, started to reveal more of his own views about life and religion to Angus, who always listened attentively to the younger man. He met the impatience of youth with silence and he replied to Burl's heated yearnings for large solutions with indifference. Angus' stoicism puzzled Burl at first but he appreciated the way his own questions were never met with sarcasm. The older man's sense of serenity started to influence Burl's behaviour. He began to sleep more peacefully. On one occasion, Angus asked Burl if he would like to come around for dinner at Minnie's place. He would make it an evening when Kakayosha was coming home from the park for a few days. Burl readily accepted.

"My little Kakayosha has an interest in all these matters. She is young, but her heart and head are open and clear. She does not know many whites, and perhaps you can open a few doors for her, of whatever kind."

"Yes - she has real natural curiosity," Burl replied. "She makes good use of my office library. I'm sure she must be a good teacher at your reserve day school."

"She is young and very new at it. But she is learning. Teaching, like fishing, takes practice."

iii

Leaning Willow, an aged Chief of the Michigan *Saulteur*, - one of the last of the rapids fishermen - was in poor health, but he still wanted to talk about what he knew. He remembered that Angus Ashabish was once attached to the people of his locality, and so he got word out from the hospital that he wished Angus to visit him, that he might talk to him about his friendship with his father and about the old ways, especially about the fishery.

"Can you get me out of here Angus? This is no way to depart. A fish should die in the rapids or on a hook."

"How badly do you want to leave?" asked Angus Ashabish.

"Oh, I think if I thought I could get up and do something out there, I might take you up on it, but they treat me well here, and a lot of Indian people come in bringing me all sorts of things. I guess I can't complain. What is bad is knowing you are probably not going to leave except through the chimney. I have been reading the whiteman's *Old Testament*. That must be a sure sign."

"Well, some chimneys are better than others. If there is anything you want me to do, let me know. Or if there is anything you would like me to bring you."

"Thank you Angus - but bringing yourself is the best thing. Sit down there, sit down. I knew your father Andrew very well you know." Angus pulled the padded chair up to the bedside.

"Yes - I know. He told me many times about working the rapids with you when you were both young together."

"Oh, I wish you could see it now. I can tell you, it was...it was an overflowing fish-basket then! And your father was good - one of the best. He was born on the Canadian side, and I was born on the American side, and we would sometimes cross to see what the differences were on the two sides of the river. We found there weren't many differences. That is how we first met. I still have a hoop-net he gave to me, and I am thinking I would like to give it to you."

"That's very good of you. I would be honoured to have it. I'm still mainly a fisherman you know."

"Yes, yes, so I have been told. It's a very different matter now I am sure. Now, would you like to hear a little about those old days?"

"Very much. We have younger people around who ask

me about these things now, and so I'll pass on to them whatever you have to say." Angus took off his jacket and then poured some water into a glass for Leaning Willow.

"Everybody 'round here knows that the whitefish were good, but when the rapids still flowed freely, did you know there was also sturgeon? But the rapids - they had to be free. Even when I was young, much of the damage had already been done on the American side. They started to fool around with canals way back when, back in the 1850s. So, the Canadian side soon became the favoured place for us, until, oh, 'bout the 1890s."

"Not much to look at now," said Angus. "It was a bit wilder then it is now when I was young. But tell me, why do you think it was such a good place for fish?"

"I'll tell you why. It was like this, you see. As long as the rapids flowed freely, the current among the rocks was strong and cold. The whitefish would tail in the fast water and feed upon flies and other good things in the water. And so they grew very fat, but because they had to work hard to hold their place in the strong current, they did not grow soft. They were firm like trout I tell you."

"And so how many might be taken in a day do you think?"

"You know, it must have been many thousands, because I can remember my father telling me that one time those in his own canoe alone hand-netted fifteen hundred fish between the hours of the early morning and mid-afternoon. And these would be between six and seven pounds each. Can you imagine how many people that would feed? If Jesus had been with us he would not have had to bless the loaves and fishes." Leaning Willow grinned and winked at Angus.

Angus listened to the old chief for a couple of hours, gently cross-examining and taking pleasure in what he had to say. Angus was familiar with many of the unhappy details of the treaties and the decline of the fishery, but he was glad to hear about the practicalities and mechanics of how the Indians of old were able to actually take the fish. And he was pleased to be able to assure this venerable one that others would come to hear about these matters.

"My niece Kakayosha is making noise about taking a few more courses here sometime. I'll be sure that she comes to see you. She'll be interested in what you have to say."

"Tell her not to wait too long Angus. Who knows when I go out the eastern door."

"I'll tell her."

"You say she is going to school?"

"Yes - she's interested in a lot of things."

"Is she a good cook?"

"She is. Her mother has taught her well, and I take her fishing when I can."

"You see that black book there on the shelf? Hand it to me will you." Angus reached for the solid but worn old volume and put it beside Leaning Willow. "I want you to give this to your niece. It's Baraga's *Dictionary of Otchipwe*. I would like her to have it. Baraga was a good man, a bit stubborn perhaps, but he did us a great many favours. One of my relatives used to take him around the river when he lived here. He helped save our language" Angus took the old dictionary and flipped through it and then sampled a few references and asked Leaning Willow how he pronounced certain words. He closed the book gently and thanked him.

"There is something you can perhaps answer for me," said Angus.

"Yes?"

"You remember that I was not so old when my father died."

"Yes."

"I was never clear on whether of not my father was *Medéwiwin* or not. Do you know?"

"Yes - he was. Fourth Order, I think. But he withdrew from practice in his last years. He would say to me sometimes: 'Leaning Willow, I want to go back further.

54

Further back.' That is all he would say. That is why I think he left his scroll unfinished. I think you have it maybe?"

"Yes - I have it. I have looked after it, but I do not understand it."

"Good, that is good. Even if you do not understand it too good, it is all part of you. There are many things we will never understand. For example now. Baraga wrote much of the Bible out for us in Ojibway. That is how I am reading the Old Testament right now. I have been reading about the great flood. I even dream about it now. This long ago man Noah, he must have been a trickster like old *Nanibojou*. How could one put all the animals of the world unto a boat and keep them alive without them all tearing each other apart? We have our own stories of the flood. Perhaps everybody was all one, long ago, and the stories got confused in the telling."

iv

Angus Ashabish's pick-up truck rolled into the front yard of Minnie Maywins's Fireweed Reserve cottage just shortly after Kakayosha had returned from Black Pebble Lake for the weekend. Kakayosha was boiling up some tea when his hulking frame appeared in the door way.

"Hi uncle. You're just in time for tea. So how was your visit with Leaning Willow?"

"He is tired. Very tired. But his mind is good and clear. That is good to see in a man of his years." Angus paused and then placed his grip bag on the table and opened it. "And he has sent you a present. Something you will like I think. It will help you with plants and herbs, among other things." Angus handed the book to Kakayosha. She turned it over in her hands gently and then opened it to the title page.

"It says it was first published in 1853. This one was published in 1878. How wonderful. I have never seen anything like this. I'm sure we don't have it in the school library."

"Hard to find. But I told Leaning Willow you were

55

interested in the old ways, so he thought you should have it."

Kakayosha laid it on the table and turned over the yellowed but sturdy pages. "Did I ever meet Leaning Willow, uncle? How shall I thank him?"

"When you were a baby your mother and father took you to see him. He thought your name was a good one. Perhaps you could visit him if you want to thank him. Time sits heavily upon those who are sick and old."

"You said he knew your father well, is that right?"

"Yes. They fished together as young men. He knows much about the old ways. I might have a picture of the two of them together. I think I do."

"I would like to see that if you can find it." Kaka got up and went to the stove and poured some tea for Angus who had taken a seat at the table. He opened the dictionary and read and drank quietly for a few minutes while Kakayosha puttered about the kitchen. Kaka paused and turned to look at Angus from the kitchen sink.

"Uncle, Joanna's been in the bush most of her life, or else with those nuns. Now she's in high school. Do you think she knows the score?" Angus raised his head from the dictionary and lowered his glasses on his nose and peered over the rims at Kakayosha.

"Did you know the score at her age?"

"Are you kidding? I remember when mom was trying to give me a talk on the facts of life. I knew them already."

"Did your mother know that?"

"Not sure."

"Sure she did. We talked plenty about you. You had a real wild streak for awhile. We gave serious thought to renaming you. We thought maybe *Bird in a Cage* might be a better name for you.

"Was I a real pain in the rear?"

"You mean you don't remember? Could have been worse. You still liked to go fishing and you still cooked for everybody without too much fuss. Your mom and me, we figured you'd get through it. But it's always harder to deal with bright young people. You probably know that from your teaching work." Kaka walked over to the corner and picked up the broom and started to work the area around the stove.

"Now where did she put the dustpan this time?"

"Top of the icebox."

"Oh, right." Kaka reached up and grabbed it and then swept up the grunge from the floor and then repeated her efforts around the doorway. Angus went back to the dictionary. Kakayosha then put her hands on top of the broom and leaned on it, looking out the window towards the lake. "Uncle...do you think....mom knew...that I was...you know...getting around a bit?"

"Oh yes...she knew. Asked me to do something about it."

"Really? Oh god!...you don't mean... not by your medicine or anything like that?"

"No. By something better. Just common sense. She asked me to talk to you."

"She did? I don't remember that. Did you talk to me?"

"Yes. You just don't remember when."

"When? What did we talk about?" Kakayosha put the broom back by the door and came over to the table. Her face was flushed and her eyes were large saucers of curiosity.

"We went fishing. She told me to talk to you. But not what to talk to you about. A man got to figure everything out for himself! Thought I would find out what you wanted to talk about first. We went out past the Chair and got some whitefish then we came back and you cooked them up for us. Then I told you both all about salmon season out in B.C. I told you about my days out there. I described the excitement of spawning season out there, when everybody watches those fish come rushing back up stream to spawn, frantic and driven. Figured then I had done my thing for your mom."

"Oh my god, yes. Now I remember. And you told how

many of them then just died right on the spot afterwards. I remember now what you said. 'They all disappeared, just like a lover', you said. I didn't quite understand that, but mom laughed her head off. And then you threw in a lot about grizzly bears lined up along the river, like baseball players taking batting practice. So that's how you talked to me about the birds and the bees is it?" Kaka broke into a broad smile and laughed. "Well, at least you had my attention, but you were probably a little too subtle for me."

"Figured from what your mom said you knew all about the birds and the bees already. Main thing was to keep you busy and give you something to think about."

Kaka picked up the dictionary again and flipped to a few terms which interested her, and then put it down again.

"I think I was lucky, uncle."

"How so?"

"I mean I didn't end up pregnant. God, it would have been so easy. I didn't do anything smart. I mean I may have known, but I didn't want to think about what could happen. I was just so...curious...and wanting someone outside of the family. And there was this guy at school who all the girls were crazy about. And he hit on me and he was really persistent."

"Natural enough. Something we all gotta go through. Its hard when you're young. Hell, its hard when you're old!" Kakayosha stood up and fetched the kettle from the stove and added some water to the tea pot and brought it over to the table.

"Then one day - think it was when I was in grade eleven - I saw Anna Bluesky coming out of the Snakepit. Can you imagine? Under age of course, but Anna always looked about six years older than the rest of us, and she was right out of it."

"Anna Bluesky? She's from Fisher River isn't she?"

"Yes."

"Lots of difficulty there. Lots of old traditional people. Lots of booze. Not much work."

"Well, about a month later she told me at school she

was pregnant, and she was proud as hell. I asked her who the father was, and she said: 'does it matter?' I looked at her and took her hand and sat her down and I told her I thought it did. She looked at me with this blank look, and when I saw that she wasn't going to answer, I felt a chill run down my spine. After that, things were easier for me. I told this guy that I wasn't ready for sex and he lost interest in me real fast. I decided he didn't really like me very much."

"What happened to Anna?"

"Not sure. But she never had the baby, I know that."

"Then you got real serious on us after that. Working at school and making plans for teacher training. That's when your mom *really* start to worry, when you make plans to go off to the Sault for a year."

"I missed her so damn much uncle. And you too. Most of the guys at the college were white, and they were afraid of me. I could tell. I mean they were nice and polite and all, but they didn't want to date me. In a group thing it was fine. That was okay. I didn't want to get involved with anybody then anyway. Nobody insulted me there - that was the good thing, and some of the white girls were really friendly. They took me seriously." Kakayosha had her eyes on the table with her head slightly lowered. Angus put his hand on top of hers and left it there until she raised her eyes to meet his.

"Took me quite awhile to find your aunt Maggie, did you know that?"

"Really? So often I felt I was somehow...outside...even when I was at a party or something."

"I know about that feeling. It was like that when I was in the army."

"I remember something mom said when I was back here for a weekend. She asked me if I had met anybody special, and I said no. Then she said how there was one thing she would never regret and that was waiting for the right man. And how even though she didn't have him that long, she had found the right one. And that she still had me. I never thought of mom that way before, but she told me how happy she was. And I remember how her face shone when she said that. And before I left for the Sault again, I looked at her from my car window, and I remember just how her face was, still shining."

"So you see then how you are both lucky."

"We're both lucky to have you. And I've had two fathers, uncle." Kaka got up and came around behind Angus' chair and put her arms around him and gave him a great hug. "Say, just how did we get talking about all of this anyway?"

"You were worried about Joanna."

"My god, yes. I must have a talk with that young lady."

"You do that."

4

On Bears

i

Two shots pried open the twilight, disturbing the drowsiness of the aftermath of supper hour at Black Pebble Lake. June and Will Bender stopped their incessant puttering about the kitchen and looked out through the window above the dishwasher, listening for more firing.

"That would be Dawson down at the dump, bet you anything," said Austin Thomas, who was sitting at the dining room table with Jack Gifford. Both men drove garbage detail for the park. Austin ground his cigarette butt into an ashtray and then fumbled in his shirt pocket for his pack.

"Yep, that's for shore," said Jack, who seldom said more than that. Like Boisant Bollard, Jack Gifford was another superannuated lumberjack who had come in from the cold and now did seasonal work of various kinds along the east coast.

"Said he'd get that bugger tonight or he wouldn't go home." Austin lit another cigarette. "Imagine that? He *would* stay out there all night too, crazy bastard." Austin walked over to the door, opened it and looked down the side of the

building towards the parking lot. "Must be Dawson alright
- truck's not there." He paused for a moment, listening for
more shots. "Bet he'll be back soon."

Olivia Wilson and Boisant Bollard were on the other
side of the room. She had started to speak in French to
Boisant after dinner one night and persuaded him to sit for
his portrait in charcoal. He was giving her the evening
promised and sat fixed in his chair by a window overlooking
the lake. They said nothing in response to the sound of the
shots. Olivia just kept working on the portrait.

Half a mile off the highway, along an old logging road
north of Black Pebble Lake, David Dawson leaned on the
front of his high-sprung, crew-cab warden truck, rifle at
the level. He had parked at the edge of an abandoned gravel
pit which now served the park as a dump, one without
fences, oddly enough. Piles of garbage-stuffed dark plastic
bags and debris stretched out in haphazard low relief across
this depression, reminiscent of pillboxes in some war zone.
In the dim light he could see what appeared to be two black
bags, almost indistinguishable from the others, slumped at
the far edge of the dump. Charging out of the bush came a
larger third one. Dawson fired again and dropped the "black
mother." She toppled in her tracks, just short of her fallen
cubs. Dawson held his position to see if there was any further
motion, but nothing moved. Silence mantled the dump.
Dawson got into the truck, revved the engine and drove
along the rough skirting road down to the far end of the pit
where the bears lay. He pulled up slowly to gauge how
accurate he had been, got out of the truck, and then pumped
a final shot into each bear's head to make sure the job was
done. After placing the rifle in the rear window rack, he got
back in his vehicle, tramped on the accelerator, and fish-
tailed his way back to the main highway where he turned
and headed south.

At Black Pebble Lake, the after dinner crowd continued to mull over the periodic sounds of rifle fire.

"Yeah - Dawson's been having a field day lately. Loves to shoot bears, he does. Told me once he could do it all day - imagine that - a Game Warden." Austin Thomas took another drag on his cigarette, settled into the easy chair by the front window and, crossing his long thin legs, stared vacantly out over Black Pebble Lake.

"Well I'll tell you, it's nuthin' like it was a few years ago 'round Mashkisibi. Bears all over the goddamn place. They came right into Mashkisibi - remember?" Ollie Finch was looking at Austin, waiting for a response. None came. "Christ, there was one day when there was twenty-four of the buggers rootin' around town. I should remember. I had to drive the truck in for supplies that day." There was a long pause. Austin still seemed far away, but suddenly he twisted his head around. He had been listening, but in slow gear.

"Funny that, isn't it Ollie? You'd think they would have been scared, what with all those people around, and the cars." He looked back out over the lake.

"Hell, it's not so funny really. When you're starvin' you just follow your nose. Just like people really - when you're out of work, you go where the money is, right? Bears go where the food is. Animal don't care much what's in its way, if it's hungry, long as it don't threaten. No sir, an animal don't give a damn where it gets its food."

"Yeah - that makes sense Ollie, that makes sense. What you think Jack?" Austin looked over his shoulder towards the main table.

"Yeah, that's for shore." Jack Gifford was still toying with his pie and coffee.

"Shit," Ollie said, "the bears have been into the dump this year 'cause the berries have been so lousy this summer. No need to go shootin' the buggers - not yet, at any rate. Been a little dry, that's all. No need to go shootin' em. Speakin' of the dump. Anybody ever hear of a goddamn fence?" Ollie shuffled his large frame into the kitchen and tossed the dregs of his coffee into the shining stainless steel sink and then padded over to the communal television. He flicked it on, moved the channels around for a moment, and then flicked it off again. "Nuthin' but bullshit." He rapped his fingers dismissively off the screen. "Well - think I'll head down to my room and do a little reading." He turned and started to walk down the hall and then did an about face. He glowered back into the dining room momentarily. "You know, there's more crap tossed around this district about game numbers. Been here all my life. Everything goes around, not in straight lines, up and down. To hear guys like Dawson tell it, you'd think the animals don't know how to keep their own numbers in check." He then turned and strode down the hall to his room.

"G'night Ollie," Austin yelled after him, and then looked back out over the water. The two loons were plying towards the near shore. "Say Ollie!" he called out.

"Yeah?" Ollie stopped in mid-stride and turned his head.

"I see you have a bottle opener on your belt."

"You noticed that. You just come down here a little later and we'll see if it works or not."

"Some liquid dessert, is that your idea?" Austin said.

"You never know - you just never know." Ollie disappeared into his room, leaving the door slightly ajar.

"Austin?" said Olivia from the far end of the room. "Would you mind taking a look at this. You too, Jack." Boisant did not move, but his eyes shifted to the two men who were getting out of their chairs. His eyes had a steel look of suspicion.

"Now that's a real good likeness young lady. Real good," said Austin.

"Now that's for shore," said Jack Gifford.

"Yes? Thank you. *Maintenant. Boisant, pour vous. Cette à vous.*" Boisant got up slowly and walked over to the easel. He looked at the portrait for a long moment, and then smiled.

"Merci mademoiselle. Merci. Très bien."

Kakayosha Maywins walked up to Burl's open office door and knocked lightly on the side frame.

"You had something you wanted me to see Burl?"

"Hi. Come on in Kaka. Yeah, I was going through some stuff yesterday in one of those boxes in the basement, and I thought you and Angus might like to have a look at something I found there. It's an old anthropological report on Bear Ceremonialism. And since bears are such a hot topic around here most of the time, it makes for good reading. There is something special about this report though. I have an idea Angus's father, your grandfather, had a role to play in it. It was published back in 1914, and there is reference made by the author, Alanson Scudder, to an Andrew Ashabish. If you want to look at it now, just take that little desk over there."

"Thanks so much. I love your office. So many neat things you have spread around it. Whenever I get stuck for topics for a new program, I like to sneak in here to get ideas. Hope you don't mind."

"Not at all. I'm glad you find it a good place. Bring yourself in a drink if you want."

Kakayosha Maywins sat down at the work table and started to go through the slightly yellowed off-print which gave off a slight mildew odour from years in the park basement.

The Eastern Cree are convinced that all living animals have souls or spirits whose good will must be secured or else they will prevent their species from being captured by hunters. Because of this belief they take pains to return the bones of the beaver to running water and prevent them from being devoured by dogs. The heads of ducks and geese, the teeth of the caribou and moose, the claws, chins and skulls of bears, are carefully preserved as talismans and trophies, and mystical paintings are placed on the skins of fur-bearing animals to appease their manes. But the customs concerning the capture and treatment of the bear have become much more elaborated.

There were notes at the back of the article of a more informal nature where the author had reproduced some of the verbatim testimony of his informants. Andrew Ashabish was identified as an Ojibwa fisherman and guide who had travelled much in the Cree country north of his own home country on Lake Superior. Andrew Ashabish:

You see it was a bit like this in older times. If a hunter while in the forest came upon a bear and wanted to kill it, he first had to approach and apologize, and explain to it that nothing but lack of food was causing him to want to kill it now. He would beg the bear not to allow the spirits of other bears to be angry. Usually the hunter would cut off the middle toe and claw of the right front foot and take them back to his campfire. He would sit down by the fire and smokes for some time, not saying anything to others, but wondering who he should ask to go out and dress the carcass. After some time he would give the claw to the person in whom he has confidence, and tells him where the bear is. This person understands what is required and takes a companion out and brings in the bear. The claw is wrapped in cloth, beaded or painted and kept as a memento.

Kaka read how Alanson Scudder then queried Andrew about the ceremonials which followed. Andrew told him that if the bear was being brought in by canoe, all the Indians would crowd the river bank and give out cries of congratulation. When the canoe was beached the young boys would crowd around the bulk covered by a blanket

66

and draw it back to expose the head. The men would then carry it up to the dwelling of the slayer and lay it out like a man. Tobacco was then placed in its mouth, and the hunter and other chief men would present smoke over it. It was as though they were all smoking together. Andrew Ashabish:

Amongst some of the people it might be like this. The head of the bear was first cut off and cooked, and then the men and boys would sit down in a circle about it. A large stone pipe was put beside the head and some tobacco put in the pipe. Then the man who had killed the bear would get up from his place and he would light the pipe and smoke first and then pass the pipe around. Each person could smoke for some time or just take one puff and pass it. After this, the bear's head was passed around and each person attempted to take a bite out of it without touching it with the hands. After that the bear is butchered and the meat given out to the people. Certain parts of the bear's flesh are burnt right then and given to the spirt to eat - this always included a small piece of the heart. The rest of the heart is at once eaten by the slayer in order that he may acquire the cunning and courage of the bear.

Alanson Scudder then asked him if he had ever killed bears. Andrew Ashabish:

A few times, when the people were hungry, but not often. We would go through some of these acts I have described, but perhaps with not so much seriousness as the older people might have done. The bones are important. They are never given away unless the bear feast is served in the lodge of the slayer. At a feast a certain amount is of food is set before each person who is obliged to finish it. If they cannot, it will be wrapped and saved until the person comes back the next night and finishes. Always, no matter what, the bones are carefully cleaned and saved, usually hung up or placed some place high where the dogs will not get at them. The people were not so worried about other wild animals getting them and eating them. That would be alright in the eyes of the Manitous. There was one exception. The skull of the bear was cleaned and dried and painted with vermilion and was then put in a safe place and kept for several moons, after which it was then taken by the slayer and hung up in a tree in the forest.

Then it was asked if these things were still done in the present. Andrew Ashabish:

It is my belief that they are not, although there may be those who do. I think the Moose and Albany Cree do not do this so much. They have forgotten the importance of these things. Some things still live in the memory. I think it is still the custom never to point at a bear, even if alive. If this is done the bear will turn and run away, even if it did not see the offender, for his medicine is strong enough to warn him of danger.

Alanson then asked Andrew about the proper form of address towards the bear:

This is depending on the time and place. If a hunter comes upon a bear in the woods, and must speak to it, he may call it *Kawipate mitcom*, which means black meat or food, and this is the bear's proper name. It will not be offended or frightened. This name may also be used when addressing it as a carcass. When one must speak to it but it is desirable not to let it know that it is being spoken about, you can use the name *Toyochk* or "old porcupine." That way it will not know who is being talked about. When making fun of a bear or joking, you call it "old crooked tail" - or *Wakiuk*! There are other circumstances. It is allowed to call the bear *Muskwa* - the angry one or the wrangler - but only in its absence, unless one wishes to anger it. It must not be called that before the carcass however.

Alanson then asked if hese things were true among others than the Cree? Andrew replied:

I have heard of these things, or similar things among my cousins, the Saulteaux to the west, among my people the Ojibwa, and the Seneca of the south. It is widespread I think.

iii

At mid-morning the next day, Park Superintendent Murdo McFadden was pacing up and down his office, phone in one hand, chewed cigar in the other. His unwiped boots were leaving large patches of mud and water on the utility carpet.

"That moose's ass! That's the tenth mother he's got this month, and then you add in the cubs...just sits out at that goddamn dump and waits...Jesus Christ, if he worked as hard at getting poachers as he does at getting bears, the money we pay him might be worth it. We wouldn't have any poachers around here...What's that?...Yeah, sure I know he's going to get moved soon, but what the hell good does that do for the system? We just give some poor unsuspecting son-uv-a-bitch our headache, unless you put him in the middle of Turkey Point or some place where he can't run amok all the time...Jesus...that would be fitting wouldn't it...Turkey Point!...What's that?...maybe...listen...here is how I see it. The wild west had Buffalo Bill Cody and we have the bloody Rifleman. Is this a goddamn park or isn't it?"

Murdo's large frame heaved about the room like a wrecker's ball searching for a wall to demolish. Warden Jan Polyanski sat in the corner of Murdo's large office, desperately trying to stifle his laughter. Jan took a perverse pleasure in Murdo's periodic tirades against headquarters, and this was a vintage performance. Jan finally stumbled out the door, by-passed the Chief Naturalist's office and fell into Burl's where he propped himself up against a filing cabinet, holding his gut, his face red. Burl was seated at his desk, unavoidably taking in the performance, more with clinical interest than admiration. The bellows from McFadden's office continued to flow across the hall in a steady stream.

"Do you know I had to go and fetch that son-uv-a-bitch out of a mud hole on the Breton Road two weeks ago?...Yeah, you read my report, sure you did, but did you read between the bloody lines?...It's after dark for God's sake, and he's high-balling it down that road, no lights on, after...you guessed it...a bloody bear. 'Didn't want to tip the bear off with my lights,' he said to me. Can you believe that? Wham - right into the goddamn ditch...what?...how often?...well I'll tell you, that's not the first time, oh no, not by a long shot. We have accident reports around here galore...what's that?...no, here's how I see it... next time, the jerk can walk out on his own and he can also pay the bloody bills."

A focused silence had settled over the rest of the office. Some ears were burning red, but others were straining to hear every choice sentence. Burl reached for his pipe and began stoking it.

"What do you make of this one Jan?" Burl asked.

"Lovely - just fuckin' lovely." Jan was grinning from ear to ear, as he plopped into a chair. "This is a telephone conversation to die for. Sometimes I love that man across the hall, bastard that he is."

"Yeah, and at times like this you want to know how to keep that man happy." Burl lit up his pipe and blew smoke towards the open window. The men sat waiting for the storm across the hall to subside.

"Murdo has a pretty good case alright," said Jan. "The guy's trigger-happy. Folks complain at the campsites now and then when bears come around, but a lot of them are the very ones who will stop on a dime by the side of the highway to feed a bear out of their window or keep food around their campsites. Most people, when you actually talk to them, realize they need to give the bears some scope. Dawson's a strange one alright." The men fell silent, waiting, listening.

"I have just one final comment on the guy," Murdo yelled. "For all the money we pay him, he's about as useful as a whole field full of one-legged ass-kickers!" The sound of the phone smashing down on its cradle ricocheted along the walls. Murdo stomped out of his office and headed downstairs to the coffee room, a chain of mumbled curses trailing behind him. The office remained quiet for a solid minute, except for a solitary ring at the switchboard. Austin Thomas's ruddy face suddenly appeared at Burl's door.

"Old Murdo pretty mad this time, eh guys?" Austin pulled out a cigarette. "Wouldn't want to be in Dawson's shoes, not for anything." Austin walked over to the window in Burl's office and spread out his spider-like hands on the sill. "You should'uv been in the dining hall last night. We were listening to Dawson shoot away at the dump. Funny guy, eh?" Austin was looking across the courtyard with very fixed attention. He half-laughed then suddenly stiffened.

"Hey you guys," he whispered, "there's a bear over near the dining hall and Felix Smith has got his rifle. He's over at the corner of the bunkhouse ready to drill it the moment it comes his way. Big bitch, too."

"I think we should keep this very, very quiet for the moment," said Jan. The men quickly walked to the main door where some of the office staff were already standing, looking over towards the bear. They all moved cautiously out onto the steps, taking a careful first look at the hedgerows for any sign of cubs. The bunkhouse where Felix was crouched was about two hundred feet away between the office and the dining hall.

"Think I'll go over there and just make sure the doors are secure," said Jan. Before he could get to the bottom of the steps the shock waves of a rifle shot bounced around the walls of the complex.

"Jesus, he's done it.'"said Burl.

"Lovely - just fuckin' lovely." said Jan. "More terminal animal husbandry."

A loud crashing could be heard in the thicket of spruce to the left of the dining hall. Felix Smith was standing now and he was looking off towards the thicket. Jan came up to him from behind.

"You get her?" asked Jan.

"Jesus H. Kee-ryste! I missed. - How the hell could I miss from twenty feet? And the bitch with her snout right up my muzzle."

Burl and the others walked over towards the dining hall. There was a blood stain on the walkway leading up to the bunk house and a trail of blood than ran across the grass and into the bush where the bear had retreated. The crashing noises had ceased. The bear was long-gone, but hurting. Felix continued to curse himself roundly.

"Shee-it. If I had ever thought I would miss, I never would have fired. If my old man on the Rock hears about this... damn! I hate like hell to say it, but I should have left this to Dawson."

"Good Lord," said Alf Anderson, the Chief Naturalist, "here comes Murdo. A few of you stand over that patch of blood there. I'll head him off and give him a story." Alf Anderson sauntered over towards Murdo who was now walking towards them from the office.

"I was just down in the coffee room. Didn't I hear a gunshot a moment ago? Is that bugger Dawson back here again?"

"You heard a shot alright, but it was Felix. He was just scaring a big black sow back into the bush."

"Is that right - well - is she gone?"

"Yeah... headed off into the bush again, pretty fast."

"Thank God some of my staff can use their heads." He stopped and looked over towards Felix and the others. "Felix!" he shouted.

"Yeah Murdo?"

"Good work...but you better hang around for awhile and make sure she doesn't come back. But whatever you do, don't shoot her. I've got enough trouble with Double-Barrel Dawson."

"Shoot her? Wouldn't think of it Murdo." Felix slung his rifle over his shoulder and started walking towards the bush where the bear had fled into the forest.

"Good man, that Smith," Murdo said to Alf. "Those Newfies are crazy as a bag of hammers sometimes, but good workers."

Felix Smith was now prowling about the fringes of the bush to make sure the bear was not lying wounded just inside the canopy. He found the trail of blood and then projected the route she had probably taken.

"All right my mother, my daughter, my little black bitch, you won't get away from me a second time, by the crucifix." Felix plunged into the wall of green.

iv

When the crew-cab from Black Pebble Lake rolled up to the door of Minnie Maywins's cabin on the Fireweed Reserve, she and Kakayosha were in the midst of dinner preparations and Angus was in the backyard setting out a jar of garter snakes around the garden. Kakayosha had promised some of her closer park companions that she would have them over for a traditional meal. Joanna led Burl, Kirsti and Olivia into the cabin where they piled an assortment of condiments and fresh bush produce on the old pine dining room table.

"Hello everyone," shouted Minnie. "Just make yourselves comfortable. Angus is out in the garden with some serpents. He's always trying to put a hex on my household here."

"Now Mom, you know Uncle Angus just practises good medicine."

"That's what he always *tells* us daughter. But how do

73

we *know* for sure. I been around that scoundrel longer than you have. He got a thing for medicine ever since he's a kid."

"Well - he told me the garter snakes would be good for your garden. Anyway, I want you to meet some folks here, including the lady who helped hire me." Kakayosha introduced her mother to Burl and Kirsti. Joanna and Olivia Wilson were already in the backyard seeing what Angus was up to.

"Mom, it was Burl here who loaned me that old report on bear ceremonies and which Uncle Angus is reading. You know, the one which mentions grandfather."

"Don't know if I should thank you or not young man. Got enough nonsense going around in Angus's head with snakes and things. Not sure we need to get him going on bears." Minnie Maywins spoke through a gapped-tooth smile which neutralized the seriousness of her words.

"Don't know if you have to worry about bears too much Mrs. Maywins. Lot of trigger-happy people around these days. Bears may not last much longer."

"That's right," said Kirsti. "We got a few people around the area who practise their own brand of bear ceremonialism. All you need is a gun."

"Thought all you folks were supposed to be protecting the wildlife," said Minnie.

"That's what we thought too Mrs. Maywins," said Kirsti.

"Everybody around here call me Minnie."

The fire had burned low in the pit in the back garden. Burl and Kirsti and Olivia had left an hour ago for Black Pebble Lake. Joanna was inside watching television. Minnie Maywins got up saying it was time for her to turn in.

"I hate to leave with the stars so bright. But I really am tired. Now Angus - don't you be filling this child's head with too much nonsense - *Midéwiwin* or otherwise." Angus and Kakayosha looked at her and smiled but did not respond, but as she turned to leave they tilted their heads slightly and winked at each other. Minnie disappeared into the slim band of darkness which separated her from the warmth of her cabin.

"Oh my, oh my! I'm such a burden to your momma sometimes." Angus got up and stirred up the coals a little.

"That was interesting about what Burl talked about up around the dams wasn't it? That Victor is sure sharp. He said maybe Victor would be able to hire me next summer if I want. That would be so neat." Kakayosha looked at her Uncle for confirmation.

"Yes. Yes - it is good. There are many reasons to go back, each person has his reason. I will work with them if they wish. There are things and places back in the bush there which may be found. Your grandfather spent much time back in that country you know."

"Did mom have a naming ceremony, uncle?"

"She did. She never tell you about that?"

"No. I think she thinks a lot of the old ways are not very useful."

"She may be right. What do you think?"

"There were probably reasons for doing things in the old days - even if a lot of things have changed now." Kakayosha held her hands out towards the revitalized coals for a few seconds.

"Yes - I think you are right. There were reasons. Good reasons."

"So - what was mom's name?"

" She was called 'The Berry-Picker'. Pretty good, don't you think.?"

"Quite excellent. Right on!"

"There is something else though which might explain your momma's attitude."

"And?"

"Where to start? I guess as far back as I can. You know from that old report that Burl gave you, that your grandfather was very interested in these things. And I became interested when I was young. So he and I talked a lot. I talked to him and my grandfather, your great-grandfather. By the way, did you know that in some old accounts, we used to always refer to snakes as 'grandfather'? I'll tell your mother that tomorrow." Angus paused and he and Kakayosha started to giggle a bit. "Anyway, where was I? Oh, yeah, so I talk with the old ones about these things. And the more you start to talk, the more you start to have new questions. I remember in the war, I got to know a Greek, and after he gets to know me a bit, he says I sound like Socrates. He gave me a little book about Plato and Socrates. Sure enough, this guy Socrates really knew how to ask good questions. Your grandfather didn't have too much time for the women folk in this regard. He was a real traditionalist - or thought he was - he wasn't mean or anything to the women - but I think your momma thought I got all the attention. And she would be right. That's why I like your mother so much. She never held it against me. But she likes to kid me a lot about it. I kid her back sometimes. Tell her she's not shaman material because she sleeps too well."

"Mom doesn't have any trouble sleeping, that's for sure. But what do you mean by that?"

"Dreams. Shamans are dreamers in the night. They don't sleep so well. That's why they remember so much. Dreams are the road into the great past of all the people. Some of the whites think this is so also. After the war a man at the Sault put a book in my hand by a man named Jung. He had a similar idea about dreams, just like us Indians."

"And what's so important about dreams? Do they teach about medicine?"

"No - not as a rule. Not about the details at least. One learns about medicine and herbs by keeping one's eyes open and watching what is going on about you. Just as you do with the children at school when you take them out for a walk. And all those who go through the naming ceremony in the old way, are sort of going through training for watching. This is the first great dream encounter - but more than that - for here one tries for a real vision brought on by hunger and want. For most people, once is enough. But it is that first early encounter which helps give the name."

"What's the main connection with plants and herbs?"

"It's like this. For those who are serious about entering into the order of the *Midéwiwin*, it is important to consider the healing power of plants and herbs. One must eventually show one's healing power with the sick and also show oneself capable of absorbing powerful medicine shot at you by another. Even if you do not want to become a member of the order, knowing about these things is valuable. It allows you to do good to others."

"I think there are a lot of stories about bad medicine as well uncle."

"Yes - that's so. In fact, when I came back from the war there was a lot of trouble down on the Manitoulin. An Indian went to trial and there was talk of bearwalking."

"Bearwalking? I've heard old people talk of that, but what is it?"

"Complicated. But it's a bit like the idea of something taking over your body. Some other living thing. And it creates all kinds of mischief. Very Catholic too. They always talking about exorcism. Something like that. Our old people sometimes talked about people 'getting-the-fire.'"

"So do you believe in such things?"

"No. It's all head stuff. A lot of nonsense."

"So what about the dreams then," Kakayosha asked.

"Well, this is where the dreams can come in. For the Shaman is a person who likes to inspect everything. He looks for meanings everywhere. He looks for things which may give him advantage over his neighbour or over evil forces. The dream-shaman is quite a bit like a modern businessman really, full of superstitions about the world and how it works. In fact, some of our best shamans have understood this. In the older times they would do pretty well in the money or trade sense for giving treatment or interpreting dreams. And some would draw the right conclusion about the world being a changed place since the coming of the whites. I know of one who was alive not so long ago who was not only a Fourth order *Medéwiwin*, but also an elder in the Presbyterian Church. He saw no conflict there. Not sure how the Presbyterian Church viewed it. They may not have known." Angus chuckled for a moment and drew out of his vest pocket the pipe that he usually had on his boat. "This man was just being careful under the circumstances. A foot in both camps so to speak - just in case the whites had more power in spiritual matters as well as economic matters."

"Does that mean a shaman has no real convictions then?"

"You ask a lot of hard questions, niece. Let me fill up my pipe so I can think of some new lies to tell you."

"Uncle Angus, you really are so bad aren't you!" Kakayosha laughed and flicked some sand at him with the toe of her moccasin. She reached for a small log and threw it on the coals and they both watched and listened as the flames slowly developed around it. Angus finally spoke.

"Each person has to try and understand the meaning of his dreams or his name. Try and recognize the gifts which are his and his alone. Some call it looking for 'manitou personal'. That's what my father called it. So it may look like a *Midéwiwin* is too practical or does not have convictions, but I see it as the gift to adjust during your life to new things. Not being too rigid. Recognize a possibility when it comes along. Just like a businessman. If you can see the wisdom of following two different paths at the same time, then that is okay. A *Midéwiwin* of white light can do that all the time."

"And of black light?"

"Then all kinds of mischief is possible. But each person is responsible for what they do. You remember all those stories about medieval knights in armour on horses, fighting for the princess? Just like that. There are lots of Indian stories about similar things. Duels between medicine men. Not always certain what they are fighting about though. Very private."

"Kind of like at the Snake Pit?" Kaka smiled mischievously.

"Hope you not hangin' around the Snake Pit niece. Now that's a place of very bad medicine."

"No - not to worry uncle. But I hear lots from Wolfie and others about it."

"Wolfie Wisdom? Oh yes. He's an okay boy - just a bit confused. Probably never had a proper naming ceremony."

" It's not that complicated uncle, really. Wolfie is just nuts."

"Could be that too. But all that aside- you're a teacher. You got to be respectable."

"Uncle, didn't you hear me?"

"Yes, yes, of course." Angus paused to take a puff on his pipe. "I'm just being fatherly. Part of my job. Anyway, what was I saying. Yes - the Indian way is a private way. That's why these scrolls I've been showing you are so tricky. I can tell you something of ones I created or have been given by others who created them, or were taught by those who had some connection with them. But if you and I went into the bush tomorrow and stumbled upon a cache of scrolls, we might not be able to make any sense of them. They were made personal, and they need a living connection between the person who created it and those who come after. That's why the whites were always trying to give us an alphabet. So we could pass things on with greater certainty. They were right in a way. But if you believe in the wisdom of privacy, then our way is more certain. It's like we have as many codes as there are people, and only one person can let another person into his world, into his experience. It's all in the symbols you see. There might be a symbol which is a bear, but maybe it has some other meaning in the scroll. There is always a private story being told of some kind."

"Uncle, tell me more about dreams. What do you do with them? Is it alright for me to ask about these things? You don't feel about women the way grandfather did do you?"

"No No. Quite the contrary. Lot of powerful women in

79

the Shaman order. Lots of powerful medicine women have come and gone. My father did not want to recognize that." Kaka leaned down and picked a ball of knitting out of the basket at her feet.

"I'm knitting you a new sweater for the fall fishing season. It has three whitefish on the front."

"That is sure to bring me good luck. Thank you. I will wear it proudly. I could use a new sweater." The sound of Kaka's knitting needles blended in with the hissing of the coals.

"It's not easy to find people to talk about these things. When I go to the Pool Side Bar or the Bear Pit people want to talk about other things. Sports, girl friends, boy friends, skidders, booze, all kinds of dumb stuff. You know?" Kaka kept her eyes on her work.

"That's not to worry about. That's what life mostly is. Dumb stuff. Making a living. Finding our other half. It was like that even in the war. Funny that. You would think when you are about to meet your maker at any moment, you might get serious. But that is not how it was. People actually relaxed and tried to get on with each other, people who in everyday life might have been at each other's throats. At the best and worst of times, people like to talk about regular, predictable things."

"That's why I like to go into Burl's office and talk with him. He's interested in all these things. Sometimes I think he knows more about our people than we do ourselves."

"Yes. He and I talk sometimes. I don't mind talking with him about our people. He shows respect."

"Did the war change you a lot uncle?"

"Changed me a lot. Opened my eyes to a lot of things."

"Such as?"

"To the dark side. Of medicine I mean." Kaka looked at him steadily but did not speak. She then turned back to her knitting."You see, there were people dying on a regular basis. And some did not know how to let go or know if they should keep fighting to live. They could not see the way out.

Sometimes a man who was nearly finished would ask me to confirm for him that he was nearly finished. If you told him he could still make it, sometimes he would fight. But if you did the honest thing and asked him to make his peace, it usually went much better. He relaxed and slid back into the greater universe - out the eastern door."

"The eastern door?"

"You remember the second scroll I gave you several months ago? That so-called *creation scroll* ?"

"Yes - I do. But I found it very puzzling."

"You were supposed to find it puzzling. That was a copy of old Loonfoot's scroll. It was created first way back, maybe in the 1840s. But you remember the rectangle? That is the material world here before us. It has openings in it to the four main winds. We enter the world from the west - from we know not where - and we leave it to the east - to where we know not either. It is all one big open space you see? And we are here only temporarily - to look around a bit. From what I have seen, I would have to say it is a good place to leave at some point. Who knows what is ahead out the eastern door. It may be much better. That is why when a man was badly wounded, I tried to get him to relax and just accept the opening of the eastern door. We leave not knowing where we are going, just as we enter, not knowing where we have been."

"And on Loonfoot's rectangle, the exits to the north and south uncle. What are they?"

"Perhaps the one to the north wind is for those who leave early in life. They are all frozen potential. And to the south. That is for the evil ones. Those who must burn. This is much like the Catholic vision. I sometimes think maybe some of what is on those scolls is Catholic."

"I will look at that scroll some more. It's all very cosmic isn't it?"

"Very cosmic. Yes. Don't study it so much that you forget to finish my sweater." Angus rose to his feet and stretched in anticipation of sleep.

"Good night Uncle. Good medicine dreams." Kakayosha returned to her work and knitted long into the night until the coals were very low.

5

At the Dam

i

Burl Manion and Felix Smith had been running timber reserve lines around lakes in the lands below the new dam for the better part of a month, making use of the fine autumn weather and the good sight lines provided during "the moon of falling leaves". In their wake, red strips of plastic fluttered from the trees. These were the markers they had placed to give notice to next winter's lumberjacks that they could not cut any closer to the shorelines. They were running the lines six hundred feet in from the high-water mark of rivers and lakes. Felix walked a course about three hundred feet from the shoreline, keeping the water body in view, and Burl walked a parallel line another three hundred feet further inland. By late afternoon they came out at the point where the Mashkisibi River, a mere skeleton of its former self, flowed into Point Lake. From here Burl and Felix could just see the top of the great dam which straddled the river about half a mile above them to the northeast, and where they had parked their truck early that morning.

"I'm beat," said Felix. "That was some tough slogging today." The two men slumped down simultaneously upon some open ground by the river and passed the canteen back and forth.

"It would've helped if we hadn't got all screwed up and walked around the same lake three times," Burl said. They both laughed, but not too hard.

"Talk about a couple of hosers," said Felix. "God, it's no wonder it's so easy to get lost in the bush. Here we are with a shoreline right in view, two compasses, two brains, and we still keep going to the left. I'll never be a landlubber."

"I don't think I'll forget the look on your face when - after the third time - we came out at Pigeon Creek and saw our lines waving at us in the face again - almost jeering at us."

"Shee-it," said Felix, "if I was already drunk, I might understand, but I just can't believe it. Look - not a bloody word to Murdo - or we'll never hear the end of it."

"I think this is probably our secret." Burl turned his head and looked off to the northwest. On a high ridge on the opposite side of the river, he could see something protruding above the trees. "Is that the old fire tower over there Felix?"

"Sure as hell is. Haven't been up there, but I flew over it once with Murdo. Goes back to the thirties, he told me."

"Feel like climbing up there my friend?"

"The pleasure will be all yours buddy. I'm going to stretch out here for awhile and catch what's left of those rays."

"Okay. If you don't mind, think I'll take a quick look up there. If you get tired waiting for me, I'll meet you back at the head pond. If you want to go back to Black Pebble, just leave a note on Rims' truck that I want to go in with him."

"Okee-dokee. But I expect I'll be doin' zees here when you come back and you'll have to roust me out." Burl got up and walked along the river for about sixty yards until he found a spot to cross over by a series of flat, slime-covered stepping stones.

"Hey Felix," yelled Burl from the far side, "if you hear that siren go up at the head-pond you better move your butt pretty fast!"

84

"I bequeath all my possesions to you," Felix bellowed from his supine position. "They're all owned by the bank."

Burl disappeared behind a thick grove of spruce bordering the sun-baked river banks at a place where a small creek entered. The going was not difficult on the grassy border which flanked the little stream. He followed its course up a slight grade to the foot of a rise where the terrain opened up into mixed forest. Burl soon came upon the grown-over scars of an old service road which he followed up, crossing a series of switchbacks, until he reached the old tower. A hawk announced its awareness of Burl's presence by rising out of a magnificent old pine which had somehow survived the years of the local timber trade. Burl watched the hawk fly off in the direction of the new dam. Half a minute later he could still see it. The bird descended and perched on top of the high metal superstructure over the flood gates.

Burl looked up at the the fire tower before him. Times had changed. It was of a design not seen for many years. Despite periodic campaigns to demolish and replace the old wooden towers, Burl knew from the office files that this one had escaped for reasons of local sentiment. It showed signs of periodic maintenance and repair. The tower was solid enough looking, and the quality of the original craftsmanship was still quite evident. A fence with a locked gate surrounded it with "No Entry" signs placed prominently on all sides. Burl fumbled for his master gate-lock key and in short order he was at the base of the old structure. A metal ladder had replaced the original wooden one. Burl shook the ladder to test it, and then, cautiously began to climb, checking the fastenings as he went. They were all sound. A hundred rungs later, Burl pushed up the trap door and stuck his head up into the small turret of a cabin, paused, and then pulled himself up the final distance. He walked around the perimeter and then pulled in and up several of the wooden shutters which could be fastened to hooks in the ceiling.

A scented warm breeze blew through the mustiness. Burl leaned on the sill and looked out over the vastness before him. It was indeed the "moon of the falling leaves" or "St. Martin's summer" as the old priest had called it. Stretched out before him was an endless mottled carpet of subdued reds, golds and greens. Thick bands of almost dark blue ran through this radiant blanket, marking the courses where rivers and streams made their way through spruce groves and bogs. These curving lines of ink were studded with ghostly white spires: poplars and birch freshly stripped of their foliage.

Burl pulled back from the edge and turned his attention to the turret. The sturdy pine flooring showed a few glitters of light through small holes but had, on the whole, survived the ravages of wind and rain quite well. The roof was intact and without rot. Bits of graffiti, mainly of the carved-in sort, graced the walls, names of past employees along with some bad limericks. Furniture-wise, all that remained was a small built-in pine desk, dusty and covered with cobwebs. He pulled out the side drawers. Empty. A wide drawer with a key hole was in the centre. Burl tugged on it gently. Locked. He looked underneath to see how solid the frames were. With some judicious prying and applied pressure the drawer was made to pop its runners and Burl slowly eased it out. There were some yellowed sheets of lined paper and a small notebook in a dark leather binding. On the cover of the notebook, in gold letters, was inscribed:

Towerman's Book. 1935. Sault Ste. Marie District.
Department of Lands and Forests
Ontario

Burl flipped through the volume, noting the regular weather record entries and short paragraphs about daily occurrences. On the first page there was a signature block which read: 'Scotty Meadows'. Written inside the back inside cover was something quite different.

I do not want you when your feet
with buoyant footsteps tread on air,
when you can smile at all you meet
and banish care.
But when days are long and cold
and cruel seems the ways of men,
when you are wearied, sad and old,
come then.

Burl closed the book, put it on the desk, and walked over to another of the shutters, opened it and secured it above. The short poem lingered in his head and he thought of how he had himself grown old, of how he had even been born old perhaps, and how he had missed, with his own compliance, too many of the joys of youth. She should be here with me right now, he thought. She should be here to share this moment.

"Damn it!" Burl blurted, as if addressing the old journal on the desk. "What have I done? I don't know the first thing to do with her." The old question surfaced again. "No - shit - what can a shrink ask me that I haven't asked myself a thousand times."

Far below, he could see Felix stretched out in the lengthening shadows, seemingly oblivious to the world. Burl walked back to the desk, picked up the book and closed the drawer. After sealing the shutters, he went over to the trap door, tucked the notebook in the front of his pants, and began his descent.

When he regained the far side of the river again, he found Felix quite asleep on the rocks, his head cradled by his bush jacket. Burl dripped some water on his forehead to rouse him.

"S'funny - I was having this dream that somebody was pouring beer on my head."

"Sorry." Burl broke out some raisins and nuts which they shared and then they hiked back to the head pond parking lot. Felix climbed into the truck and turned over the engine.

"So if I see Murdo, I'll just tell him you've gone native once and for all, shall I?"

"Yeah - you do that Felix. Tell him I'm organizing all the bears of Northern Ontario to descend on Black Pebble Lake and take vengeance on Dawson."

"That could get you a promotion real fast," said Felix.

"Take care then. I'm going to walk up top of the dam and see if I can spot those guys."

ii

Standing at the base of the high metal head-frame works where the hawk had landed earlier, Burl looked down and along the curve of the dam, its mass softened by the early October sunset, so that the sloping concrete slabs took on some of the colour tones of the surrounding billows of Precambrian rock. This great concrete structure had that about it, Burl pondered: it had been successfully fused with the local landscape. The old protestant hymn, with its invocation to "build your house on a strong foundation" had, he thought, been followed here to the letter. The effort before him was worthy of comparison with a few of the well-designed summer homes which dotted the north shores of Huron and Superior. Some, in fact, had been designed by Frank Lloyd Wright for the elite of Chicago, and he had contoured them to the Shield rock in a similar way. Behind both types of architecture lay considerations of power.

The boreal world had quickly come to rest in the pre-twilight. Down below, at the base of the dam, where only a few months ago hydro crews had been conspicuous, the trucks were gone; the men were gone; the river was gone. Behind the dam, the head pond was imperceptibly filling out the contours of a the new Lake Mashkisibi. Only one real concession to the old order had been made: stingy trickles of water still issued forth from the main sluice gates which protruded out from either side of the dam like the paws of some latter-day Sphinx. It was as though two persistent sores afflicted the circulatory system of this great megalithic creature. From the top of the tower of the main headworks, two lights stared down like the bulging eyes of a Preying Mantis, inspecting the two wounds in its own flesh.

Burl turned around and walked over to the other guard rail and looked out over this new lake. A year from now, the land he was looking at upriver would be swamped by at least another two feet of water for a distance of some eighteen miles and for a width of three. Two loons swept in overhead from the south and carried out over the head-pond and then landed. The pair dove and surfaced thirty yards further away. Having contemplated their prospects, they called once and then flew off again to the east in search of a real lake. Burl reached into his jacket for a cellophane package of cashews, ripped it open and crossed his arms on the railing. He looked at the package more closely:

Les Noix C'est Notre Affaire
Our Business is Nuts

Far around on the road which ran along the eastern shore of the head pond, Burl could see Angus's pick-up parked around Mile One, its windshield reflecting the low sunlight like a beacon.

iii

"I'll tell you something, Victor. I know an old man at the Sault who has been dreaming about the great flood of the Bible. He thinks Noah has something in common with *Nanibojou*."

"Really? I wouldn't have thought of that. How so?"

"Thinks Noah is some kind of *trickster* for being able to save all those animals on one boat." He looked at Victor who scratched his chin for a moment. "I think he might have it wrong. Floods keep coming and I think the *trickster* might be the Minister in charge of Hydro."

Victor and Angus had passed the last seven hours probing the country around the perimeter of the head pond as part of Project Rising Water. They had been selective in their survey, examining places where ancient hunters and gatherers might have chosen to stay or work. Victor was anxious that Angus tell him as much as he could about this stretch of the Mashkisibi in the little time remaining before the head pond started to spread its fingers out where standing water had not been since the retreat of the last glaciers several thousand years ago. The two men were sitting on a large slab of rock taking a snack and looking out over the sterile stretch of water where they could see a lot of deadheads breaking the surface. A gleaming white gull was perched on one of these protruding tree trunks close to the shore and it shone like silver in the oblique light.

"You know," said Angus "I think if we're going to bring this lake back to something living, we have to get ourselves a midwife."

"A midwife?"

"Yes - I think so. Maybe we should go and visit some people on the Manitoulin first. Folks I know down that way."

"Now why's that, Angus?"

"Well, the way I see it - after drowning the land like this - its having a tough time recovering. It wants to get born again, but it doesn't know exactly how or why. So it holds back and just suffers. And you see, on Manitoulin, they had a solution for this kind of thing." Victor's expression now encouraged Angus to continue. "It went something like this. They tell a story on Manitoulin Island about midwives. When a women was in a prolonged labour and there didn't seem to be any hope for the child, somebody went and got some owl's eyes which had been dried. These were then given to the woman who was told to swallow them. The child, on seeing them, would be frightened and would make vigorous attempts to escape." Victor looked at Angus for a moment and then they both burst out laughing. "So you see, we've been walking around the rim of this artificial lake here for hours and nothing seems quite right. It just hasn't adjusted properly. Its even dangerous to go motor-boating here because of the way those darned deadheads keep floating up to the surface. And then there's that release of mercury from the shore line which probably doesn't do any good for the fish either. So the forestry guys tell me. Lousy fishing so far. Seems to me we need some owl's eyes to send down to the bottom, see what happens."

"Well, you may be right. But those would have to be mighty big owl's eyes." Victor and Angus chuckled again and then fell into a reflective silence that Victor eventually broke.

"If you still have some time to spend around here over the next few days, we should think about walking further back into the bush and see if we can find some old river banks on higher ground. Maybe that way we can at least give re-birth to some of the people who lived around here a long time ago." Victor pointed towards a ridge about a half mile to the southwest. "Over there might be a good place to start."

"Okay. I got time for that. Let's do that tomorrow." Angus was thinking about scrolls. "If nothing else, might see some grouse or moose." Angus pulled out his tobacco pouch and tossed a liberal amount into the head-pond. "This lake needs all the help it can get."

6

Dreams of Commerce, New and Old

i

Burl Manion settled into a window seat. He could just barely see Kirsti Kallela and her uncle walking over towards their truck in the parking lot. They vanished around a corner. Family duty had not weighed upon him too heavily in the past, but this particular year he would rather have stayed here in Thunder Bay for Christmas. Kirsti's family was everything his was not. "Thank goodness," he whispered to the window pane. Burl smiled, recalling the way two days ago they had all six piled into her Uncle Paavi's sauna, and how he was not sure how to behave; and of how delighted Uncle Paavi was on realizing that his guest was not just all seriousness and ideas, but could also hold his Scotch. Kirsti had plied him with coffee the next morning, trying to conceal his hangover from Uncle Paavi, all part of the status game, she had told him.

This early morning flight from Thunder Bay to Toronto was not full and, by a stroke of good luck, the aisle seat next to him remained unoccupied. A watered down muzak version of *Silent Night* filtered into the cabin. Absurd, he thought. He was recalling his trip to Winnipeg in late

October where he had gone to work in the archives. Most of the larger department stores, it seemed to him, were busy promoting Christmas sales even before Halloween was over.

Burl lowered the flip-down tray in front of him and rooted through his briefcase for his note paper and the *Group of Seven* card he had bought to send to Kakayosha Maywins. The card was large format, displaying a reproduction of J.E.H. Macdonald's *The Tangled Garden*. Looking at the brilliant colours and composition of the print, he thought about how, since her arrival at Black Pebble Lake, Kakayosha had conquered hearts and minds, including his. She would come into his office and go through his book case, looking for what she called "interesting stuff." On one occasion she had grilled him about the significance of a particularly dry and chart-laden report on the archaeology of a rock shelter at Charleston Lake, some distance north of Kingston. "Is this stuff important?" she asked. She borrowed it and read it all. "What did you think about it?" he had asked her when she brought it back. "Mind-blowing" she had replied. Kakayosha then told him she was going to develop a new children's programme about rock shelters. She did, and later expanded it into a larger series called *Early Peoples Playing House*. Burl took out his pen and started to write.

> Dear Kaka:
> Here I am on the "big bird of non-everlasting flight."
> Thank goodness for that at least! I wanted to get this card
> to you before I left, but - you know what happens! This is
> a painting done somewhere in Toronto - I know of gardens
> much like this. And since you asked me last month where
> I am from, this will give you one idea. Lake Ontario of
> course, is not nearly as grand as Lake Superior.

He raised his eyes from the notepaper and looked out the window. The early morning sky was cold and clear. The views over Lake Superior might well be outstanding today.

"Sir? We're going to have a short delay this morning.

Shouldn't be too long."

"Yes - alright, thanks." It was starting already. Complications. He looked back at the notepaper and tried to focus his attention on the incident in November. Why had she so abruptly walked out of his office that day? Or maybe she hadn't. Maybe he really was just imagining it. Then there was the fact that when he had mentioned it to Kirsti, she had not replied. Instead, she had offered to play a new piece for him. No clues there. Burl turned back to his letter and resumed writing.

The last time I saw you, I did not give you a very good answer as to where I am from, but now I am in a better position to do so, since I am right in the middle of flying there for Christmas. You will be surprised to learn that I was born at an old Indian village called "Tai-ai-ay-gon." This was an Iroquois or Huron village along the route of the "old Toronto Carrying Place" as it was called back in the seventeenth century. Some think the people there were Senecas - Iroquois from present New York State. Anyway, this was the route along the Humber River from Lake Ontario up to Lake Simcoe. Father Hennepin and La Salle both mentioned the spot in their writings. By the early eighteenth century, the Iroquois were gone, but some of your people were coming down here from the north shore of Lake Huron, from Mississagi River Mouth. The situation around here now is all a bit like the situation at the Sault and Thunder Bay in some ways, only on a larger scale. Here the Europeans eventually built their best homes right on top of the old Indian village. When I was a kid I used to deliver the Globe and Mail to the home of the man who owned the Toronto Maple Leafs. His place was right smack in the middle of old Tai-ai-ay-gon, along with a lot of other fancy houses. When you go down to the canal at the Sault, it is a bit like that, except there it's mainly industrial structures that are on top of where the Indian village used to be.

Burl paused and looked up at the stewardess who was preparing people for take-off.

"Coffee when we're in the air sir?"

"Yes. Please." Burl turned back to his table and read over the letter as it stood so far and realized he was delivering a lecture rather than being chatty. On the other hand, he thought, she will probably like it. He decided to carry on.

When you asked me 'where I am from' however, I cannot help but think that the honest answer would be to say - from my childhood - for when I walk along the banks of the Humber now, with its well appointed paths, and flood control devices, and regularly cut meadows, I do not see these things as much as I see what I remember from childhood. I see the place as it was before the flood, before the flood of 1954 that is. Then it was still a bit wild and rural and overgrown. The pockets of forest were thicker, and in the mornings, pheasants would come up in numbers to strut about our back lawn which opened up onto the valley below. There were ponds in the woods where young zoologists could capture tad poles in jars, and there were thickets where young adventurers could build forts and get poison ivy if not careful. There were patches of damp ground where skunk cabbage and bulrushes still could grow and real snow still fell on the dirt road into the valley. Sleds and toboggans would be thick on that slope on a January afternoon. The dirt road led down to only a few farm houses scattered here and there across the flats, ones owned by Chinese market gardeners, who still drove horses and wagons. There were sunsets of fire which seemed to last forever and raccoons, lots of raccoons, nightly prowling in hope of garbage neglected. Some years there were scarlet tanagers or indigo buntings, but always robins and starlings and squirrels. And on Sundays, there was church. There was always church.

How much does she really want to hear of all this? he asked himself. Burl looked at his reflection in the window portal. He then put the letter aside, leaned his head back, and closed his eyes. Sleep did not come. He thought about the quiet pocket of upper class real estate which encased the former Tai-ai-ay-gon, the way it jutted out into the valley with such a fine command of the river below. This would indeed have been a strategic place in those ancient times. The tip of this neighbourhood - the Point - was known to his childhood comrades as *Dead Man's Bluff*, and one of the rites of passage for any boy worthy of *belonging* was to scale that bluff, climb over the chain link fence into the backyard of the current resident nabob, and scoot out onto the street by whatever route one might choose. He wrote again.

When I was young there was great wealth in the "new" Tai-ai-ay-gon. There was a community club with a tennis court and lawn bowling greens. The tennis court was converted into a natural skating rink every winter. There was a club house where I was taken - very reluctantly - to kindergarten. And beneath a grove of trees at the east end of the tennis courts, there is a granite boulder with a plaque, placed there by the local historic sites board, to honour the vanished Iroquoians of Tai-ai-ay-gon. The plaque is tarnished and not very visible to the public, but I always read it when I walk by that way. And often when I was young, I wondered: "where did they go,where are they now?" I determined to go north. And I subsequently met you and many others, and I am grateful for that. It is possible that someone else from Tai-ai-ay-gon, back in the 1600s, met somebody from your area, for purposes of trade, or - who knows? - perhaps for marriage.

Burl put the pen into his breast pocket and read over the last sentence a number of times. Yes - that is fair enough an observation he thought. The Sault was definitely a place where tribes from far and wide converged during the spring sugar-making festivals. Marriages were arranged.

The stewardess was distributing fresh coffee again. Burl took another cup and looked through his window. Intense blue met the horizon which stretched above Lake Nipigon to the north. *Lake Nipigon.* Just the name brought back another memory: that of his first exposure to *Paddle to the Sea* at the old library on Bloor Street, a warm and friendly building where his parents regularly took him as a child. How unlike the church that old library was. What else should he tell her?

> There are many other aspects of the Humber of course. There were many mills along this stretch back in the last century and there are still some signs of them. Hurricane Hazel changed the course and nature of the river when I was young - when I was still delivering newspapers. Even the ruins of the abandoned mills almost disappeared as a result - but not quite. They had been built with floods in mind after all. Water was the miller's business in many ways. The Chinese market gardens disappeared after the flood and were built over by new houses, often bought by refugees from the last war in Europe. The old dirt road into the valley was paved over, the old swamps dried up, the forests were thinned out - and the pheasants disappeared. Commerce grew. You have probably heard people call Toronto "Hog Town" and perhaps it was destined to be so. Way back in 1632, a Franciscan named Sagard recorded a definition for the word "Toronto" in his Huron Dictionary. He rendered it as "much or plenty, applied to persons or things."

Burl put the letter aside again and eased the seat back a few notches. Out the window portal he could see that the aircraft was approaching Sault Ste. Marie from along the southern edge of Lake Superior. He could see the sharp outline of Whitefish Bay directly below him. Halfway up the eastern shore, he could see the dark patch of Flat Island, and much farther up, he could make out the rugged outline of *The Island of Ghosts* - Mashkisibi Island - guarding the corner of the lake like some medieval castle. He leaned back and drifted off into a light sleep.

"Sir? - Sir?" Burl opened his eyes. "Sir - would you mind doing up your seat belt please. We're coming into a little bit of turbulence." Burl pulled himself up and could see through fast scudding thin cloud cover the last of the north shore of Lake Huron. Manitoulin Island was directly below. The airplane veered slightly to the south and followed a course straight down the middle of the Bruce Peninsula. He placed the unfinished letter on the tray again and considered where he should go with the finale.

> I really should close here, before you doze off. Just a last word on some other remnants around the vicinity here. The clan usually gets together, along with a big bunch of suits and other corporate types, at a well known restaurant on the edge of Tai-ai-ay-gon, all for a first class pre-Christmas pork-out. I can normally do without this sort of thing, but the food and the atmosphere is good. So when you and your family are doing moose, we will probably be doing turkey or venison. When I get back to God's country, I will have a few historic photos of the Humber Valley to show you and Angus. I'm rather looking forward to walking around old "Tai-ai-ay-gon" once again.

Burl added a few pleasantries of the season and folded the sheets into the card, and then sealed it for mailing at the Toronto Airport.

Around five on a mid-December Saturday afternoon, the extended Manion clan began arriving at Dalton's Mill. The cobble stone walkways inside and out were an obstacle to some of the elderly; but to a person, this was the only place to be at this time of the year. The reigning matriarch, great aunt Hilda, was fond of saying on these occasions "There is really nothing at all vulgar about this place, is there dear." It was customary for a great retinue of accountants, clients, lawyers and other associates of the family, to attend this function as well, which was not anything so democratic as an office party, but more of a *mixer* followed by a sit-down dinner. There were no formal invitations extended: one merely *arrived* as a matter of tradition.

The gothic shell of the old Dalton Mill stood exhausted on a flat at the edge of the river, obscured by tall dark oaks and willows punctuated by the occasional birch tree. Sumach bushes had encroached upon the building which had the forlorn appearance of some bombed out factory or apartment block from the First World War. The sandstone walls were thick and helped to explain its long survival. Time and flood had worked to leave it ever higher and drier, for the course of the river was now a good forty yards away, another partial effect of the 1954 storm. Burl Manion stood looking up at it as did the woman at his side. They were at the end of the little trail which led down to the river and to the plaque which explained the significance of Dalton's Mills.

"What a contrast with Mashkisibi No.1" Burl said to his sister Willa, who had never been in Northern Ontario.

"Mashkisibi No. 1?" Willa arched her eyebrows.

"I've brought along some slides to show you. It's the big new power dam on the Mashkisibi River which has been thrown up over the last few years. You'll love the colour. I took them in the fall."

They walked back up to the main building and into the

Grist Room and went over to the cash bar. A distant cousin, one soon to be married, swooped over and dragged Willa off to a corner. Burl looked about and took in the details of the spacious room. It had high ceilings, broken by the criss-crossing of large dark beams of oak. The stone and half-timbered walls displayed the heads of several species of game animal, most not seen for many years in southern Ontario. A large open fire place was in full operation at the far end. Scotch in hand, Burl walked over towards the large window which looked out over the ruins of Dalton's Mill. From this height, one gained a much improved view of the upper portions. He detected a presence behind him, pre-announced by the smell of cigar smoke.

"Well Burl, down from the north woods eh? Good to see ya. Good to see ya. Put'er there my boy."

"How are you Mr. Bentley? Good to see you again." Burl said, responding with as firm a handshake as he could muster. He had learned that businessmen like Jim Bentley practised their handshakes. Anything smacking of less-than-firm was enough to induce discreet eyebrow raising. Bentley's grip was firm but fleshy, a reflection of his general build and demeanour, the expanded body having gradually given way under the relentless pressures accruing from too many noon hour deals. His choice of a loud checkered vest merely reinforced his overall physical dilemma. The smile was infectious however, and because he was what he seemed, Burl did not entirely dislike him. Within limits, he thought, Bentley knew how to enjoy life.

"Fine my boy, just fine." Bentley smiled the universal smile of the perpetual salesman. "You're lookin' mighty fit, I must say. Look - I was talkin' just last week with some of my friends in the mining industry about the kind of things you've been doing over the last few years - you know - wildlife management - culture - preservation - those kinds-a-things? - and I was tellin' them that we need more of that sorta thing - not just in the schools and in government and the foundations - but everywhere - ya know? I mean the more the merrier, right? - and you see, my point is, if it got to be the kinda thing to do in industry, well - there's no telling where it might lead."

"We're talking value-added in a social sense here are we Mr. Bently," said Burl, who was trying not to think too much about the fact that Jim Bentley described nature and culture in the same way that one might describe commodities on the Toronto Stock Exchange.

"Call me Jim. We've known each other too long. Yeah - 'social value-added' - that's a good way to put it. Now you just think of all the jobs, Burl. Just the thing for those young people enlisted in the arts and sciences in universities and the community colleges. Its those areas where we're feeling the pinch a bit, you know - as some of the traditional areas of employment dry up. They're dried up for the moment at least, although I'm damn sure they are going to open up again. Dammit - this country has just got too much going for it for them not to - know what I mean? Now - I've always believed in this culture-thing - never had much time for it myself - too busy out on the stump selling construction vehicles - but that's another story - anyway, I still believe in it, and I believe in this country - even *Kweebec*. Those people are good people down there, just get a bit confused sometimes, that's all. But we need these cultural things and environmental things, and some people to keep the rest of us remembering just what it all costs, especially the young." Bentley punched out the last words with a reinforcing finger which he jabbed, staccato-like, into Burl's chest. "Cause you see, they're the ones who don't remember the depression or the war or anything like that." Jim Bentley paused to take a sip of his rye and ginger. The plausibility of what he was saying to one side, Burl felt that he better understood the key to Bentley's success as a salesman. He was good, he had to concede.

"Wildlife is very important Burl. No doubt about it. It takes time to master knowledge of it doesn't it? - someone like yourself fer instance - I know that it takes time to learn what you know - and I respect it - yes sir! And if there aren't some people like you around - to - to sort of keep the prod in - well - more than one country has gone down the drain, right? Didn't one of those old French philosophers say something like that?"

"Rousseau I think, Jim."

"Right - Rousseau - I remember that now. Can't stump *you* can I." Jim Bentley turned away for a moment and went into a brief paroxysm of coughing. Burl quickly looked about the room to see what other familiar faces were about. Jim Bently turned back to him, slightly flushed.

"No sir. Business is just not enough in this country now, especially in view of the way the unions are taking us straight towards anarchy."

"Anarchy?" Burl looked at Jim intently.

"Yes my boy, anarchy - and with a big 'A'. My God, just lookit the strikes we've had in this country just the last half year. How many work-days are we gonna lose over this riff-raff at the head of some of the unions? Now - I'm all for unions - don't get me wrong - but we can't afford some of these kinda demands. Inflation is too high as it is. And it's not like the old days - not like the depression when people didn't have a pot to piss in - everybody is eating pretty well these days." Bentley took another sip then turned away to clear his throat again, his voice starting to suffer from some rasp. He coughed a few more times before turning back to Burl.

"Well, what do you think Burl, am I right or not?" The cigar in hand was poised, the drink in hand was poised.

"I think you have probably hit it pretty well on the head, Jim."

"Sure I have. And I don't tell you how to go about your business, do I? Takes years to learn what you know, and I respect that. Now, what I was really going to tell you Burl, when I started all this, is that these friends of mine in the mining industry, they've been thinking it would be good for them to do some sprucing up of their corporate image, you know what I mean? That is, I mean business knows when to change and get its act together - when to adjust. How should I say that better? Business knows when change is in the air. You know that anyway. You study change, right? So, with all this talk about environment and softer amenities and cutting down on growth - all good things in their own way - good things - it occurred to some of us that up in those areas where the mines are, and where the reserves are, there is a lot to be learned in a preliminary kind of way. You know - inventory - assessments - impact studies - that kind of thing. And rather than wait for all kinds of pressure to come down from above, we all think that it would be good to take on the responsibility voluntarily. Prove to everybody that we take responsibility as well as profits. Prove that we are *good corporate citizens* - isn't that the phrase these days?" Burl, while taking a slow sip of his Scotch, marked these words, stressed so carefully by Jim Bentley.

"Now Burl, here's the pitch, - are you ready for this? - there just might be room for a wildlife-biologist-type in all of this, someone with a bit of savvy and experience in the field - someone like you and I might both know - right? - someone who could take a good look at the holdings of a given company and come up with some short-term and long-term suggestions. 'Policy alternatives' to use the language of you government boys. It could all work into some good 'p-r' experience and perhaps be a good stepping stone for someone if need be."

"Sort of natural history with a 'p-r' slant, is that it?" Burl asked.

"Yes, yes, that's it exactly. Something to convince the public that we've done our homework on both sides, and are not just a bunch of rip-off artists." Bentley's speech and manner struck Burl as being totally without guile.

"I'll have to give all of this some thought, Jim. You certainly raise some interesting questions." Burl polished off his drink and wondered if somewhere along the line he had actually missed his calling, and if he should not be in the diplomatic corps.

"Good, good. You keep this in mind and mention it next time I see you - which I hope will be long before next Christmas."

"Look - I see someone over there I should say hello to - its been a real pleasure chatting with you again."

"Me too Burl, me too. You look after yourself. Give me a call sometime."

"Thanks - I'll do that." Burl shook Jim Bentley's hand again, with even greater firmness than before.

"Oh, and Burl - those squaws leaving you alone up there?" He put his cigar in his mouth while giving the ritual wink.

Burl hesitated in mid-turn, looked at Jim, paused, and then winked back. Jim Bentley shuffled off to the cash bar. Burl looked into his glass at the remnant ice-cubes and rotated them for a few seconds in a slow circular motion. There was something familiar about all of this. It was near the surface of his memory. It was something Chinese. He walked over to the cash bar after Jim Bentley had joined a small group of the relatives. Yes, it was Chinese. It was something in the *Recollections* of the Grand Court Historian of the Han Dynasty, Su-Ma-Ch'ien. That venerable ancient had described the perils accompanying writing official history for the Emperor. Apparently the penalty reserved for court historians who drew the wrong conclusions was castration.

iii

On the shores of Smoky Lake, some sixty miles northwest of Mashkisibi, members of the local Indian Band had been hacking out a clearing in the black spruce on the strength of a winter works programme grant and a hope. Before Christmas, Burl had been volunteered by Murdo McFadden to go up there the following January to assess the wildlife conditions of the area and prepare a short report for the

Chief. Dugah Beshue's cousin, Warren, had mentioned to his schoolmate Neenaby, that his uncle was trying to develop a lodge in the bush as an economic project for some of the Band members. Neenaby had mentioned it to his teacher in Mashkisibi, and the teacher had told Murdo, who then approached Burl.

"That's quite a loop of conversation," Burl said to Murdo. "Talk about a bush telegraph."

"Those are good people up in there, Burl. As a rule the Chief up there doesn't put up with any bullshit. Been in there a few times in fire season. It's a place where fifteen and seventeen year-olds lie about their age in order to get on with the fire crews. I look the other way if I can."

When Burl arrived at the shore of Smoky Lake he could see a small group of people gathered in a clearing nestled in the curve of a small peninsula . A few others were standing around a fire by the shore, and a third group was out on the ice working a number of fishing holes. Burl walked towards the first. As he approached he could see that some were dressed in bush jackets and some in city overcoats. Everybody had paused and had fixed their eyes on him.

"Burl Manion from Black Pebble Lake," he introduced himself.

A thickset man in a plaid bush jacket walked over to him, his hand slowly extending. He wore no gloves and had a round and radiant harvest-moon face.

"Ben Bigsky," he replied. "Murdo told me you would be coming in. Welcome to Black Spruce Lodge - lodge, *I hope* - that is!" Ben Bigsky introduced Burl around to the assembled, made up of engineering consultants, government economic development officers, the band lawyer and a professor of recreation studies.

"This is where we bin thinking 'bout puttin' the lodge," said Ben Bigsky. "There are a couple of other sites under consideration, but just 'bout everyone, includin' me, thinks this is the best. Glad to get your views. Mostly we been talkin' about all the ways that money can get screwed up in putting a project like this together. Our lawyer, Jack Holtmann here, is gettin' a pretty good handle on things however, and I think we're going to be in business by summer."

"Glad to hear that," said Burl. "Murdo told me a bit about what you'd like me to do."

"Expect you don't want to hear too much about what the rest of us have been going on about here for the last couple hours. We need the wildlife information though, in case we can do something in that direction. We know enough about the fishing here. Its damn good - and no bloody pulp mills to bugger up the water. But not so sure about the animals. We might try and sponsor some hunting here if it looks any good."

"In that case, I'll do some bushwhacking over the next couple of days. I've wanted to get in to see a bit of this area for some time anyway."

"Good, good, but first, let's all go down to the fire. The boys have been fixing us some fish for lunch."

Burl fell in with the Chief and the professor, a woman named Marcia McCallum. She was tall, slim and never quite at rest. She emitted energy as though the fate of the world hung on the events of the next five minutes. Her attire was practical and revealed the scars of many past treks in the bush.

"What's your interest here, Marcia?" Burl asked for openers.

"My department has worked something out with Ben by way of a special training program for tourist guides. Now - I am sure you must be wondering - 'what do the locals here have to learn about hunting and fishing from us?' The answer is - 'nothing' of course - but the program is very business-oriented and aimed at customer service." Ben Bigsky broke into the conversation.

"My son Ben is over at the fire, along with his cousin, Warren," he said. "Both in the first year of the course." Ben then ushered his guests onto the beach.

"Hey you guys, this here is Burl Manion. Going to do some scouting out of the wildlife around here. If he wants anything or any help you give him a hand, okay?" The young men nodded and then started to dish out the freshly caught whitefish along with wildrice and carrots.

Everyone settled down on the smooth logs which had been arranged around the fire. Looking down the shoreline, Burl thought he could pick out the peak of a small cabin about half a mile down the lake. A slight whiff of smoke was curling out of the roof. Ben Bigsky Jr. then sat down next to him, meal in hand.

"Looks like you folks have some company on this lake," Burl said to Ben Jr.

"Belongs to my old great aunt, lady from our reserve, Josie Fisherwoman. She been up here for quite a number of years. That's how we learn about this place, from her. She not like the reserve anymore, ever since her husband die. She tough though, and teach us lots of things, and look after the young girls too, when they start to change and stuff. Anything you want to know about herbs and roots, she can tell you."

"How does she get by when there's nobody else here?" asked Burl.

"She just does. But we leave lots of fish and vegetables for her when we leave, and we pile up the wood in the autumn so she always have good wood supply. My dad tried to give her a two-way radio system, but she didn't want it."

"So have you and Warren been out in the bush around here much?" asked Burl.

"Some, but not too much lately. Mostly working around the lake when we here."

"If you guys want to go out on survey, let me know. This is darn good food by the way."

Burl went out on his own for the remainder of the afternoon. Returning along the shoreline where Josie Fisherwoman had her cabin, he gave it a wide berth, not wishing to intrude. Standing in a thicket of Jack Pine he took out his German-made World War II field glasses. These had been a gift to him from Albrecht Boeker, the German war vet and baker in Mashkisibi. He trained them on the cabin. The place was small but cozy looking, with well chinked log walls. There were distinct signs of what was probably a garden facing off the south wall. He could see three fencerows, and between them, stakes here and there raised their heads above the snow. Placed at the centre of this garden there was an unusual scarecrow-like creature. There was something familiar about it, but Burl could not quite place it.

That evening Warren and Ben Jr. told Burl they were anxious to do some bushwhacking with him and so they decided that next day they would do a broad sweep of the area with each man walking at about 100 yards from the other. They would record any signs of wildlife they saw and notice the way in which branches had been browsed by moose or deer. The land north of Smoky Lake gradually rose towards higher, windswept ground where the snow was not quite so deep and was crusted over. After a day of steady hiking, they returned by a course to the south of the lake bringing them back past Josie Fisherwoman's cabin once again.

"We go in and say hello, make sure she's okay," said Ben Jr.

As they approached the cabin the door swung open before Ben had even knocked. A slim, elderly woman, dressed in bright calicos of many colours and leaning on a cane, beckoned them to come in. She had a wide smile and asked them what had taken them so long. Tea and biscuits were already set out on the table. Warren introduced Burl Manion to her and then explained what they had been up to and where they had been.

"So young man, you've seen a bit of our country around here. What do you make of it?" Josie Fisherwoman was looking at Burl.

"Quite a few moose and deer. Lots of rabbit. Looks like

some pretty good fires have swept through the area north of here over the years. Pretty good berries I imagine."

"Do you like rabbit stew?" Josie was still looking at Burl.

"You bet. One of my favourites."

"Good, good. Ben - when you fellows get back - tell your father to bring everyone up here tonight and we'll have stew. And we can talk about this here lake as well."

"So you catch rabbits now and then Josie?" asked Burl.

"Even old lady like me can catch rabbits around here", she said. "Some of my ancients were called by the old traders 'the people of the hare'. That was a good name for them around here."

"Perhaps the lodge should serve rabbit stew to the guests" said Warren. Josie was looking out the window over the lake and seemed lost for a moment. She then turned back to her guests.

"Maybe Warren. Maybe you have a good idea there," she finally said. "Many years ago my father told me about his father. He used to work now and then for a survey man from the east named Sinclair. He gave me something this man Sinclair wrote later, and he said much of it was based on what his father had told him. Would you like to see that?" The young men all nodded affirmative.

Josie told Ben Jr. to pour more tea and then she hobbled over to a small shelf where she kept a few personal items, including a bible in the Ojibwa language. The cabin was remarkable for its sparse economy. The chairs and couches were comfortable and well-padded, there was a kitchen table, a pine stand with a record player, a few cabinets, some throw rugs, a fireplace and a stove. There was no television set. Three well cured bear hides were stretched upon the walls and there was a large cabinet with glass doors containing a great assortment of small jars, each one labelled. Josie returned to the kitchen table with a folder from which she drew an off-print, dated 1867, and set it before Burl, and asked him to read it aloud. Burl looked it over and then started.

As the hare lives upon the various kinds of small brush that is to be found growing up in the track of great fires that sweep over the country, hence brush is the staple food product of the country, manufactured and prepared by the hare, in the way of putting flesh on itself; and in order to have plenty of small brush food for the hare, the Indians set fire to the brush from time to time which sweeps over an extent equal to a township or county at times. Then in seven or eight years, this will make what is called good "rabbit lands" after it grows so thick that a man cannot make his way through it without using both hands to push the brush aside.

"You know, I can really believe this", said Burl. "There were a few places today where I ended up walking up some stream beds and the undergrowth was really thick. And sure enough, I saw plenty of rabbit in those parts."

Josie Fisherwoman turned to Warren and Ben Jr. "Now tell me you two, are you going to work with the Chief in this lodge business?"

"I'm in for sure," piped up Warren. "I couldn't spend enough time around here."

"And you, Ben?" she asked.

"Not sure, Auntie. Not really sure. Lot of things getting into my head from school and I just haven't figured it all out - 'course I'll help my Dad anytime he wants while things are getting started - but long-term, not sure." Josie got up and fetched a few more biscuits from the stove and added a little more water to the metal tea pot.

"Did I ever tell you how things were still done when I was a girl?" She brought the tea pot and biscuits over to the table. She did not wait for an answer. "The young men and women were sent out at certain times for a vision quest. That was important in getting a name too. Expect you never went on one of those did you, Ben?"

"Can't say I ever remember anything like that, Auntie." Ben picked up another biscuit and so did Warren.

"There is a point of land about a mile up the lake here where it used to be done lots. Little tent be put up and young person sent there to spend time until vision comes. Not s'pposed to eat anything, but sometimes parents pack a little food and tell them if they really have to, to go ahead, have some. But best visions come without food. An old woman like me would tell the young person before they go out there - 'go without food, that you may learn what to do with your life' - sometimes it work, sometimes not."

That evening, Chief Ben Bigsky led his delegation of visitors to Josie Fisherwoman's for the meal of rabbit stew. On the way over to her cabin, Warren Beshue conferred briefly with Marcia McCallum, and then walked over to Ben Bigsky and urged him to consider this as a business expense, that it was market research, which could then be written off, and that Josie could be reimbursed for the service provided. Chief Ben looked at him hard for a moment.

"Nephew - you been smokin' too much *Kinikinik* or something? - thought we were just going up to Josie's for a nice social time?"

Before the meal began, Ben Bigsky asked if anyone had seen Ben Jr.

"Not to worry Ben," Josie Fisherwoman replied. "The boy is down the lake aways, on *personal* business. Told me he probably not be back for a day or so."

Ben Bigsky looked hard at Josie for a moment, and then turned back to his guests. He knew Josie had more information than she was telling, but he also knew better than to ask.

7

Mashkisibi Evenings

i

A double line of moderately-lubricated underachievers formed up, gauntlet-like, in front of the open motel room door. Wolfie Wisdom's brother, Willy, was mounted precariously on a Harley-Davidson, and was revving it up with great ceremony. He suddenly gunned it straight into the large double bed room. "Parteeeeeee!" he bellowed as he made his triumphal entry to the cheers and clapping of the crowd. The owner had long ago learned that it was better to join them than fight them. He knew who was who, and later he would bill whichever one of them was the most gainfully employed. Based on past experience, they would collectively pay, with a little extra thrown in for his trouble. Burl Manion had been watching from the other side of the street. He shook his head knowingly and moved on towards his favourite retreat at the Falcon Crest Hotel.

There were only three patrons in the Pool Side Bar. Burl ordered a Scotch-on-the-rocks. On the other side of the hotel was the more popular Bear Pit Room, a cavernous place with its large dance floor. It was already jammed and moving to the sounds of *Frig* - a new group from Duluth which had taken the young of the town by storm. Burl sloshed his Scotch around in his glass, staring at it as if waiting for some significant residue to suddenly settle out. On the far side of the room the bar-maid was chatting with a couple who were draped over each other, obviously in a sort of love. A shadow moved across Burl's table. He did not turn to acknowledge the person who slipped quietly into the chair on his left.

"So you ask me to the pub, and then ignore me. So that's how it is eh? - okay, okay - I'll get over it." Burl kept looking straight ahead over to the other side of the pool.

"Do I know you?" he asked in a detached tone.

"No - I'm just a flooze, looking for a free drink."

"Sure flooze. What will it be?"

"I'll have whatever you're drinking."

"Do you really want water?"

"Fallen on tough times, have we?"

Burl caught the barmaid's eye and flashed a "V" sign.

"So what's the matter? Feeling lonely tonight or something? Everybody else is over on the other side dancing up a storm." Kirsti Kallela put her arm through Burl's and leaned her head on his shoulder.

"Noise is what I call it - and you know I'm not much for crowds. But what's your excuse?"

"Well - I just thought I would go on the prowl, and see if there was anything more interesting in here. And I was right - there was - although he's a bit jaded."

"I'm glad you have that Finnish trait of liking Scotch!" Burl teased. "Its no wonder you're so popular at the Finnish Club in Thunder Bay."

"There are *many* real old world gentleman over there, I will have you know - many anxious for my favours. I shall run off with one of them one of these days, and look after him for ever. And I will inherit all his buried money. Then you will be sorry you didn't look after me better." Two Scotches arrived at the table.

"Cheers!" Kirsti clinked her glass with Burl's.

"Buried money? I think we can drink to that then."

"Meanie. You'll pay for that." She frowned at him, but her look was mischievous. "So - before we get too snapped up - are you going to take me dancing in the Bear Pit?"

"Naturally," Burl said, "but first you have to tell me some more about your grandfather and his connection with the utopians of Northern Michigan. Your Uncle Paavi didn't get to tell me everything that morning on the way to the airport."

"I can tell you a bit, but not a whole lot. You'll just have to come back for another visit and get it from him first hand. Uncle Paavi's very funny when he talks about it. My grandfather worked in the Hancock area in the mines - that's where my dad and uncle were born. They all moved to Fort William later. But Uncle Paavi told me he remembers meeting this man back in the 1920s - a member of some kind of weird organization called the *Hiawatha Villagers* or something like that."

"And this is where Harvey Booze comes into it?" asked Burl.

"Yes - this guy Harvey Booze had been a part of it - *Harvey Booze* - isn't that a neat name? Especially for a preacher."

"A preacher?" Burl raised his eyebrows.

"Yes - or evangelist, or something. They were all tied up with socialism and populism and radical money theories. Uncle Paavi has this old book by a man named Mills which they were all very big on. I think its called *The Product Sharing Village* or something, written in the 1890s I believe. Uncle Paavi sometimes takes his copy down to the Finnish Club to show his friends. They all like to sit around down there over pancakes and compare notes on the best form of government. Most of us Finns up here are all communists and radicals and co-operators you see."

"Would that include free love?" Burl slid his hand into Kirsti's. She grinned at him.

"That's only known to us Finns." She squeezed his hand.

"So why else are you all commies?"

"I think it probably has a lot to do with the first Finns who crossed the pond. They were all poor. Many had lost their farms and were out of sorts with the authorities, including the church. But these utopians in Michigan were not Finns, they were more English types from around Manistique. But their ideas really interested the immigrant Finns over there. Actually, *any* alternatives to government interested them. That's why my Uncle Paavi has that book."

"Well, all I can say is, *Harvey Booze* is a heck of a name for a radical socialist land reformer of religious persuasion." Burl raised his glass to Kirsti. "Here's to Harvey Booze."

"Shall we dance now? I told you your story." They made a move to leave the Pool Side Bar just as Wolfie Wisdom came in to set up his sound equipment.

"Hey - you corn-holers really know how to hurt a guy. I come in and you start to leave."

"We'll be back, Wolfie - just going to the dance floor for awhile." Kirsti waved to him.

"Nuthin' but amateurs over there - nothin' but amateurs, I'm warning you." Wolfie looked at them, his mouth slightly twisted, his eyes already glazed. Then he grinned his infectious endearing grin. "Alright - guess you have to see and hear and prove to yourself that they're nuthin' but rinky-dink imitators. Hey - you guys come back later. You're good people, man. Damn good people."

Kirsti and Burl moved arm in arm down the dim, timeworn hallway which led to the Bear Pit Lounge. They peered into the great cavern, straining to see over the bulk of Freddy the Bouncer whose presence was passive but mildly threatening to any not familiar with his good nature. In the swirling smoky light Burl finally picked out the unmistakable facial silhouette of Felix Smith. He was seated at the head of a large table, apparently the temporary headquarters of Black Pebble Lake Park. They slid their way through the throng and up behind the table and eased into the overlapping circles of conversation from a standing room only position. Uncharacteristically, Olivia Wilson was among those at the table, and even more unusual, she had an escort. Kirsti tugged Burl with her over towards the couple. Olivia introduced her young man as Karl Zimmerman. When the next slow dance started to flow out of the speakers, Karl led Olivia authoritatively out onto the floor where he turned her hesitant movements into something more confident.

Kirsti turned to Burl."Well?"

"I dance only in my mind really - not in my heart."

"Precisely," she replied. "But I'm going to change all that. Just you wait."

Kirsti and Burl moved toward the crowded dance floor where motion was more valued than form. They entered into the swaying and gyrating spirit of the Bear Pit Lounge and were swallowed up by the strobes and by the mounting rhythms of *Frig*. Burl Manion had a knack for turning fast dances into slow ones. Kirsti was hanging around his neck when *Frig* shifted down from moderate rock to a mellow version of *Misty*. They pulled a little closer and when it ended Burl guided Kirsti over to an empty table for two.

"That was nice," Kirsti said. "I could have gone on like that forever. I like slow dances."

"Shall I get you a beer? Ours are over at the other table." Burl made a motion to get up.

"No. Not right now. You get one if you like."

"I'll just look at you instead." Burl had his back to the dance floor. Kirsti was looking over his shoulders checking out the crowd.

"You know something? Victor is brilliant, but he's not very social is he." Kirsti made a statement more than asked a question. "He hardly ever comes here with the gang. Do you think he doesn't really like us very much?" Burl did not reply for a moment. Kirsti turned towards him as though to prod him into a reply.

"I think he has his priorities. He's like a lot of archaeologists. Drawn to endless discussions about artifact-types and their meaning. Also to Irish music, beer and women who like to be dominated."

"Wow! Say again! Where did that come from?"

"Just long exposure. Have I over-generalized?"

"I don't know, but I thought you two were pretty good friends. That sounded a little harsh."

"Wasn't meant to be. Just accurate. Perhaps I should rephrase. We certainly get on well, and work together well. I think we respect each other. But friends? That's a special category. I don't think I would ever confide in him on important things. Not the way I would with you for example. Friendship is one of those rare things that just seems to happen now and then. Do you agree?"

"Perhaps - yes - probably."

"Well - you tell me. Do you have many friends?"

"No. Not too many. You. Uncle Paavi. An old girl friend from college."

"You really mean that?"

"Yes." Their eyes met and neither looked away from the other.

"So, you can't have too much problem with what I'm saying then. I'm sure Victor feels the same way about me. We're just not *close* in any emotional way except for work-related things. I don't know much about his private life really, although I hear a few things."

"Like he keeps a scorecard?" Kirsti kept her eyes on Burl's.

"A scorecard?" Burl looked at her, eyebrows raised slightly.

"Yes."

"We're not talking about hockey, are we."

"No. Not about hockey."

"I wouldn't know about that."

"I thought men talked."

"Some men talk. But I would probably be the last person he would discuss that with. I'm about as unlocker room as they get." Burl looked past her over towards the table of the Mashkisibi crowd.

"Yes. I know. I like that. Its very sexy." Burl looked back at her and then he rolled his eyes towards the ceiling, fluttering his eyelids.

"He's never come onto me. Not really."

"Kirsti - do I really want to know about this?"

"Just thought I'd mention it. So then, what's all this about him dominating women?"

"You're very curious about this aren't you. That's what I hear. He's rough on women. Also he's one of those who goes through personality changes when he drinks. Maybe that's why he avoids this place. You would have to give him credit if that's the case, don't you think?"

"True. You always look for the good in people. I like that."

"I'm just not a really good scuzz source. You should probably bounce this off some of the other women in the office. They track these things constantly. Women talk don't they?"

"Some women talk."

"*Touché*," said Burl. Kirsti laughed and poked him in the ribs. Karl Zimmerman and Olivia Wilson swirled by their table and Olivia waved at Kirsti and Kirsti waved back.

"But what if I raised it with somebody in the office who was *on* his scorecard? That could be really embarrassing."

"Depends on why you're asking. It *might* be embarrassing, but since you're getting all involved in soap-opera stuff here anyway, its a bit late to be thinking of proprieties. If you *did* ask someone who was on his scorecard, you would probably know soon enough. Misery loves company. I mean if you asked someone about it they would probably assume you had got burned yourself."

"I think maybe I *won't* ask around about this. You can be my confidential source. Besides, what if Victor ever found out I was asking?"

"Yes - he might assume you were feeling neglected," Burl said. Kirsti started to giggle.

"So tell me one more thing. Does he have a sense of humour."

"Not a real deep-down, side-splitting, rapier-like sense of humour. Nothing like mine, that is to say. His laughter is measured more at the expense of someone or something. And if he's had one too many, he doesn't laugh at all. You probably don't want to be around him in that situation."

"You mean he gets violent?"

"I mean he gets violent - so I've heard - but *only* heard."

"Anything else I should know?"

"I don't think he goes around stabbing people in the night. He just has more focused things to do with his time as a rule. He's ambitious and has a lot of things on the go. Project Rising Water is just one of the things on his plate. He goes drinking one-on-one with the local member of the legislature sometimes, and any other higher-up bureaucrats he can find. Spends most winters in Peru on some important digs. He's going somewhere, professionally. He's well connected."

"You don't mind me asking you about all these things do you?"

"Yes."

"Jealous?"

"Yes."

"Good." Kirsti turned her head and watched Olivia moving through her private world of discovery. "Shall we join the others again. I see a few spots at the big table."

They shuffled their way along the edge of the dance floor and sat down next to Felix Smith who was next to his wife, Rita. Felix was in his usual animated state.

"Now I tell you my friends, this might be one strange evening before she's all over," said Felix, beer in hand. "Sure as Rita and I come from St. Jones-Within, I look over dair and who do I see but Rory O'Flanigan. Now what in de name of Mudder Superior is that son-uv-a-bitch doing here and not at de Snake Pit?" Kirsti leaned over to Burl and whispered to him how she thought that after a few drinks,

Felix's Newfoundland accent always seemed to take on added vitality. Warden Jan Polyanski looked over in the direction where Felix had nodded.

"Damned if I know Felix," said Jan. "Don't think any of us *wanta* know do we?" Jan said.

"Now ladies, I know dis askin' quite a bit," said Felix, "but if that boogger comes over here and asks you to dance, we men will be obliged if you does it. Odderwise, he gonna come after one of us. Now, the only good ting I can say about him is that I never heard of him beatin' up on any women, so I think you'd be alright."

Joanna Beardy looked over in the direction of Rory. "He kinda cute looking. I'm not afraid of him. He ask me to dance, it'll be okay." Jan Polyanski looked at her until her eyes met his.

"Joanna - you bin suckin' on too many of those bottles your daddy collects."

The band started up again and the floor filled, but Burl and Kirsti stayed at the table to hold it for the others.

"Do you know that guy?" Kirsti asked.

"Who? - Rory? - no - not really. Been introduced, but expect he wouldn't even recognize me, which is fine by me if I understand Felix correctly."

"I've heard from a few people that he can be really bad news alright."

"He sure looks like he works in the mine. Those are real muscles he's got. I met him in the Snake Pit when I was there with Wolfie. Not sure what possessed me to go there at all. Wolfie got him laughing so much though, that I don't think he was thinking much about picking a fight with anybody. Still, Wolfie told me, without being too obvious about it, to make sure I did him a favour or two. Wolfie's not *totally* oblivious to reality. So I gave Rory the last half of Wolfie's pack of cigarettes when he asked for a smoke."

"That was clever. You did them both a favour then." Kirsti laughed.

They turned their faces from each other and looked

out at the seething mass of dancers. Through the opaque smoke-mist the crowd resembled the rolling waves of Lake Superior in a storm. Crest rose upon crest until overwhelmed, all were dragged under into a peaceful oblivion.

"Wonder if he's married or ever was?" Kirsti asked in a slightly puzzled tone.

"Who? Wolfie?"

"No silly! - Rory O'Flanigan."

"Don't know. Might do him good, if he isn't. But then again..."

"What?"

"Did you ever hear what they say in Italy about marriage?" asked Burl.

"Bet they say a lot of things in Italy about marriage - especially the Pope."

"Well - some wry observer said that marriage is like a besieged city. Everybody who is inside wants out - and everybody who is outside, wants in."

"You trying to give me a hint or something?" Kirsti poked him in the side.

"Hell no! If I were to marry, it would have to be someone like you."

"Thanks - I think."

"But just consider - can you imagine, if that applied to a man like Rory? Supposing he got in, and then wanted out. I think he would probably figure a way, and the way he chose might not necessarily be any too pleasant."

Kirsti's eyes scanned the room, trying to spot Rory. The music died and the lights brightened a little. She could see him sitting at a table by the wall with two other men, his eyes fixed on a jovial fellow halfway across the room who was holding forth like an entertainer, keeping the rest of his party in steady laughter. Rory was not smiling.

The Black Pebble table filled up again. Burl nudged Kirsti gently and pointed to a tall figure who had appeared at the side entrance to the dance floor where he had started talking with the bouncer. It was all six and a half feet of Rex Mathews, one of the local constables, although he was out of uniform. Burl and Kirsti could see the two men look momentarily in the direction of Rory O'Flanigan. Rex Mathews then moved over to the bar where he ordered a drink and sat watching the crowd and chatting with the bartender.

"I have an idea everyone can relax," Burl said.

Over In the Pool Side Bar, the evening gradually wore itself out. Wolfie Wisdom had been playing to a steady crowd of about twenty and he had fallen off his musician's stool three times already. In a space of less than a month his new sound equipment was showing battle-scars from random collisions with its owner or the floor. Each tumble from his perch brought a new stream of obscene one-liners from Wolfie, which in turn induced counter-observations from the pool siders. With his fourth collapse the crowd howled with ever greater delight, one akin to that expressed by patrons at an underground cockfight when they sense final blood. The room was in chaos. Wolfie's accompanist on guitar was a large woman named Lorna, and she was leading them on now with obscene gestures of her own. From the audience an equally corpulent patron yelled: "Hey honey, why don't you go on a diet, then you could handle that little twerp a little better!" Lorna let the insult sail over her head for a moment and grinned back at the audience which was now busy transferring its lust for ridicule from Wolfie Wisdom to her. She raised the volume level on her microphone a few notches and raked out a couple of brittle chords in order to get the crowd's full attention. Lorna paused and struck a dramatic posture, helping emphasize the sudden silence in the room.

"Sweetie," she called out, "if I wanted to hear an ass-hole talk, I would fart!"

Pandemonium broke loose. The victory was hers. Wolfie was clutching his sides in a combined fit of laughter and cursing, unable to resist the delectable nature of the well-timed comeback, but also unable to cope with having been so thoroughly upstaged. His lack of self control now translated into a body-convulsing, shivering cackle, an exaggeration of his strange mode of laughter, and it quickly brought the audience's attention back to him. He became the subject of their renewed laughter and derision. It was not perfect, thought Wolfie, but it was something.

ii

In May the evenings are long in Mashkisibi. Felix and Burl were walking down the old logging road which led to the rustic old Otter Slide Lodge, musing over one of their favourite mutual appreciations: the similarity of the local landscape to parts of Newfoundland. They passed the lodge and took another short path which sloped down into a thicket of pine, spruce and poplar. This grove gave some shelter to the lodge from the full force of the north wind off Lake Superior. Dusk was suddenly upon them, that unmistakable moment on a long summer evening when one realizes that the world has wound itself down for another day. Or almost. Something scurried off to the right. Felix was onto it in a flash with three rocks.

"Dumb son-uv-a-bitch - I'll get you, you, you little bugger!" Felix sent his third rock crashing into the head of the hen with a thud that sounded like a damp twig breaking. They were slow, these spruce hens, not at all like the Ottawa valley partridge which, though larger, were also more elusive. "You've got to get them in the head. If you don't you'll bruise the meat all t' hell," Felix said matter of factly. In fifteen seconds the bird was de-headed and plucked. "Did it in twelve seconds once," Felix apologized, "but this one is pretty young." Felix stared at the bird in his hand as though contemplating a purchase in the supermarket. "Shit - I don't know why I do that sometimes. I don't really feel like eatin' right now. When something runs in the bush, I get this goddamn urge to see what it is - and if its good game - I gotta kill it - I just gotta kill it, you know? And sometimes I think about it later, and it really makes me wonder, you know..." Felix's voice trailed off. He turned and looked off through an opening in the trees where some traces of twilight penetrated to the trail. Felix could just barely see Lake Superior flickering through the tangle and it was as though he was looking for some kind of signal, a sign, a lighthouse, or some source of guidance such as a fisherman might seek when approaching the fog-bound coast of Conception Bay. A great confession seemed to lie latent within him, but he did not ask Burl to be the priest to pry it out of him. Instead he turned on his heel. "Ah, the hell with it," Felix said, and promptly headed back up the trail towards the lodge. His thoughts had turned to lobsters, the thousands of lobsters that he had helped his father catch around Harbour Grace. It seemed incongruous when Felix, withdrawing from his sudden introspection, turned to Burl and expressed a wish for a meal of fresh lobster. "None of that fast-frozen bull-shit."

Burl chose not to reply. Walking in the rear, his eyes were on the pathetic naked corpse which only a moment ago had been picking food from the forest floor. It was swinging to and fro from Felix's hand and Burl felt himself transported back to the ranks of some late medieval procession of mendicants somewhere in Europe. Ahead of him walked the Monk Superior, hood over his head, as if to prevent his looking out at the world. In his hand he was swinging a small bell, such as might have been rung in order to warn town folk and peasants encountered along their way of the impending advance of the Black Death.

125

iii

"Can you help a fellow out boss?" Burl fished in the side pockets of his bush jacket for what change was there.

"Here you go my friend."

"Thank you sir, thank you."

Street life was customarily brisk on a Friday evening in the Sault. Burl carried on toward the Algoma House, his tote bag over one shoulder. He was looking forward to hooking up with Victor Simpson for a beer and showing him a couple of chapters of the history report he had been working on in his spare time. He ducked into the pub room of the Algoma House, sought out one of the preferred round tables, one with a soft terry-cloth covering. He plunked down his tote bag on one of the high-backed, padded wooden chairs. He signalled the barmaid for a couple of draft and sat down, his eyes slowly adjusting to the hazy light. He could see the bartender fill up a tray for the heavy-set woman with the bad back who had worked at the Algoma House for years and who was on speaking terms with all the regulars.

"Thank's Rose." Burl thought about how easy it all was for him. Unlike the man on the evening street outside, life's little extras posed no difficulties. They had always been easy. Having the price of a beer was a given. Burl thought about the possible genealogy of that panhandler. Then he thought of Farmer Jones and his clever money-making mode of survival. Were these men connected in some way? What works for one, clearly does not work for all. The face of the man outside resurfaced in Burl's glass. Dark, worn, dishevelled, fluid - yet strangely undefeated. Where did he go at midnight? Farmer Jones' ancestors in earlier centuries, were known as the *gens de terre* - the men or people of the land. By the old French fur traders sometimes called the *O'pimittish Ininiwac*. Burl nursed his ale reflectively and then reached over for his bag, fumbled around with the contents and then pulled out the brown envelope which had "North

126

of Superior" written on it. He drew out the manuscript and flipped through to a particular passage.

> The *Gens de terre* who lived north of Mashkisibi, resorted to the Sault on occasion for the fishing, for ceremonials, for marriage-arranging, sugar-making, and for news and conversation. An English trader, Alexander Henry the Elder, encountered them in 1767.

> Such is the inhospitality of the country over which they wander, that only a single family can live together in a winter season; and this sometimes seeks subsistence in vain, on an area of five hundred square miles.

Burl slipped the pages back into the envelope again. He attempted to reconstruct the possibilities. For reasons of economic necessity, these hunters and gatherers had eventually come in from the cold, into the even colder city. But some could not entirely leave behind one fixed idea: that food was to be shared. In the cities of the Europeans, they would have reasoned, surely food was just the same as coin, or "made beaver" or the dried whitefish which they used to employ as currency. So, when in the later twentieth century street, a large, smiling unrepentant figure, confused since youth, lumbered towards a stranger - any stranger - in the old familiar way, hand outstretched, the man was appealing to him as just one more fellow tribesman - a brother - one searching no doubt, as he was, for "spare change." And if this stranger had come upon some first, surely he would share it with him, as they would have shared a deer in the old days.

Such optimism seemed insoluble, no matter how often it failed to provide results or only induced looks of contempt. "Why do you give them money?" some of his friends would ask him. The actual shift in Burl's sensibilities on this point had come some years before, after he had first ventured into the north country. The moment of his conversion remained vivid in memory. It was on another

Friday night when everybody in the Sault was out on the town, most packed along Queen Street. In that throng it was difficult not to have at least fleeting eye-contact with several hundred people in a very short time. The difficulty, for those paying attention to such nuances, was to distinguish true eye-contact from that which was merely a random and accidental crossing of eye-paths. On that singular evening, on the opposite side of the street, and a good forty yards away, walking in the opposite direction, a veteran panhandler had somehow picked Burl out of all that fluctuating, noisesome, Friday-night swell of humanity. Two men passed each other on opposite sides of the street, one oblivious and the other not; but - and this was the point - the panhandler immediately crossed the street and came up behind Burl to put the touch on him. Burl had been vaguely aware of all this happening out of the corner of an eye. It was the most amazing performance of this type he could recall - and it was well worth the shelling out of some coin. Indeed, their eyes *had* met, if just ever so briefly - and the ever alert forager - trapped in his wilderness analysis - *had* been correct. He had read the lay of the land and positioned himself well, like a lone wolf hounding a herd of caribou. Which one should be cut out? He had selected Burl, amidst all that hurly-burly, as the one to hit on, to be selected. He was the vulnerable beast on the edge of the herd. Thereafter, Burl had resigned himself to, if not the dignity, at least the legitimacy, of panhandling. He saw it as an extension of an ancient tradition in which real survival skills and a long-perfected moral practice came into play. It was in part the *nin wabas* as rendered by Father Baraga: "I survive the night."

iv

Angus Ashabish walked into the kitchen at Minnie Maywins's. Kakayosha was finishing up the dishes. Minnie and Joanna had gone off to the Fireweed Hall for Wednesday night Bingo.

"Hi uncle. There's still some coffee and apple pie here. Like some?"

"You betcha. Fishing not very good today. I could use something alright."

"Where did you go?"

"Up past the Chair. Probably why fishing so lousy. Didn't throw in much tobacco. Wanted it for myself." Angus winked at Kakayosha as he sat down at the kitchen table where Kakayosha had been reading. "See you been lookin' at that report on bears again."

"Yes. Sure is interesting. Glad Burl gave it to us."

"I got thinking about that today. We should do something to thank him for it. Any suggestions?"

"Well - mom and Joanna will be off to Bingo again next Wednesday. Why don't we invite him over here and you can tell us all about the *Midewiwin* and what you know about bear ceremonies. Anything you want to tell us that is."

"Will you ask him at work?"

"Of course. What shall I say?"

"Tell him I want to tell you both some things about my long quest for visions."

The following Wednesday evening Burl arrived at the appointed hour. Minnie had prepared whitefish and vegetables in the backyard and they all took food together. Minnie was in good humour and warned Burl not to take anything Angus said seriously. "Otherwise, you gonna have nightmares rather than visions." Joanna pleaded with Angus to hex the numbers at the Bingo Hall so that she and Minnie would win lots of money.

"So you see how it is?" said Angus, after Minnie and Joanna had left. "Is it any secret why we medicine men are in such poor standing now? We are seen as mere fixers of games. 'Charlatans' - like so many of your men of the cloth in older times used to call us." Burl and Kaka looked at Angus but responded only with suppressed smiles. The familiar Angus grin slowly surfaced and covered his jaw. "But has it ever been different? So first, I am going to show you my scrolls. Kaka has already seen some of these, but you haven't, Burl. I hope you will find this valuable. Scrolls have been getting out of our hands in recent years, and so it is better you hear from me what they are all about. The reason I am so interested in working with Victor on his rising water project is that I hope we will find more caches of these out there in the bush. He has promised me that if any are found, they will be given over to me first on behalf of Fireweed. 'Not strictly legal' he tells me, but then again he says, 'what is?' I like the way Victor thinks."

The evening passed more quickly than Burl wished. Esoteric knowledge flowed out of Angus and he reviewed the many levels of advancement through the *Midéwiwin* order. "Kaka knows enough now to be a first order, but she has not decided if this is really for her, am I correct niece?"

"Yes uncle. But I like what you've taught me about plants and stuff over the last year or so. Just not sure my mind is right, my... my attitude perhaps."

"It's good to hear you say that. This is not a decision to be taken lightly. We do not baptize babies the way the whites do. We encourage young people to come to things in their own time." Angus then turned to the kitchen table and began to point out and explain the patterns on the creation scrolls, on the teaching scrolls, on a scroll of the *Ghost Medéwiwin* and on the *Sky Scroll*. "These were all left to me by my father." Kaka and Burl looked at them with reverence.

"Is it alright to pick them up?" asked Burl.

"Yes. I keep them in the cellar in a corner where there is some humidity. It's just like old books, you know. A bit of oil from the fingers helps keep them supple. And I roll them out every so often, so that they do not stiffen too much."

"Did grandfather do these?" Kaka asked.

"He probably did. He would have copied them from

older ones. Since you are good with your hands, I thought, if you wish, you might want to begin copying these onto new bark. It is good way to learn about them, as you do the copying." Kaka ran her hand slowly over the creation scroll, as though she was reading brail. She felt the fine grooves on the scroll, made with some distant knife so many years ago.

"Now," Angus said, "I should tell you. In times past, and even today, some Indians believe people come in three parts. There is the *wiyo*, or physical substance of the body; then there is the *udjitchop*, or soul - and it is this that travels after death to the Land of Souls - that is, in the west. And then there is the *udjibbem,* or the shadow, which we believe is earthbound for a period after death, and it lingers near the grave. That is why food is left out after death near the departed, to give sustenance in the journey to the Land of the Souls." Angus went over the more obscure symbols of his *Ghost Midéwiwin* scroll. Then he turned to a scroll his father had given him. "This is called a *Sky Scroll.* It is very personal. When I returned from the war, my father, Kaka's grandfather, had passed on, and I never got to learn all that I needed to learn about this scroll. And without such a personal guidance from somebody familiar with its creation, much is lost. I have only a small understanding of this scroll. But my father Andrew was a man of great medicine, and you both know that from the article on bears."

"Angus, I suppose it's to be expected, but Hollywood and everybody else is interested in bad medicine. Can you tell us anything about that?"

"Yes. Bad medicine lurks like a skunk in the back woodshed of the higher orders of the *Midéwiwin*. Down near Lake of The Woods I once met old Dog-in-the-Sky. He said: 'No one should know bad medicine - it should be off the earth. People die off fast enough anyway.' Once when I was in the Sault I watched a karate match. It's a bit like that. You have the power, but if you used it all you would have a mess on your hands. There are beliefs about it. It is something like those boomerangs Victor makes for you people on the weekend. If you send out bad medicine it may come back to you months later and do you in, or perhaps do in your family. Many people take this very seriously. There are people down at Fisher Creek Reserve, very traditional people, who are still under the shadow of this kind of thinking. That is a very poor reserve. Not like us here at Fireweed. I think I've told you about that business of bearwalking on the Manitoulin just after the war. I remember meeting people who knew all about it. They were very distressed about it all."

8

Roadside Ceremony

i

Low bands of dark cloud streamed in off Lake Superior in steady succession, just thin enough to filter the sunlight and distribute it in broad shafts. These shifting columns cast an eerie glow over the forest country around Mashkisibi which for the past week had been ablaze with autumn colour. From any height of land along the coast, the hills to the north, south and east, all took on the appearance of a seething mass of dying coals sliding down into Lake Superior.

No moose would last long near any road at this time of year, even though it was illegal to hunt from the highway. *Moose-lust* had a curious way of suspending all local legislation. It was open season and in the north country even the park lands were available for the shoot. The call had come in at 7:30 a.m. "Two moose down near the north boundary." No details provided. Jan Polyanski and Burl Manion jumped into the half-ton in order to check out the report, on the chance they were roadkills. If the animals had been victims of traffic, hunters-turned-scavengers would soon be all over them like ants if the flesh was not too badly bruised. They arrived to find ten vehicles already pulled up on the shoulder of the highway just beyond the north boundary.

"Do you believe in universals, Jan?"

"As in *joints*? "

"No. As in *scientific laws* or *values*."

"A few. The speed of light - the power of money maybe - why?"

"I think sometimes its the attractive power of any spectacle of carnage that is the oldest one," said Burl. "Maybe its some aspect of the collective memory, some kind of resurfacing of an ancient need by the group to gather round the bloodied beast that has been brought to its knees. I'm not *judging* all these people here. I do it myself."

The cow lay about thirty feet from the edge of the road, half-concealed by a bush. A few feet from the cow, a calf hung in a heap over a rotting log. Two marksmen? Or had one man shot both and allowed a partner to claim the calf? That would be illegal. But it would be tempting, a cow and a calf together. A hunter might not see another animal all weekend - and the calf-meat was superb. No one would know the difference, and besides, the calf could not get on without its mother. It could all be rationalized as humane.

A local hunter in new bush clothing was leaning over the cow, proceeding to dress it. The bag of gases had been punctured first and a stench, familiar to all hunters, farmers, ranchers and meat-packers, hung tenaciously in the air. There was an objectivity to the performance, such as might accompany a demonstration by a master surgeon before his class. The onlookers were mute but their attention fixed on the lesson at hand. To be sure, these watchers lacked the ritual involvement of the hunters and gatherers of old, who better understood why they formed a circle around a fresh kill.

Jan and Burl quickly confirmed that the animals had not been shot. They were dead owing to an unfortunate intrusion into the cow's habitat. Accustomed to leading the calf down familiar trails and old skid roads, out onto the highway where they might catch some breeze, especially in the blackfly season, this path had become a routine, even after the passing of the high season pestilence. Here, the highway crossed their route to a small lake where there was good marsh. She had carried the calf for months, given birth, and now it showed all the characteristics of becoming a fine bull of the future. This was all arrested potential. Burl sought out the eyes of the calf, large mirror balls fixed on the trees just over its motionless shoulder. These globes were all that still lived, for in them was reflected some of the continuing world of motion.

Burl rose from where he was kneeling by the calf and walked over to the cow and then agreed with Jan that this had been a double roadkill. The calf must have been directly beside the cow. The driver of a large camper with New Mexico license plates was talking nervously with some of the other bystanders. The front end of the camper was seriously damaged, but no one appeared to be hurt. A provincial police car moved slowly past the line of parked cars and pulled up in front of the camper.

Burl's thoughts trailed off to Duino, on the Adriatic Sea. Several years ago he had visited the castle there where the great poet had spoken for all scenes like the one before him.

> And yet within the warm and watchful creature
> is the care and heaviness of a great melancholy,
> For it also clings to him always, that
> which often overcomes us - memory:
> As if once before the thing for which we strive
> had been closer, truer, and the relation
> infinitely tender. Here all is distance,
> there it was breath. After the first home
> the second is hybrid but open to the winds.
> Oh, the beatitude of the *little* creatures.

Burl's reverie broke and he looked towards the camper and then beyond the edge of the crowd. He was slightly startled when he saw off to one side, almost in the bush, the figure of Angus Ashabish, pipe in hand. Three months had passed since he had last seen Angus at the wharf, but only one fact now came back: their discussion of clan affiliations. Angus had told him he was of the Moose Clan. Angus was slightly bent over, preoccupied with lighting up a pipe which he then passed over to a young man next to him, a young man unknown to Burl. It was no ordinary pipe. Abe waited for Angus's eyes to meet his own, and they each touched their caps. Burl decided not to intrude on their ceremony.

Abe and Jan got back into their truck and returned to Black Pebble Lake to file their report. They passed the debris from another trailer which had been demolished four weeks ago, still visible in the bush near Three Mile Hill.

"Shit - are they ever going to clean up the rest of that mess?" asked Jan. The vehicles involved in this earlier mishap, a truck and a car, had long since been towed away, but the car's trailer had been more or less reduced to kindling. There was little left to remove as local two-legged scavengers had quickly come and picked the site clean of anything useful.

"Been a funny summer traffic-wise" added Jan. "I think the cars and trucks have been moving marginally slower this year. Beefed up highway patrols I think. But you know what else?" Jan looked at Burl.

"What's that?"

"I would say there is a hell of a lot more of those special tourist vehicles on the roads now. And they just really slow things down. That's why roadkills come in various species."

Burl nodded in agreement. Every conceivable type of rig was making the rounds, if one cared to make a systematic survey. There were smooth, glossy, air-craft-styled, bus-like mobile homes; there were rickety home-mades, somewhat resembling mobile junk-yards; and there were older back-to-the-land type vans, stuffed with sleeping-bags and all apparent worldly possessions of the occupants. There were small cars which had little power on the hills; and there were large tractor trailers which came sailing through with little regard for anything or anyone. The patience of drivers habitually wore thin as they dallied with the solid white line. If the recent vehicular dead were buried on the sides of roads, in the same way that the fur trading voyageurs of old had buried their comrades adjacent to the customary waterways, the effect would be dismal - an endless series of crosses along some great *via des morts*.

ii

A few days after the roadkill incident Burl drove to Mashkisibi for a meeting at the Lands and Forests Office, one called to consider the need for a publicity poster campaign to inform the public about hunting season issues and roadkill policies. After the meeting he went over to the town library to spend a few hours clearing up a few things related to his historical manuscript in progress. About mid-afternoon Olivia Wilson came in and took a place at a table in the art book section. He was reminded of the morning meeting and the decision made to contract out some original art work for the poster campaign and that he had been asked to look after that end of things. Olivia had done very well that summer doing illustration work for Kirsti and the Chief Naturalist. Why not? he thought. Burl got up and walked over to her table where she had spread out a number of books on English art, including several dealing with J.W. Turner.

"Hello Olivia. How are you getting along since leaving us?"

"Oh! - hello Burl. Just fine thank you. I didn't see you when I came in. I'm sort of at loose ends these days. My folks can't really afford to send me off to school right now.

Guess I will hang around Mashkisibi this winter and try and save some money."

"I see you are into one of my favourite artists in a big way." Burl pointed at the open book on Turner.

"Really? Yes - I think he does wonderful things with light."

"I think maybe you've learned something from him. I could see it in some of the things you did for the park this summer."

"Do you really think so? Thank you - that's such a compliment."

"That raises a question. How would you like to do a little more contract work for me over the next few months. It would be more art rendering. Wildlife related."

"I would really like to do that. What's the topic?"

"The unnecessary death of animals. Which is to say - roadkills. Tell you what. I'll send you a contract in the mail this week, and perhaps next week we can meet at Kirsti's office at L and F here in Mashkisibi. She's working out of the office here over the winter. We can all talk about the project then."

"That would be wonderful. It was so great working for her last summer. I would like so much to see her again." Olivia turned her face up to face Burl more directly. He noticed a bruise around her left eye.

"I'm sure you don't have to stand on ceremony with Kirsti. You can call on her anytime. She would tell you that if she were here, I'm quite sure."

"Burl?"

"Yes?"

"I need to...I mean...I think I need to...to...thank you. Yes... thank you very much." Her face lowered again so that she lost eye contact with Burl.

"You're very welcome Olivia. Call me in the meantime if you have any questions. Alright?"

"Yes...I will...thank you."

Nine

Old Erkki

Burl Manion was on the road early. Murdo had asked him to talk to some of the local bush farmers south of the park about their views on hunters using their land during the fall hunt. Most of these farmers were hunters themselves and had no objections as long as they came to see them first. The agricultural land parcels were odd units, carved out of the bush during the inter-war years and later, mainly by Scandinavians who had escaped from the mines and who understood how to squeeze the Shield country for crops and pasture. Many of them now lived beyond the reaches of electricity, largely by choice.

One of these bush farmers on Burl's list to visit was a reclusive old Finlander who was seldom seen by anybody. Murdo had scratched some details on a topographical map indicating the way to "old Erkki's" place. Turning onto a primitive overgrown trail which ran off the little used Shelagh Mine Road, Burl followed it for about a mile until, over a slight rise, it threatened to dissolve altogether into lush second-growth meadow. A wind break of trees became visible around what his map indicated as the last turn before coming to Erkki Siiralla's property.

Burl stopped the car some twenty yards beyond the wire

139

and post gate, cut the engine and rolled the window down. After easing back a few notches in the seat, he peered out the window through a gap in the windbreak towards an almost indiscernible homestead planted well back among a grove of spruce and poplar. The cottage was set back some thirty yards from the fence line and it gave off an air of abandonment, dispelled only by a tell-tale wisp of smoke rising from the metal chimney and by clear, but unbroken, glass windows. The latter randomly caught the light of day through the canopy of trees. Reflections of leaves played across the panes like ghost ball-room dancers. There was scarcely a sound except that of a breeze rattling through the poplars. The pungency and warmth of the mid-August afternoon mixed with the stillness, started to act on Burl's brain with narcotic effect. Drowsiness filled the car by a steady osmosis and he succumbed to the tranquil earth-tones which engulfed him and eased him away from his task. His eyelids grew heavy as stone. Leaning his head back he slid into quick sleep, one replete with those fantastic dreams which often frequent the head of the cat-napper. He found himself in some damp dark wine cellar, surrounded by people he did not know, all jabbering in French and packing furs into file cabinets. Burl awoke with a start, aware of a voice calling a repeated request. The words had first been part of his dream, incongruous as they were, but they defined a road back to the world of the quick.

"Vud-you lika bita Scoytch?" came the question, quite steady, and softly spoken. Burl turned his head towards the car window, still not quite awake.

"I haff Scoytch in za cabin. You velcome to some."

Against the sky, the man's face was like an eclipse of the sun, surrounded by the penumbra of a straw hat, much the worse for wear. Burl stared for a moment at the backlit hovering face at his window, awaiting the return of his mind to full alert.

"Scoytch ?" Burl said softly, not sure of exactly what it was the man was describing.

"Yah, yah, Scoytch. I always have some Scoytch. You are velcome."

"Yes, yes, thank you!" Burl said. "That would be very pleasant." He slowly eased himself out of the car and shook hands with the troll-like figure before him, and introduced himself.

"Oh yah," said Erkki. "I know Murdo for long time - yah. So you are verking for him, yah?" he paused.

Burl nodded and said that Murdo wanted to get his opinion on hunters and to know if he had any difficulties with them.

"And I am called Erkki" he said. "I am living here at Vitefish. I haff Scoytch if you like. You come this vay." Erkki held open the wire gate and advanced up the roadway towards the cabin, beckoning Burl to follow. "So, yah. I haff a few hunters come in here. They are okay. I am glad for the company sometimes, and they usually leave me a bit of meat if they get something." Burl followed Erkki into the dim cabin and saw what he had already anticipated, a half-empty bottle of Scotch on a table by the large stone fireplace. The cabin was one of great warmth and craft, demonstrating the touch of a skilled carpenter. A set of black wooden skis stood in a corner, criss-crossed by ski-poles. Framed photographs hung on the walls, but not so many as to create confusion. Along one wall was a large four level pine shelf with glass doors filled with long-playing records.

"You vant ice perhaps?" he said.

"Yes - some ice would be good, thanks."

"Yah. Around here ve always haff ice. It is only for a few veeks that ve *don't* haff ice." Erkki's face broke into a wide smile. "I make the joke, yah?" Erkki walked into his kitchen area and opened a pine-panelled door which disguised the refrigerator.

"I see you like music, Erkki." Burl pointed towards the wall.

"Ah, yah, music, it is good, yah? I do not listen so much now, but sometime - long ago - I bring many records from old country - after za war. And I get some here at Thunder Bay. Mostly classical I haff.... I don't know what the young people listen to now. Mostly I haff classical here." Erkki handed a glass to Burl. "Sometimes I see some old ones at secondhand store.To your goot health! - your name again is?"

"Burl - Burl Manion. And let us drink to Sibelius, then."

"Sibelius. Sibelius. You know Sibelius?"

"Yes - I am very fond of Sibelius. Especially the fifth."

"Oy, oy, oy! So. So - I must to show you some pictures I haff then, and I vill play some of my old records for you. I have much Sibelius. You sit down at table and I will get some pictures for you. But first, you are looking at those pictures on the vall in the corner." Erkki disappeared into a back room where Burl could catch occasional glimpses of him rooting around in a trunk and through desk drawers. The old Finn became more animated in his search, knowing what he sought was near at hand, but just where?

Burl wandered over to the photos on the north wall. His eye first caught one of Sibelius in old age wearing a broad, Spanish-looking, brimmed hat, and standing on a porch with the famous American conductor, Eugene Ormandy. There were rumours about Sibelius and Scotch - rumours connecting drink with the fate of the mysterious eighth symphony which had never been found. Some say it had remained only in his mind all those many years when his pen lay still on his composing table - during what came to be called "the great silence." They were long years when Sibelius seemed to be waiting among his beloved pines at Järvenpää only for death.

Burl looked carefully and hard at the other well-framed photos under glass which were arranged in no particular order but which were mainly pre-1945. On many there was some writing, but in Finnish or German. One picture now held his attention for it looked vaguely familiar. The inscription bore the name "Mannerheim." Marshall Mannerheim? It read: "Erkki, von Gustaf Mannerheim." The picture showed a ski patrol clad in white, the men bearing rifles.

Erkki shuffled out of the bedroom, clutching an array of pictures and loose photographs. He nervously spread them on the kitchen table with a certain reverence.

"More Scoytch?" he asked

"No - my drink is good - thank you."

"So - you come over here and I explain you."

"Erkki - tell me about this photograph on the wall here first, will you? This one right here."

"That picture? - yah. That is important picture for me. That is early in vor with Russians - yah. And here, you can see is the great Marshall Mannerheim. Ah! such a great man he vas. He vud come and meet vith us and tell us ve must fight even more hard. All of these men, they ver my friends for three years about - yah." Burl looked at Erkki but Erkki's eyes were now looking out the window, fixed on the leaves of a nearby aspen, his mind bending with the boughs under the weight of memory.

"Yah, yah....three years I think ..."

"And then?" said Burl.

"And then - then comes trouble...." Burl could feel the darkness in Erkki's words and he moved over to the table in order to change the subject.

"So - what have we here then, Erkki?"

"Here ve haff pictures of my friends and comrades before the vor and during the vor. And some of my family on farm near Helsinki. Yah." Burl paused over them, picking them up one at a time. There were many winter shots of skiers in white along with some in which young women were shown on the arms of various members of the ski patrol. Burl glanced over to the corner again at the pair of well preserved wooden skis.

"Erkki, are you in any of these pictures - I can't tell with the headgear these men are wearing!"

"Yah, yah. I am there. Here I am for instance, in this vun. You see? - yah?"

"Yes - yes - that is you for sure. These are all shots of the Finnish Winter War ski fighters aren't they?"

"Yah, - you know about that? - Ve gave the Russians a good fight, that is true. Ve did okay - yah. And you see this vun over here. That is Mannerheim again. He used to come and see us ven he could. Ve all loved him. He vas not afraid of anything. Not even Hitler." Erkki picked up the picture of Mannerheim and held it closer to the lamp hanging down over the table and then put it down slowly again. "You look at the others now, and I vill put a little vud in the stove." Erkki turned around and moved across the room. Burl could see him putting a handkerchief to his eyes.

The photos were a mix of military photos of the Winter War with others of musicians and assorted family pictures. There was one of a symphony orchestra and a young female violinist. It was inscribed: *Liebe Erkki, von Saaro Maki.* Another showed Erkki with this same Saaro Maki at a beach in the summer of 1937. Others showed a farm with stacked sheaves of grain, a cart with horses, a family picture in a well-appointed farm kitchen, young men on a soccer team, and others of day to day events.

"Do you mind if I also take a look at your record collection over there?"

"Yah, yah, sure. Please you do. They are quite old, and I haff not listened to many for a long time. If you like, ve are playing some."

"How do you play records out here beyond the electricity?

"I haff batteries and also little generator which I set up. Do not use much. Gasoline generator." Erkki pointed out the back window to a little shed. Burl could see a number of other out-buildings. There was a small barn, an ice-house, and a little cabin with a metal chimney. It appeared to be a pine sauna building and it was located not far from a small natural pond. The wood working on the buildings was just as well executed as that of the main cabin.

Burl turned back towards the shelves of music. Some of

the records were very old, kept in large folios containing 78 RPM recordings made before the war. Most were of foreign origin, Finnish labels, and some of the more familiar German *Deutche Grammophon.* The rows were rich in Sibelius Grieg, the Dane, Nielsen, and many of the German classics. "You must like music a lot Erkki. Do you play an instrument?"

"Yah. Vunce I play, many years ago, but not for long time now. Ve all played back in old country. Every veekend ve vud play at the farm house, or later after ve move to Helsinki, ve haff people come over for music. That is how I met Saaro - in Helsinki. She vas at the University studying music. Her father vas friend of my father. I play trumpet sometimes, and in military band."

Burl pulled the heavy folios out one by one in order to inspect the cover of each. It was rare to see such old recordings now unless one visited garage sales or the basement holdings of antique or used book dealers. He stopped when he saw a pre-war Norwegian edition of the Sibelius violin concerto. On the cover was a beautiful young woman posed by a large boulder along a fiord. The cover advertised *Saaro Maki* with the Oslo Philharmonic. Burl eased the album back into its spot and refrained from saying anything. Something had gone disastrously wrong with Erkki's life.

Ten

Remembrance

i

Like most northern towns, Mashkisibi had its own traditions and ways, but it shared with many other frontier communities the notion that it mattered little where you were from or what you had been. The proprietor of the Cypress Cafe, Ardo Kulduhn, was fond of saying: "You may have been camel dung in the past, but here the air is fresh once again - at least for awhile." This brand of tolerance extended even to that signal day of Canadian tradition, Remembrance Day. Since the end of the Second War, the town had, like much of the country, become something of a dog's breakfast of nationalities, a home to people from the four corners. There were immigrants from Italy, from India, and from the Middle East. There were people from "the Rock" seeking to make a new beginning in mining in the aftermath of the Belle Island closings. There were local Native peoples who now worked more in town than in the bush; there was a patchwork of seasonal transients just moving through - so they thought - but who stayed, took jobs and even started families; there was a mix of other "new Canadians" who sensed opportunities outside of the larger southern cities where their compatriots tended to gather; there were the restless young from the south, keen, for the usual reasons on escaping home and testing out life in the "big north." Finally, there were the Germans and Austrians and East Europeans. These last represented some of the oldest of the new arrivals. After the prisoner of war camps of Northern Ontario had been emptied in 1945, some of the internees applied immediately for "landed immigrant" status. Following a brief visit home to Europe to pick up the pieces of whatever was left, they quickly returned, having confirmed that in the old country there was nothing left but ashes, ruin or shame.

The Legion Hall was the meeting place in Mashkisibi for all who wanted a civil drink, a place to remember the old days, or a place to talk about the present and the future. For some it served as a refuge where they did not have to talk at all. A former Russian or Lithuanian officer might be seen taking a glass with a former RCAF pilot or a German foot soldier. All were bound by memories of a bad time and individuals rarely gave offence. As November 11 approached each year, an understandable clannishness set in, and the men and their wives or companions might seek out the company of their own a little more frequently; but at the Legion, it tended to remain business more or less as usual.

Mashkisibi No. 1 was not the only nostalgic show in town. On almost any night of the year, a person who walked past the rear annex of the town bakery, a pre-fab structure operated by two former German prisoners of war, might find another kind of assembly. This annex was the apartment of Albrecht Boeker and Freddy Schultz, and it was known locally as the "rear oven". It had become the informal meeting ground for many of the Central and East Europeans in town, a place where they might reminisce, listen to music, drink, sing and lie to themselves about the past. It was not so much an apartment as a miniature Bavarian beer hall. All were welcome there who wished to enter into the spirit of the place. A supply of ales and other bottled items was always on hand. Displayed in Albrecht

Boeker's impressive home-made cabinet were his other valuable items, particularly his recorded music and tapes. There might be as many as ten men and women packed into the "rear oven" on a given night. Albrecht and his friends were particularly fond of having young people join them - young people who, of course, knew nothing of the war. They helped fill in the vacuum of lost families and reminded them that, despite everything, there was still a normal succession; and when the young people asked them about the war, they tried their best to explain, even though they could, and sometimes, would not. Burl Manion was not a stranger to the "rear oven" and he had gradually adjusted to the normal pattern of performance at these sessions.

"Burl," Albrecht would say, "later tonight, or maybe next week - after we haff had a few drinks - I am going to tell you things that it is hard for me to tell you. Things about the war which nobody knows but me. But you are a lover of music - you are interested in the same things we are - I know. But I am going to tell you things not about music." Burl had stayed the course on several occasions, long into the morning, having nursed his drinks carefully so as not to be the one to fall under the table; but Albrecht never would speak about those things. He would be on the very edge, there was a visible yearning to speak etched on his face, but that last drink would always put him to sleep rather than activate his tongue. He could not be made to air the dirty German national linen piled so high in the closet of his memory. Burl eventually decided that Albrecht probably could not speak about these things. To press him, he thought, might be, as they said at the Legion, to "give offence." Instead, Burl entered into those areas of Albrecht's lost world where he was more welcome. This was the world of music and comedy. The spirit of the old cabaret and the music hall, these were the memories which kept Albrecht and his friends going in the land of the victors; and they were overjoyed when the children of the victors would join them, and not judge them. And they were even more pleased when the young demonstrated some understanding of that world.

"Burl! How I wish you could have met my friend, Leo Lismer." Albrecht splashed some rye into his glass and then, with eyebrows upraised, asked Burl if he wanted more. Burl declined. "There is ice over there in the little refrigerator. But you know that - you haff been here before I think." Albrecht laughed. "So goot to see you again, so goot. You haff not been here for awhile." Albrecht often referred to Leo Lismer. Burl had heard this same hope for their meeting expressed at least twenty times in the past. It was like a refrain for Albrecht.

"That man could sing I tell you. Is that not so Freddy? - Freddy - reach me the Lismer tape there. It's just above you on that shelf - yah?" Freddy Schultz got up and pulled out the familiar and well-used tape from its place of honour.

"I re-tape these for Albrecht two or three times a year," said Freddy Schultz. "That is how often he listens to it. But it *is* so very good. I agree. I too, knew Leo Lismer. He was a beautiful man, so beautiful, and such talent...yah."

Burl thought of Erkki out in the bush and his beautiful lost Saaro. And he thought of Kirsti Kallela, who had come here once with him, but was not comfortable, and told him later that she preferred not to return. Albrecht always asked after Kirsti.

"So now we play the tape. I listen to this tape of Leo almost as much as I listen to the great Richard Tauber. This tape I am making in 1956 when Leo visited us here in Mashkisibi. Leo had with him a recording he had made in old country." Freddy turned on the large and impressive reel-to-reel tape machine. "So - here we haff him singing Lehar - you know him perhaps? Hungarian? - yes? - goot. This is *Dein ist mein ganzes Harz*, a very great favourite with us in the old days. How you say in English Freddy?" With his hand, Albrecht appealed to his companion, who had a better grasp of English.

150

"I think that would be - *My Whole Heart is to You* - I believe that is it." said Freddy.

"Yah, yah, that is it. I have here a translation - English and German - and that is it. Yes, Freddy is right. And so you are taking this now Burl, so you can follow the words. Now soon we listen. But first, a little toast. To all my good friends here. Skol!" Everyone clinked glasses and Burl could see that there was moisture in the eyes of all the Germans.

"And shall we have a toast to Leo?" asked Burl. "Does he come back to visit now and then?" Albrecht looked to the others for a brief moment and then became sombre and held his glass chest high and paused, and then he put one hand on Burl's shoulder.

"Burl - I must tell you, with great sadness, that Leo does not come here anymore. He is in North Bay - in the asylum there. He could not...he could not...how do you say?...come to terms? - Yah! Come to terms. It has been a long time since we saw Leo here."

"I see," said Burl. He paused and looked at the others. "Then we must drink to hope for his recovery." The Germans looked at each other and then all rose to their feet and raised their glasses with poise, with something like the long-forgotten discipline of the ranks. They all toasted with feeling in their voices, and drank to hope for the recovery of Leo Lismer. The room fell silent for a moment and then Albrecht reached over to the machine, flipped a switch, and turned the volume up. A clear and unshrill voice filled the room with a familiar melody. Burl followed the translation Albrecht had given to him.

> My whole heart is yours!
> I cannot live without you -
> I am like the flower that fades
> without the kiss of sunshine!
> My sweetest song is yours,
> for it springs from love alone.
> Say it once more, my one and only love,
> say it once more: I love you.

Lismer's rendition went on for several verses and at the end everyone clapped and wept unashamedly. Albrecht then filled everyone's glass again. The Germans muttered in low tones to each other, nodding and smiling. Stephan Strauss, a tall quiet and still handsome man, who did not say much, but who was often there, always joined in the singing, for he loved music as much as any of them. Burl had heard from veterans at the Legion that Strauss had been a young SS Officer, captured early in the conflict. He remained standing after the others had sat down. Everything was uncharacteristically quiet.

"Yah...yah...and at the asylum in North Bay, Leo Lismer fades away," said Strauss, more by way of a whisper.

"Haff some more Stephan, haff some more. Everything is okay," Albrecht said, as he put his hand on Stephan's forearm. "Now, Stephan and everybody, we are listening to some Richard Tauber, and then I haff a surprise for you Burl, because you like women so much I think - and that is - we will listen to the young Elizabeth Schwartzkopf - ohhh - she was so beautiful, so beautiful...." Albrecht's voice tailed off as he momentarily vanished into the world of 1940. He moved over to his cabinet and pulled out one of his large folio albums, folios like the ones at old Erkki's. In two days it would be November 11. Burl watched Albrecht handle the folio with reverence and he suddenly remembered his promise to old Erkki that he and Kirsti would drive out and bring him in to the Remembrance Day service.

ii

The eleven o'clock ceremonies were scheduled to take place at the town memorial. This would be followed by presentations at the Legion Hall to the winning students for their essays and poems on the theme of Remembrance Day. After three, the lounge in the Legion Hall would be open. The other drinking establishments in Mashkisibi would be open as well, unlike those south of the French River which complied with the law. In Mashkisibi, the local tradition was that if veterans did not deserve to have a drink on Remembrance Day, then when did they? The Provincial Police looked the other way. There was nobody to complain. It was also the tradition that on November 11, at the Legion Hall, the men and women appeared in whatever uniform they chose. During the rest of the year, members of former axis powers usually had the good sense to appear in civic attire. The one exception was that members of the Indian sub-continent Imperial forces were welcomed in their turbans year-round, by special by-law.

In some of the other bars in Mashkisibi, a man would be more careful about how he displayed himself. There were establishments where, even at the best of times, one would find people anxious to give and take offence. The clientele in these places was often composed of people with no experience of war, but who yet entertained a strong desire to speak with their fists. They often held strong views on right and wrong, on history, and on economics; and while they drank much, they read little. The sources of their opinions were not at all clear, but those opinions were usually received, and seldom changed, but above all, they were held tenaciously. They were often held by people with a hard edge, like the rock many of them broke daily, and only rarely were they ever seen at the Legion where a certain decorum was required and expected. Rory O'Flanigan was never seen at the Legion.

The Command President of Mashkisibi No. 1 entered the Legion Hall and started to walk up the centre aisle towards the stage. He was a chunky man in his sixties with a well trimmed beard and he made use of a gleaming oak cane. He smiled at people as he walked steadily up the aisle. At the first row he stopped to shake hands and have a few words with a very elderly man sitting in a wheelchair. He then mounted the stage, called the gathering to order and extended welcomes.

"Friends, we have had many good submissions from the students this year, as we always do. And as usual, it has been difficult for the judges to select the winners. Now I think we will call all of those up who are to receive awards, and after that, our first prize winner in the poetry division will read aloud her prize winning poem." The President then called the students from junior and senior school to the stage and announced the name of each one in turn, described the contribution each had made, and presented each with a book. He then called for the first prize winner in poetry.

"It gives me great pleasure to call Olivia Wilson to the stage, who graduated from High School last spring, and to ask her to read her poem to all of you here today."

Olivia was pushed up and out of her seat by Joanna Beardy and Kirsti Kallela, both of whom were sitting next to her. She made her way slowly to the stage. The crowd fell silent and waited for her to begin.

"Thank you. I feel very honoured. My poem is called 'The Idea of War in Autumn, in Algoma' and it is dedicated to the war dead." She paused for a moment to let the room become still. She then read in a firm and impassioned voice:

Pilgrim trees were Roman Legions:
Green companies, moving singly and together
Into forever.
Young men, soundless
and without memories of marbled cities
eased themselves eagerly into the dark frontier.

Visions of confusion:
before the final falling on the last breeze,
before the shadow of the hawk obscured the light,
before the descent, each saw the height
and himself only as a line
on some imperial design which no longer held.

And so,
the gentle letting-go,
the dissolution of firm footprints,
the rising waves of a blood-red sea.

Olivia folded her script slowly and stood and looked at the audience and then bowed ever so slightly towards the Command President. He came over and grasped her hand and thanked her.

"They are not clapping because it is too sad," he whispered to her. "It is not an occasion for clapping - but you have done a very wonderful thing. Thank you so much. You must continue to write poetry. Promise me that?"

iii

The proceedings were adjourned and the crowd broke for lunch, moving to the long tables which had been set in the main hall. After the meal, people started to trickle out the door or into the pub room where the afternoon was passed in conversation over darts and beer. Burl was sitting with Murdo, Kirsti and old Erkki who, after much prodding, had been persuaded to come, dressed in his Finnish Winter War uniform. Many comments were heard about what a fine figure he cut. When they had driven out to get him, Kirsti sat him down in his cabin and trimmed his hair, beard and mustache. When she told him, in Finnish, that she was studying violin and that she intended to play for him sometime, there was nothing he would not have consented to. He put on his recording of the Violin Concerto of Sibelius for her while she was applying her scissors art.

In a corner of the pub room of the Legion Hall the Germans had been having an animated, but civil, conversation with some of the Canadians. They had been taking turns in buying rounds for each other. The Germans restrained themselves from breaking into song as they would do at the "rear oven." Albrecht was always careful to make sure that none of his compatriots got out of hand, and he would gently usher any out the door if this was a looming prospect. Such a time was approaching in once case, and Albrecht began the exit procedures for his friends by proposing "one last toast: to the end of the war." All at the table got to their feet and raised their glasses and then Albrecht, with Stephan Strauss, who always maintained his composure, no matter how drunk, escorted the source of potential embarrassment out of the Legion onto the main street of Mashkisibi. Stephan, having been a ranking officer, and looking authoritarian in his uniform, organized the men in formation in front of the Drugstore, and from there they all goose-stepped down the street towards the bakery. Murdo, Erkki, Burl and Kirsti were on the porch of the Legion watching, as were many others on the street. Erkki looked at Burl and sighed with some resignation.

"You know, I am remembering when Hitler came to Finland. It vas Mannerheim's birthday. That vas 1942. He vas old man already, but still leading us in fighting. People here do not know so vell how it vas in Finland then. Ve ver in difficult situation you must understand. Ve ver - how you say? - *caught in the middle?* - yah - very difficult."

11

Columbus

Kirsti Kallela had been sitting in the train coach, intermittently reading a not very good mystery and eyeing the few other passengers who got on. She leaned her head back, closed her eyes and let the book flop closed. How nice this will be, she thought. I'm glad Uncle Paavi liked Burl. Five days doing nothing with someone I like, even if it is the dead of winter in La Prest. A sly smile played around the edges of her mouth as she recalled Burl's awkwardness when she had suggested she join him on his little holiday. "Its just an instant idea," she had said, when he looked nervous. "Thought you might like some company. I kind of need a break myself from Mashkisibi." Kirsti smiled more firmly when she remembered the soft look of terror which shone out of Burl's eyes, a look she had seen in other men's eyes: fear of commitment. "I would like that," he had finally said. "I'd even thought about asking you, but I didn't want the office wags to have such a ripe opportunity - you know?" When she grilled him on his meaning he said, "Well - they'll talk of our 'dirty weekend' and so on. Bad office politics. One never has any private business in Algoma." Kirsti opened her eyes and put her hand to her mouth and turned towards the window in order to stifle the laughter which threatened to burst out of her. The memory was too priceless. She had let him get in deeper and deeper. "I mean it wouldn't be a 'dirty weekend' he added. "I mean - they might think it was - but it wouldn't be - I mean - we wouldn't - that is..." She remembered leaping in to torture him in his tracks. "Wouldn't it?" she said, turning on her full vixen look. "What's the point of my going along then?" Burl had buried his face in his hands and then come up laughing, relieved to see that she was laughing too. "You're such a Scandinavian imp" he had blurted out. You must be descended from elves." She had slid up to him and put her arms around him and then breathed into his ear: "Well?" He had said, "Well yes - if you really want to come along." She whispered, "Not good enough. Try again," clutching him a little more tightly. "Yes - I want you to come with me," he said. "Finally - you got it right," she said as she leaned back and put her finger on his nose. "I'll make the arrangements," he said. "I'll book you a room at the La Prest Inn and a train ticket." Then she had shocked him when she said: "I'll book a train ticket. But it will be cheaper if we share a room, don't you think? Cheaper and warmer."

Kirsti's image in the train car window next to her arm came back to meet her and she felt a flush run through her body. "My god," she whispered to herself, "I wonder if my face is as red as I feel." She could see Burl exiting the station door and walking towards the coach and she gave a little laugh which was louder than she intended. Soon he was standing beside her in the car.

"I thought we might be the only two on the train at this time of year, but I see there are a few others," Burl said as he leaned down and gave Kirsti a soft kiss. He stuffed a bag into the top rack and placed a thermal cooler and another bag on the seat opposite, and then sat down. "You look a little flushed. You feel okay?"

"Never better."

"I'm looking forward to this. Have been all week."

"I'm glad. So am I." She asked him what was in the cooler.

He told her and she did an imitation drool. Burl opened it up briefly so she could inspect it.

"Burl?" He looked at her. "How long have we known each other?"

"Let's see. Six - maybe seven months?"

"I feel we've known each other all our lives."

"You too?" He got up to put another bag on the rack above.

"Burl, it's not too late for me to get off. I imposed myself on your little holiday. If someone did that to me, I would be really ticked off." Burl looked down at her, his hands still on the baggage rack above. Kirsti had folded her hands in her lap, her mouth was neutral and she was looking at his chest rather than his face.

"You try and leave now and I'll tackle you in the aisle."

Two hours later the train was snaking along a difficult route through the great canyon, a route which later engineers, it is known, would have rejected. In winter the gorge took on visual qualities unknown to the summer crowds which filled the tour coaches or to the folk on the autumn specials going up in search of moose, fish and carpets of hillside colour. This January day was one of grey upon more grey, reinforced by billowing streamers of snow which rose in waves from the sides of the train. At certain exposed elevations, the chasms below remained completely obscured. The combination of rough terrain and snow-laden winds moving up through the river valleys from Lake Superior induced a variety of hostile effects. In more open areas the mood was sometimes that of a dust storm in some remote desert. When the canyon walls closed in again, claustrophobia could set in from the too-close proximity of the trees. When the forest was at such close quarters to the train, a passenger could see tall stands of spruce bending under long capes of snow. The train would then disappear between these columns, as though running the gauntlet, the trees resembling some alien force of helmeted ghosts against which there could be no victory. Now and again the train passed a solitary Native trapper about to wade single-handedly into the first platoons of that fantastic army. Such austerity must have been forbidding to the prisoners assigned to the stark and isolated camps of the canyon during the second war. Men and dogs had patrolled the tracks - who could tell what lay to the west or east?

Late in the afternoon, Kirsti leaned her head on his shoulder and dozed off. Burl had decided to make the winter run to La Prest out of curiosity and for a change of pace. Little had he suspected that it would become a real holiday. There were only eight other passengers on the mix train, all spread out randomly in the one passenger car. Towards the front sat a black couple from Detroit, apparently a minister and his wife. For the last half hour or so they had been engaged in an animated conversation with two of the train's crew. There were two other couples travelling together, seated a few rows behind the black couple. A well-dressed man sat across the isle from Burl and Kirsti. From casual chit-chat with him, Burl learned he was an industrialist from Norway, seeking out new sources of wood supply for his furniture company.

Snatches of conversation continued to reach Burl from all directions in the car. Rather unintentionally, he pieced together profiles of most of the people on the coach. The preacher had a deep, resonating voice and a confidence attended his remarks. From the body language of the two couples a few rows behind, Burl determined that the preacher's performance was the cause of some gossip among them. These tourists were also American, for they talked in mid-western accented tones, but now and then their conversation became hushed. Burl sensed that the minister and his young wife were mildly frustrated with the attitude of the two members of the train crew. Their energetic way of urging solutions to the ills of the world had little effect on the easy-going conductor and porter. Neither would be rushed into adopting any hard universal conclusions. The railway men spiked their comments with casual references to how things "were done" in this part of the country or in "other" nations of the world.

Darkness had closed in on the train. At about 5 p.m. the conductor got up and took an empty seat closer to Burl and Kirsti and pulled out his walkie-talkie. When he got up he was stone faced. He paused, and then walked towards the front of the car, looking at his vest watch as he wove his way from seat to seat in the swaying car.

"Folks!" he yelled, "I'm afraid we're going to have a delay. We'll be stopping at Cowie Junction for the night. There's a bad snow blockage on the tracks ahead and it will take some time to clear it up. We'll be putting you up at the Moose Head Inn, and of course there will be no charge to you people." The passengers indulged in some whispered mumbling, but no one it seemed was in any great hurry to get anywhere. As the engine started to brake, Kirsti woke up and Burl filled her in. Ten minutes later the train ground to a halt at Cowie Junction, population forty five.

The passengers and crew filed into the warmth of the Moose Head Inn, the proprietors of which were not accustomed to such sudden patron demand in mid-winter. They might put up a hundred people in the hotel and outdoor cabins on some weekends in the fall, but otherwise, business was local and the hotel got by on the strength of bar room receipts, mainly from winter work crews, loggers and a few trappers. The rustic lobby provided a welcome refuge from the cool steel and the dark, snow-bound night. The conductor said that he would look after room arrangements and then directed everyone into the main lounge, known as the Burnt Rock Room. A fire roared in a five-foot high stone fireplace. The hostess, a large jovial woman, recognizing a windfall when she saw one, quickly placed everyone at table while carrying on amiable small-talk. The few locals at the sit-around bar, their evening tranquility shattered, broke their conversations and watched as the room filled.

In one corner, a fortyish-looking man wearing a tweed overcoat and a working man's cap sat nursing what appeared to be a glass of water and reading a slim book. Despite the warmth of the Black Rock Room this man still wore his gloves and seemed oblivious to the stirring all about him. The newcomers had all shuffled into the haze-filled room and settled themselves at the empty tables. Burl and Kirsti looked about and found themselves caught in the piercing eyes of the silver-haired man who was now waving them over to his table.

"Come over here my frands. Sit - haff a beer."

Burl and Kirsti walked over and stood before him.

"Thank you - if we may. We don't like to intrude."

"Haa! How CanAY-dyun! - I don't vant to intrude - dats de good ting with this contree. You sit - you sit. I am from old contree, as I am sure you can tell. Over dair, zat is all ve evair do - intrude - but that is vat life is - ya? Life is intrusion. But over here - all is distance, yah? Vot you tink?" Burl and Kirsti were a bit nonplussed and nodded, not quite prepared to get into an animated philosophical discussion on national character.

"Yes - I think there is something in what you say," said Kirsti. "There is certainly lots of distance in these parts, especially when there is trouble on the train tracks."

"Yah - is not so uncommon along zis part. So - vot is your name may I ask?"

"Burl - Burl Manion. And this is Kirsti Kallela."

"And I am being called Columbus."

"Columbus? That is your first name or your last name?" asked Kirsti.

"My last name. But now it has become like my first name. Sometimes tings change, yah? First, ven I am born in old Slovenia, I am called Gustav Kolyumbic. But everybody here tells me zis is too difficult - zat I should change my name to make it easier. Vell then, you see, I am coming to the new vorld after the vor, so they all say - ve call you Columbus. A nice little joke, yah?" Burl grinned and agreed it was a good choice.

"You live around here then, do you Columbus?" Burl asked.

"Vorking for the railway, yah. Ever since the vor I am vorking in zis area, not always for za railway, but much of time. I do some trapping sometimes. Haff little cabin in za bush." Columbus wore the trademark red and black checkered bushman's jacket.

"We're over from Black Pebble Lake. I study animals as well. Going to La Prest on business. " Kirsti kicked Burl under the table.

"Black Pebble? Yah, I haff been over zair. Sometimes I go to Mashkisibi, go shopping and visit Legion and see some old frands. I haff frands zair from vay back. Some I arrive on same boat to Canada with many years ago."

"Know any Finnish women?" Burl asked. Kirsti kicked him again.

"Not vomans. But one Finlander. Yah - but I not see him for long time. He not come to Legion the vay he used to."

"Would that be Erkki Siiralla?" asked Burl.

"Yah, Erkki. Erkki Siiralla. You know him zen?"

"We met last summer. I go and visit him at his cabin sometimes, and sometimes Kirsti here plays the violin for him."

"Yah? Is so? Zat is nice. So you are a talent. Zat is good. Erkki, he vud like zat for sure. He like music lots. On boat from Hamburg I am remembering, he often vanting to listen to music in the lounge where they haff phonograph record player. After the vor, ve both end up in Hamburg by chance you see. Me, I am from old part of Austro-Hungarian Empire. I am born near Malavas. Then, ve in Slovenia become part of Yugoslav Kingdom after first vor - and zen - zen all the trouble begins. Nothing but trouble I tell you."

"You were there during the last war then?" asked Burl.

"Oh yah, but not as soldier. In 1941 Hitler comes into north of Slovenia where I am then living, and most of us taken off to Germany to vork in factories and such. If you had a house, that goes to Germans as vell. Lose everyting.

But I decide to vork in factory rather than join army. I was lucky. Most had no choice. Then after vor, I go back home but I see vat is happening. I saw Tito moving to take over for communists - I cannot blame him - nothing but chaos everywhere - ve needed order - for sure ve did - but I for one, could not stay. I saw that it vud be just more of same - one strong man with blood on his hands replacing another, yah? Maybe a different *ideologishe* perhaps, yah? But not so much better. I am remembering vat comrade Djilas from Montenegro used to say: 'in politics, all that is well, is soon forgotten.' So - when I still could - I am going up to Hamburg and get on boat. This is ver I meet Erkki, coming from other direction. He tells me he has relatives around Lake Superior. I tell him - I vant to go there too - for although I have no relatives zair, I am reading about this contree in old Slovenian books. I tell you someting. Ven Hitler come in, ve could not read Slovenian anymore. Not the children, nobody, not anyone. So anyvay - ve go togezair - Erkki and I - which is nice when you are in strange land, yah?"

"So why to Lake Superior for you? Asked Kirsti.

"Vell - as I am telling you - when I am young, I am in Malavas, and there, ve are having famous priest in nineteenth century. He vork with the poor and the peasants - and then he go to America and vork with the Indians and write books about zem. He wrote very good dictionary of Indian language. Some of us read about this in school. After vor, I say to myself: why not go vair Baraga vent?' - Yah? And so I say -yes - and so this is how I come here."

"I know a bit about Baraga, would you believe that? In fact, I have seen his picture in a little church over by the lake on one of the Indian reserves. It's a very fine picture. And you know something else? There are also these wood carvings there made by him."

"Yah - yah. I know vot you say. I have been zair too, soon after I am arriving I meet somevon who knows this, and he is telling me how to get zair. I have gone back now and zen, although I am not religious man now. When a child I vas, but the vor finish all zat. But vay back, ven the priest come over here, it vas still possible to be religious - yah? But perhaps I offend you. Perhaps you are both religious. I mean no disrespect. It is just not possible for me anymore, zat is all I mean to say."

Burl could see over Columbus's shoulder the man in the tweed coat talking with the barmaid. She went back towards the bar, but pointed at the piano as she went. He could just make out her saying to him, over the din of the crowd, "Have a go if you like, Sir." He rose from his chair and walked over to the vintage upright in the corner. He nervously looked about the room then took off his coat and gloves and placed them on a chair before sitting down on the bench. Soon the room was filled with an energetic rendition of *Down Town* which was then followed by applause as he started to walk back to his table, coat in hand.

"More!" someone shouted. The call was quickly echoed. The man tipped his working man's hat and went back and sat down at the piano again. This time he played a complicated, but rhythmic, piece from the classics.

"My God, he's good," Burl said to Columbus.

"Yah, very goot. I haff seen him here now and then over the years - just for a day or two - and then he is gone again. He keeps to himself, but is very friendly also. Haff not heard him play piano before. That is Bach I think he plays now. So very goot. Who would think Bach in here?" The man rose, gestured to the crowd and then went back to his table to general applause.

The businessman who had been sitting opposite Burl on the train was at the next table talking with the black couple from Detroit along with the conductor. There was a lull in the conversation and Burl leaned over towards them.

"Why don't you pull your table in here. I want you folks to meet one of the locals here."

"Right - thank you. Good idea," said the man from Norway, who then got up and oversaw the readjustment of tables and chairs.

"Your name is...?" he asked.

"Burl Manion. And my friend Kirsti. And you?"

"Anders Johannasen. I am with the Oslo Furniture Company. Happy to meet with you."

"And this is Columbus," said Burl. The others all introduced themselves around.

"What would you folks like to drink?" boomed the friendly voice of the hostess, who by now had pitched in to give the waitress a hand.

"Just a ginger ale for the two of us, thank you," replied the preacher.

"These ones will be on the railway, Rhoda," said Will Busineau, "and of course, one for Columbus here."

"How you do Vill? Haff not seen you for long time," Columbus reciprocated.

"Getting some furs this winter are you Columbus?" enquired Will Busineau.

"Not too many, but a couple of nice fishers. They should bring in a few dollars." Columbus smiled at the others. "You haff seen fishers before?" he asked, looking at the black couple. "I am sorry, your name again is...?"

"Somers...Washington Somers, and this is my wife Julia." Columbus nodded to her and extended his hand.

"Only fishers of men I think, my friend - we bein' church folk and such. What is this 'fisher' y'all talking about here?"

"Is nice animal for fur, is zat not so Burl?" exclaimed Columbus, looking at Burl for confirmation.

"Yes," said Burl. "About this long." He stretched out his hands. "You know about weasels? Well, it's a large kind of weasel, with good black fur, a fur that is much in demand."

"You don't say now. You don't say. Well - we have lots of weasel-types down where we come from around Detroit, but most of them is dressed as politicians. Difference is, they usually take our skins - not the other way around." Everyone laughed.

"Vell, I tell you my frand, ve haff a few of those type of veasels up here too," said Columbus.

"Oh, I'm sure of that ... sure of that," said Washington Somers.

Rhoda Roussain brought the drinks to the table and mentioned that it was good to have a full house in the dead of winter.

"It's good to have a full house at anytime of the year, Rhoda," countered Will Busineau, the conductor. "Besides, it's getting damned cold out there."

The windows of the tavern room facing the tracks framed portions of thick icicles. They caught and refracted yellow light from the bulbs which ran in a row along the centre of the porch roof, giving each window the appearance of a peep-hole into some underground cavern.

"Then you are a businessman, Mr. Johansen?" Burl enquired. "Taking a look at our forests over here, are you?".

"Yes, correct. My first time looking at how you are doing things over here. I am still so amazed about how long the distances are. I feel as though I am travelling since last month."

"And you see" said Columbus, "you haff not gone so far from the Sault yet, and you are still not far north, yah? And snowbound still. You may not get vair you are going this year even." Columbus grinned and winked at Burl.

"Sure. So - if that is the case - then I think this is as good a place as any to be stuck. We have much to drink, it is warm, and the gentleman over there can provide us music. Is there anything else we need?" Anders raised his glass to the table. "Skol!"

"Skol!" the others echoed. Anders Johansen was seated next to the preacher.

"Do I understand you to be a man of the church then, Mr. Somers?"

"Yes sir, that is correct. A man and woman of the church-active, to be more precise. My good wife and I, we work as a kind of team - attempting to take the word to wherever it is most needed. We don't make too much of leadership issues in our church. It rotates so to speak, and all the brothers and sisters may approach the pulpit if the spirit so moves."

"Yes, I see. So it is very democratic your church, yes?" Anders queried.

"Yes sir, that is how we see it. Everyone should be free to talk about God as they may have experienced the light."

At another table the other two parties of Americans were sitting with the train engineer and the brakeman. One of the Americans was quite fascinated by the two mounted heads flanking the main doorway into the lounge. One was a moose and the other a caribou. Above the door and between the two heads there was a sign with a fancy gilded border which read: "We Don't Give a Damn How They Do It In The South!"

"Y'all have pretty good moose huntin' around here I guess?" asked the American.

"Pretty fair. Pretty fair." said the engineer. "It's a real bugger if you hit one on the road though, even with a truck. I could tell you a few stories, I'll tell you. I'm only too glad to have the hunters get 'em."

"Sure would like to get one of those suckers. Wha'dya think Harry? Wouldn't one of those look good over my fireplace in Chicago? Tell me sir, would you be able to refer me to a huntin' guide in this area?"

"Sure I could," said the engineer. "There's one right over there at the table by the wall behind where those folks are sitting. Name's George Tawab. Knows the land around here very good. If he's not interested, he can tell you about others around the area. Quite a few Indians who will take you out. Or perhaps Columbus over there at the next table might take you out as well."

"That a fact now."

"I think George has left his card and some literature out in the foyer there. You could pick it up," the brakeman added.

"Think I'll just do that right now. Be right back. Harry - buy these good people here another round will you? And buy a round for the other table too, Harry."

Burl got up from his table to fill the popcorn basket and when he returned he found the discussion still going strong on religion.

"Do you have members of your church up here, Julie?" asked Will Busineau.

"Not so far, but we had a call from some of the Indian folks north of La Prest, that they would like to meet with us. That's why we are on the train now. Ours is called the New Alliance Church of the Redeemer."

"Yah, yah, that sounds just like the old times, when Baraga came over in last century. Ve haff people in Austria raising money for Indian missions over here back then."

"Who was that again sir?" asked Washington Somers.

"Father Baraga. Burl and I were talking about him a little time ago. He vas a Roman Catholic from old contree working around Lake Superior, more than one hundred years now. Some are vant to make him a saint."

"You don't say now. A saint you say? That's something our church does not have much to say about, being low church and all. We have lots of sinners however," said Washington Somers and everyone laughed.

"Mr. Somers," whispered Columbus, "you see zat man sitting over in za corner wit za papers and pen? His fadder used to be connected wit zat church of Baraga's." Columbus was pointing towards George Tawab, a heavy-set man, who was just getting up from the table by the wall and folding his papers under his arm as if to leave.

"Say George?" called out the engineer, Fred Palmer.

"How you, Fred?" George Tawab waved to him.

"Good, very good - look, George, just before you leave, there are some folks here I want you to meet." George Tawab walked over towards the table where the Americans were sitting.

"Ladies, gentleman - welcome to Cowie," he said.

"George, these folks are from the States and think they

might like to go huntin' for moose some time. Thought you might be able to help them out."

"Glad to meet you Mr. Tawab" said the one called Harry. "Obliged if we might be able to make some arrangements with you sometime."

"Everyone call me George here. You gentleman been in the bush much before?"

"Some, George, mostly in northern Michigan."

"Close enough, I would say. Tell you what. If you take my card and pick up the literature out front, you can send me a note about when you would like to come. You probably know about our hunting season and regulations up here. If not, I can send that to you."

"Very good, George. Would you join us for a drink?"

"Thank you, but no, I think I've had my fill for the night. Gotta stay sobre or else I'll jump into that open patch in the Montreal River for a swim." The people at the table sat silent for a moment. Then George Tawab burst out laughing, revealing the full force of his smile. The others laughed as well, but only Fred Palmer laughed from deep down, having seen George Tawab pull that one on strangers before.

Columbus had been watching the negotiations. He leaned over to Burl and said "Now zair is one bush-smart man. You get lost in bush, you vant to be vith him, for sure. He goes back long vay around here. His fadder, his fadder's fadder, you know what I am say? You find his name in za old church register by za lake."

"And his name again?" asked Burl.

"Tawab - George Tawab."

"Yes - I think I have heard that name from my friend, Angus Ashabish."

"Sometimes I am meeting him in za bush where I least expect to find anybody. Sometimes he stop at my cabin and ve take tea and fish togezair." Washington Somers watched George Tawab move away from the table and shake hands with the man in the tweed coat before he left the pub room.

"So - I zink, Mr. Somers," said Columbus "you might have trouble saving zat man's soul."

"Why is that sir?"

"It's already been saved. The man knows vot he believes and vy he believes it." Columbus winked.

"Must be that some of his country kin are not so sure, since they been writin' to us for some time now. Talkin' about a crisis among the people."

"Yah, yah, no doubt. But George - he is different matter. His soul out there wiz ze animals."

"The animals?" asked Washington. "That sounds quite pagan to me, sir. No real redemption is possible at that level. Don't mean a person may not be well motivated and all, but in terms of feeling the inner light, doesn't seem likely to me."

"Yah - but you see, maybe za light may mean something different - like a full stomach and feeding the young children. I too can believe this, because I haff seen zis in za old contree. Thousands of people scratching around in za ruins looking for a full stomach. You find an old crust of bread and zat is za light as you call."

"You have the advantage of me sir. You are talking about your experience of the war I believe. I do not disagree with what you say there, I am sure. That was your experience of things."

Columbus waved to Rhoda and ordered another round for the table. Julia Washington had said little but was following the discussion closely. Kirsti and Burl had been watching the duel as though it were a ping-pong match.

"Columbus," Julia interjected, "do you think the Indians of these parts have an idea of the evil one as well as the light? Perhaps the devil, or something like that?"

"Yah! Of this I am sure, Mrs. Somers. Of this I am sure. For some people, he is alvays hiding, vaiting to get zem when they do not expect - or after they have committed some great insult or violence against somebody. For others, he is not so hard to find. For instance, in za bottom of a bottle like zis. Yah?"

"Quite so Columbus, quite so," Julia nodded in agreement. "Perhaps we are not in such disagreement then. Do you believe in the devil, Columbus?"

"Oh yah. I haff met him many times. For me he is not hidden at all. For me you do not have to look under za rock for him or beneath za mountain or in za bottom of za lake. You just haff to join a political party or za army, or perhaps just look in za mirror."

"What do you recommend then?" asked Julie.

"Better to - how you say in English? - 'to live wit za devil you know, zan wit za one you do not know' - better to talk to him now and zen, radder zan ignore him. Zis I tink is vot the Indians do. They haff many devils scattered around in za bush and in za rivers, not just one big devil. And they recommend you get to know zem, and maybe even give zem present some times. Devils get lonely too."

Nobody rose to the bait of that statement and all were saved from having to do so when Rhoda Roussain appeared at the table announcing that, for those on the train, dining tables had been set up in the side lounge. "After dinner, you folks can pick up your room keys at the desk."

Kirsti and Burl took their leave from Columbus and the others and slid into a small table for two which had a card on it saying *Mr. and Mrs. Manion.*

"Oh, isn't this sweet," said Kirsti, smiling broadly at Burl, and fluttering her eyelids. "They've looked after all the little details. I wonder how they knew. Me without a ring and all."

"Very discreeet of them, don't you think?" said Burl, who looked rather sheepish.

"I can hardly wait to see *our* room." Burl felt himself losing this joust. He picked up the menu. Kirsti reached over and pulled it down from his eyes.

"I think maybe Columbus is right, you know that?"

"How so?"

"Do you have something in your eye?"

"No - I don't feel anything?"

"Let me take a closer look." She reached over and gently spread the flesh above and below one eye. "Oh yes - there it is. I can see it. I do believe that... yes... I do believe that the devil is in your eye."

"Is he a friendly looking one?"

"Very. I think I would like to get to know him better."

Twelve

By the Fire

i

Kakayosha Maywins led a fatigued quartet along the crimson-dusk beach of Superior. In the lengthening shadows it stretched out ahead of them in a great curve to the northwest where half an hour earlier the sun, masked by a band of cloud, had sunk into the lake like a pillar of flame. There was no longer any clear line indicating where the sky ended and the water began. It was the conclusion of a day inspecting shore life and whatever else time had dragged up for view. Kakayosha led them higher up on the beach ridge, into a series of the circular cobble depressions encountered here and there on isolated stretches of the north shore. Walking was difficult on the round unstable stones and eyes were fixed downward. Kakayosha was the first to point to a fire flickering about a half-mile ahead. Its minimal glow began to exercise an influence on the hikers akin to that of the flame over the moth.

"Looks like we'll run right into it," said Burl. "We have some food to share, and who knows, perhaps there is something already cooking."

"Lead on," said Kakayosha. Alf Anderson grunted in

agreement and Felix Smith suggested they regain the beach lower down for easier walking. A single figure gradually added itself to the low fire light ahead. The smell of wood smoke drifted down the beach to greet the party.

"Hmmm, that smells cosy," said Kakayosha, beaming a smile at Burl.

"Oh lady, I do think you are right. Perhaps we should send you in first as kind of a peace offering. What do you think fellows?"

"Get out! If I go in alone, I eat alone," she laughed as she pushed Burl towards the water.

"Okay - we all starve together then. Looks like I have to do all the diplomatic work around here."

"Right Burl. That's why we brought you along," said Alf. "After all - you're the guy who asked the local member for Mashkisibi at the annual Christmas party if he smoked dope." Felix had moved into his cross-country trekking stride and pulled away from the others. Forty yards later he yelled a "hello" to the man by the fire and gave him the high sign. The man responded and slowly rose to his feet.

"C'mon in," the man called out. He was standing in a fixed position waiting for a face to emerge out of the ambiguous light. "Didn't expect to see anyone hoofing it along here at this hour." The man was tall and slim and had made himself a comfortable nest at a point where the beach widened out considerably, divided by the estuary of a small stream.

"There's three more behind me," Felix said. When the stragglers arrived the man asked them to pull up a log and then they introduced themselves around. Kakayosha had already recognized the man as Professor Simon Russell from the Sault.

"Good to see you all. Well, I have some coffee left here, and could make some more, and as you can see, I have a good mess of whitefish. Didn't catch them myself of course. I leave that to a fellow named Angus down there at Tawab's Cove. He gets the best darned whitefish I've ever eaten."

"He sure does," said Kakayosha. "I know him well. He's my uncle."

"You don't say now. Well, you're a lucky one." Simon kept his eyes on Kakayosha and cocked his head slightly. "Now, I think we know each other don't we? It's... it's... don't tell me yet...I'll get your name."

"Kakayosha Maywins," she said.

"Yes...now I remember. You came to see me some time ago about doing courses in the Sault next fall." Simon Russell paused to stoke his carved pipe. His craggy features were reinforced by the flickering light from the fire.

"Still think I'll go to school at the college in the fall," Kakayosha offered. "I'll take a year off from my teaching at the reserve - and probably starve instead."

"Good, good, I'm glad to hear it. Not about you starving, of course. If you decide to take history, we will probably see more of each other. Come and see me before the school year begins if you like." Simon Russell then looked at the others. "Now let me ask you if you have eaten anything tonight?"

"Not so far, Simon," said Felix. "Our camp is down the way a bit, but we do have some things we could set out here."

"Good, that's just fine. We can throw everything together. We'll just put on a few of these whitefish here, unless you folks have a special way you want to cook 'em up?"

"Would you like me to cook them - Indian style?" Kakayosha asked.

"Sounds good to me. I'll show you what I have in my box here - if you need any extras."

"Okay - but just relax. I'm going to go along the beach and up on the ridge to gather a few things, and then when I come back I'll fix you the best whitefish you've ever had."

"I'm not about to refuse that offer." said Simon. "Is it not too dark for you to see?"

"With my trusty flashlight here I'll be alright. Know pretty well what I'm looking for." Kakayosha pranced into the dusk.

177

"I guess maybe there's nothing to do then but to pour some coffee and perhaps add a little to it, if you gentlemen wish. Looks like otherwise we're in real good hands."

Simon Russell pulled out a flask of Scotch from his knapsack and offered to "add a little." A book lay face down at Simon's side, along with a few note pads and pens and a guide to the geology of Lake Superior.

"Good place to do a little reading out here isn't it," Alf Anderson said.

"It is. I've been doing a bit of rock hounding today, but there's nothing quite as good as getting back to a fixed place and just relaxing. If there are no people around, then a book will do very nicely as a companion. Mind you, it would be hard to find a book that could grip you as much as this shoreline. There is something utterly haunting along here, and I can't quite say what it is. At any rate, I decided not to bring a mystery along to read...it would be kind of redundant."

"So what's the book?" asked Burl.

"Its an old archaeological book I've been meaning to read for some time - thought it might kind of complement the setting, although it's not about North America."

"You've got that right," said Felix. "We got a lot of archaeologists mucking around out here. Wish I had a quarter for every moment of agony some of dose buggers have caused me." Felix's face broke into a wide grin revealing he wasn't totally serious. "Mother of Jeezus. Last summer, I had one-a-dem clowns workin' for Victor trying to buy wine for de crew on a local government purchase order. The accountant had a shit-fit!"

"Yeah, Felix - you're just jealous 'cause you've finally found a bunch of people who are actually crazier than you are," said Alf, who was bent down, stoking the fire. Everyone laughed as Simon started to fill their coffee cups.

"So then, I gather that you're with the park, is that right Felix?"

"That's right Simon. All of us here. Myself, I joined up

after workin' the mines north of Mashkisibi for a bit. Came here after the mine closings away in Newfoundland. It's not for me though, workin' under da ground. I needs air."

"Thought that voice of yours had a shade of Newfie twang about it. Well...you've certainly found the right solution then."

"Yes sir. It would take the Russian army to get me away from here now, I tink."

"Do you fellows know of many caves along this stretch?"

"There are a few for sure," said Felix. "Some out towards de *Devil's Chair*. That's what everybody calls it. Bunch of shoals down that way. Place gives me the shakes though. Don't go out there 'less I really have to. Local Indians feel the same way."

"Then there's the *Devil's Warehouse* a little further on," added Alf.

"I've prowled around some of the caves in southern France - the ones where cavemen left art on the walls. Those have rather piqued my curiosity about caves generally, although I don't do any real serious caving."

"I know some pretty good caves a bit further south," said Felix, "but I don't think you're going to find any damn paintings in 'em. Maybe some old stashes of booze. That is...if I haven't been there first."

"Not a chance of that then," said Alf.

"Yeah - guess you're right about that," said Felix. "Sorry professor - you're probably too late and shit-out-uv-luck."

"That's alright," said Simon. "I've been tryin' to cut down on my drinking anyway. This pipe will probably kill me fast enough, if I don't talk myself to death first in front of my classes. But perhaps you fellas would like another shot of Scotch - I'm only trying to cut down you see - not quit altogether." The men laughed and Felix angled over towards Simon.

"Don't mind if I do professor." Felix held out his cup to the offering hand. "When you're in Mashkisibi next, you come around and me and the wife will fix you up a mess of lobster down ta the cabin. I just got a load in from buddy at ta mine who's after comin' back from Newfoundland wit a supply. Good as hell, I'll tell you."

"That sounds good Felix - I would like that - thank you." Felix took a sip from his strengthened coffee and looked out at the lake for a long moment and then walked towards the edge of the water. There was no sound but the hissing from the fire for the lake had fallen into a dead calm.

"Think I'll stroll along the beach with this for a bit - see you all a little later." Felix eased himself out beyond the unstable light of the hearth and the others watched as his back disappeared into the rising darkness. The professor broke the spell by stirring up the flames into a burst of rising sparks.

"This *Devil's Chair* - now where would that be again?" he asked.

"About six miles in from the highway by an old logging road" said Alf. "Or, if you want to really test yourself, you can hike from here along the shore line. Its near an old fishing port and lighthouse, both abandoned now for quite a few years." Alf had pulled out a small note pad and started sketching a diagram for Simon Russell.

"Would that be a name given by the whites or the Indians, do you suppose?"

"I guess you could say both," said Burl. "It was an important site to the Indians, and the name reflects a certain sense of evil, although I can't say if the term *devil* is really appropriate or not. You would want to ask Angus about that I think. There have been lots of names for that headland, some of them quite ribald. It was called Gargantua by the old French voyageurs, and the name stuck to the fishing port later on.

Kakayosha suddenly appeared out of nowhere, her hands full of herbs. "Everybody still hungry, I hope? Just give me a few minutes more."

"Hope you don't think this will get you off from writing my exams, Kakayosha."

"Oh darn! You're no fun professor," said Kakayosha. She squatted down by the fire and set about her food preparations. Burl had been fussing in the back of his knapsack for a folder with some maps.

"Ah - here it is. Thought I had this with me," said Burl. "Take a quick look at this Simon. It's a copy of a portion of a map which Alexander Henry made when he came through here in 1775." Simon held it out before the fire and Burl flashed Kakayosha's flashlight onto a section of the map. "About that headland just south of where the Chair is he has written right on the map 'a remarkable high Rock laying at a small distance from the shore, it is said by the Indians to be the residence of some evil Spirit, the rock being hollow with an opening into it.' So there you have it. A genuine reference."

"I'll have to read up on old Henry," Simon Russell said. "I teach mainly European history." Simon Russell bent over the map again and then raised his head, folding it up. "And did you find everything you were looking for, Kakayosha?"

"Got it all. We're gonna feast good here." The men watched her flying around the fire, all efficiency.

"And so would you recommend that book of yours there Simon?" asked Burl.

"If you have a keen interest in such things, then yes, I would. It's by a woman named Mary Boyle. She used to spend a lot of time in south France inspecting the cave paintings there and she knew some of the important scholars such as the Abbé Breuil. He was one of the ones who first got into the caves in the Dordogne. It's not an easy book to find now. Most of the modern books on archaeology are rather cold, full of statistics, theories, charts and models. That's the way things move now. But some of these older scholars, they wrote from the heart and guts about what they found, and they didn't think emotion was a dirty word. Quite often it had cost them a lot in terms of

181

time, money and private life to gain the knowledge they sought so much. And then also, there were other factors. In the first half of the century, there always seemed to be some bloody war going on to complicate things. It was not so easy as now when there are a lot of universities and more money floating around and better chances to go and do field work." He paused to stoke his pipe. "But there I go - lecturing and sounding like the old fart that I am."

The smell of the cooking fish now started to envelop the beachcombers. Felix reappeared with a superb sense of timing and Kakayosha, kneeling by the fire, started to serve up the meal. Plates were passed around and sounds of appreciation filled the air. When everyone had finished Simon stood up and looked out at the smooth glass of the surface of Lake Superior. A quarter moon had broken through the twilight and cast a perfect reflection on the water. "You know," he said, "looking at the stillness of this lake reminds me of history itself."

"How so?" asked Kakayosha.

"It's because the goddess of history, Clio, is reputed to wear a seamless robe," he said.

"Now just what would dat be all about Simon?" Felix asked.

"Well, at its root Felix, I think, is the idea that you can't have an explanation of the past or of any specific series of events, which excludes any relevant evidence. So that the best interpretation of the past - or as we like to call it - *historical explanation* - will be that which admits as much of the knowable evidence as possible. And of course, *new evidence* can always be admitted at any time."

"Is it a bit like dis den, professor. If Constable Rex Mathews nails me for drunk driving - and I go to da slammer on da charge - and then I hire a good lawyer to get me off - cause I in fact hadn't had any booze - and I could prove it - that would be what we are getting at here?"

" In a nutshell, Felix - excellent - in a nutshell," replied Simon.

"Son-uv-a-bitch," Felix blurted. "Wait 'till I tell Rex this one."

"And do you think that Clio does indeed wear a seamless robe?" asked Kakayosha. The professor looked at the fire for a moment, and then began stoking his pipe.

"I'm playing with my pipe in order to buy time. It's an ancient custom with academics. Yes... I think so... tattered to be sure, but still seamless." He paused to light-up. "But it's certainly not a very fashionable robe these days. Some believe it's so moth-eaten as not to be worth putting on anymore." The professor chuckled and then looked at Burl: "What do you think about that?" There was a long pause. Burl was looking into the fire with great intensity.

"I think the robe is seamless too," said Burl, "but it also comes in an infinite set of sizes, colours and fabrics. Most people do not want to wear it very often, unless it suits some narrow purpose, and when they do, they usually only want a robe of the greatest lightness and transparency. One which allows them to see through it to the very ends of the universe. It has been a very popular robe with dictators though. They seem to be especially comfortable in this kind of robe because it confirms every bit of nonsense they have inherited from their father or have come to believe, by whatever route. Others, more fashion-conscious perhaps, wish something a little heavier and more colourful, while still others prefer something tight-fitting in a very dark colour, closed at the front and back. Many religious leaders have been seen wearing this last type over the centuries." Burl paused. "Sorry, I'm, becoming very pompous here." Simon Russell had taken it all in with great relish.

"Go on Burl, go on," he encouraged.

"Well - on the more practical level - many politicians have been seen wearing robes of many different sizes, cuts and colours, changing them regularly, sensing the content of history to be like a kaleidoscope, or like the changing seasons perhaps."

"One of the odd things though," Simon said, "is that there doesn't seem to be a whole lot of difference between the kinds of robes worn by the rich and poor - on a qualitative scale. You will find the well-to-do quite as likely to pick a robe of tattered ideas out of the sale-bin as much as the poor person. And you may find a downtrodden worker wearing a most impressive robe just as fine as that of a well-educated and universal man."

"Yes, I agree," said Burl. "It's a world of everyman. I think that's why I enjoy talking history with a Newfie hoser like Felix here, just as much as I enjoy reading Gibbon." Burl fed a piece of driftwood onto the fire and everyone laughed, and Felix laughed the hardest. The laughter subsided.

"Now who da hell is dis guy Gibbon, Burl? Does he drink beer at da Snake Pit?"

"He might, if he was around, but more likely at the Legion Hall. Gibbon was a man who wrote more than he should have about the Roman Empire a couple of hundred years ago."

"By Jeezus, I think I been had here... I'm not that bloody old. For that, I think I'm after having another shot of da professor's Scotch." During the laughter Simon Russell passed the bottle over to Felix. There was a momentary lull in the conversation which was suddenly broken by the brilliance of a shooting star which fell out of heaven and seemed to plunge into the very centre of Lake Superior.

"Far, far out!" exclaimed Kakayosha. Everybody got up and moved away from the fire towards the beach and then stood at close attention, hoping for a repeat.

"You see," said Burl, "even that was instantly absorbed by the seamless gown of the lake. Simon is right." They all moved back again around the fire.

"Yes - I like your way of going about this," said Simon, "but tell me one thing - who is the tailor? - or should I say - the tailors?"

"There are only a few main tailors I think, many of these also being of a religious bent. But then, there are a lot of factory-outlets pushing better or worse designs. Now and then some independently fabricated robes appear on the market out of non-union shops, Scientology or Mormonism for instance. But they are rather rare. Some robes have a lot of resilience however, such as the one designed by Hegel or Muhammad. The Marxian imitations of Hegel were not nearly as good as the master's though. Too many dropped stitches."

Simon chuckled heartily. "That's good. Remind me to use that in one of my lectures."

"This is getting pretty heavy, you guys," said Kakayosha. "I am not sure I know what you are all talking about anymore. Who's Marx and who's Hegel?"

"You must forgive us Kakayosha" said Simon Russell. "Burl and I are running the risk of becoming frightfully boring."

"For me, I kinda liked the story I heard as a kid in church about Joseph and his coat of many colours" Kakayosha said. "Do you suppose one should wear a robe like that? You wouldn't ever give offence that way. Although I think you have to know a bit about where you have come from if you are going to make sense of other things around you."

"Amen," said Simon. "Perhaps you have pre-selected your essay topic for next year."

A log exploded into a shower of sparks which floated up into the night like fireflies. The philosophy lesson ended and all sat, eyes fixed on the flames, which warmed but did not instruct.

"Do you want to move over to our camp and go back with us tomorrow Professor?" Kakayosha broke the long silence.

"Thank you, but I plan to stay out another day and track further south."

"I suppose we should be leaving you, and getting on down the beach to our camp. I hope you have a good hike tomorrow," said Alf. "If you find anything unusual, I would be glad to learn of it. Drop into the Naturalist's Office at Black Pebble anytime."

"I'll do that Alf - a pleasure to meet you. All of you. Look - before you go - I want to just read you a short passage. I think you will like it - and it fits our setting here so well tonight - may I?" The professor held out his pipe like a conductor's baton.

"Please do - that would be so very excellent," said Kakayosha.

"Very well. Here it is then." Simon fixed a small reading flashlight on the page. "This is Mary Boyle speaking, back in the nineteen thirties, after she had visited the cave paintings of France."

The longer we travel the more entrancing will be the journey, centuries will fall behind us like autumn leaves, time will lose its significance, and nationality will have no meaning, the absorbing epic of humanity will unfold, until we stand in a universe beyond the dreams and genius of any single race, and look outward over the ocean of the unknown.

Kakayosha sat down again on a large rock next to the fire. Nobody spoke for a long time. All were looking quietly upward towards the stars which were emerging into a magnificent display spread across the great bowl of the night sky. "That was so beautiful," said Kakayosha. "Please read it again."

"Yes - that is pretty good isn't it? - There's something for everybody there - no matter who you are - no matter where you come from." Simon read it again. They sat for a few more minutes, listening to the fire beating its small heart against the vastness of the universe. Felix got up but did not speak.

"Thank you for the company and the thoughts," said Burl, rising to his feet in turn.

"Don't forget to drop around in Mashkisibi, Professor" said Felix. "The wife's as crazy as I am, and she can cook up lobster like nobody's business." Felix shook hands with Simon. Everybody picked up their gear and Alf gave Simon his card.

"Goodnight," Kakayosha waved a long goodbye as she backed slowly away from the fire and into the shadows. Burl followed her, bearing the flashlight.

Simon Russell watched them disappear into the night, like the elements of an interrupted dream. He suddenly felt exhausted, more tired than he had ever been before. He gazed after them, straining his eyes, until they were nothing but muffled sounds. He lifted his eyes towards the stars again, where they mixed with the sparks rising from a new log on the fire. The sight suddenly provided the most wonderful comfort. This was a setting anyone might crave during his last moments on earth: cave-warmth, wombal, eiderdown-like mystery, regained at the end.

"No person should part from the scene in a clinical manner - let there be the soft light of Altamira and Lascaux - let there be people bearing flowers - gentle Cro-Magnon - you knew that already, didn't you?" Simon was speaking to the stars. He got up and walked down to the shore where no water was lapping. Just a perfect continuum from solid to liquid. He stood and looked up until his mind started to bend and then walked back to his neatly arranged lean-to. He reached for his sleeping role and unfurled it, slipped off his boots and then worked his way into the bag. He then reached for his journal notebook and turned to the next blank page where he penned a new date. Under the heading of "Lake Superior: Glacial Beach, Lake Minong" he wrote:

I used to be alive to the things of the mind, like my young friends. Ideas burned like fires in the night on black hills. And we? We fed them with the winds of our young passion. Oh, the brightness of those flames - and such a heat! I have been peering through the flames, trying to see below the floor of the hearth, trying to see what supports all of this frenetic motion; but I cannot see any sub-structures. I can only feel the present, tottering on piles sunken in quicksand, and the water rising to wash the flimsy spars out to sea.

Thirteen

The Night of the Dog

i

Olivia Wilson had just turned twenty. It was well known that she had been the recipient of a stern and unbending religious upbringing in a town which gloried in the midnight revel. From age twelve, her trademark had been a Labrador Retriever, a friendly beast going by the name of Blackjack, a dog that accompanied her everywhere. In the summer just passed, girl and dog had for the first time become a trio. Karl Zimmerman had been Olivia's first real boy friend. Open about her affection at the beginning, she began to take great precautions in her meetings with Karl Zimmerman after having brought him home to a more than cool reception. Two weeks after this awkward encounter, she had been informed matter-of-factly by her father that "he was not for her" and that she was to cease to see him. Through the complicity of her friends at Black Pebble Lake, Olivia managed to continue the relationship, even declaring once that she was staying over at Black Pebble Lake for some weekend camping with her co-workers. There were no secrets kept for long in Mashkisibi. One late summer Monday morning, Olivia appeared at work bruised about the jaws. She told Kirsti Kalella, very privately, that it was not the doing of Karl Zimmerman, but said no more.

On a September evening, Olivia Wilson and Karl Zimmerman returned to her home at about midnight, both somewhat tipsy. To no surprise, they found Albert Wilson waiting on the porch. Olivia had quickly backed Karl Zimmerman down the walkway and told him to leave, not wishing to embarrass him again. He pleaded with her for a moment to come with him, but she insisted on doing things her way, and he withdrew, but not before a few barbs were hurled at him from the dimness of the porch. Albert Wilson then remained silent as Olivia moved passed him and into the house. He followed her into the living room. Blackjack bounced over to Olivia and she nuzzled his head. She could see the light of the reading lamp reflected in his eyes. Albert Wilson coldly announced that if she continued to see Karl, he would have no choice but to force her to shoot Blackjack. This ultimatum hit Olivia like an unexpected fist in the stomach. She stood up sharply but still slightly bent over, eyes straining, trying to get air, and then sank to the floor in a fit of quiet whimpering. Her father stood silent for a moment, savouring his victory, and then proceeded to feign a slight sense of mercy.

"Very well then, we understand the gravity of the situation," he said. "Be repentant and go to bed and we will not speak of this again. It will not be necessary will it? Neither of us wants to see Blackjack harmed, do we?"

Olivia gathered herself off the floor, grabbed Blackjack to her body and held him tightly until her father disappeared. She shakily mounted the stairs to her room, Blackjack trailing behind her. She fell on the bed and cried quietly until a form of sleep claimed her. Much later, she got up and went to the window and looked down at the familiar wooden, castle-like, doghouse she had made for Blackjack many years ago. Her father had helped her to build it. "That was the one and only thing we ever really did together," she whispered to the dog who was standing beside her below the open window.

In the days following the receipt of the Blackjack ultimatum, Olivia's behaviour remained outwardly unchanged except that she insisted Zimmerman stay away from the house completely. The lovers met in the restaurants or bars, along the beaches, or in the bush. Then on a perfect autumn late afternoon, when the land was mad with colour, the couple strolled out along the coast. They walked on, oblivious of time, past the old fishing village, past the sheer rock at the cove with its ancient red ochre paintings, past the last signs of anything, and then out onto a long, curving beach which would have taken them towards the Devil's Chair. They followed the path of the moon as it rose and then hung suspended over Lake Superior, blinking through high thin clouds like a serpent's eye. When a sudden breeze of cooler air caught Olivia in the face, she quickly turned to Karl and said to him - "tonight." When he hesitated, she said it again, a little louder - "tonight." She encouraged Karl to take her meaning in the only way he could; and there on soft green where grasses encroached upon the dunes, with the scent of pine and water everywhere, he gathered her up in his arms, stretched out beside her, pulled his coat around them both and gave her all the tenderness he had, and they kept each other warm. An hour later they stumbled, rather than walked, back towards the town, intentionally taking forever, all the while cursing the inconvenience of sand, laughing at their bodies, toasting the moon, delighting in being quite drunk on themselves, and holding all in contempt who rushed by in cars on such a night as this. Karl was content and happy and he told her so.

The lovers finally came out of the bush at the end of a street on the edge of town which led towards Olivia's home nearby. Albert Wilson was waiting for her under the porch light, as she knew he would be. Her nerves tightened and she turned to her lover and fixed a look upon him that Karl would later describe to Kirsti as "both tender and foreign." It was not just a look of gratitude or joy. It was a look given by one full of dark knowledge to one who is not. Then she had said to him:

"You must leave now - I'll be alright - you are precious to me - it will blow over soon - leave now for my sake and yours." He took her in his arms and kissed her deeply. He then reminded her that he would not tolerate a second attack upon her. She assured him that she could handle things, but if he got violent again, she would come to him. Karl then backed away slowly and shuffled off backwards down the street with a periodic wave of the hand. She returned his wave and watched him disappear into the woods like one of the old French *coureur de bois*.

Olivia listened to Karl's footsteps fade and become those of her father who had started approaching her from the porch. Olivia could also hear the familiar jingle of Blackjack's collar tags and the shuffle of her mother's feet. It was all too familiar to Olivia. This time Jean Wilson had been bludgeoned onto the scene, a reluctant extra, inwardly yearning to return to her kitchen to see if, perhaps, she had left the kettle plugged in.

"The family that kills together, stays together," Olivia whispered to the trees. Moonlight congested the swaying, witness pines which lined the driveway. She turned slowly and looked fixedly at her mother. Jean Wilson's eyes went down even lower where they could not meet those of her daughter. Poor pathetic creature, I could almost feel for you - but you have been such an accomplice to your own destruction. These words went through Olivia's mind. She yearned to articulate them, to say them aloud, but as so often before, something held her back, perhaps a submerged recognition that her mother's main fault was an unrepairable weakness of spirit and a lack of luck.

Olivia turned towards her father, determined to stare him down. An uncontrollable quiver suddenly ran amok through her neck muscles and upper chest and then spread to her whole body. It was as though an icicle ran the length of her, from the top of her head to her feet. She gazed past her father to Blackjack, tethered on the steps, whimpering his pleasure at seeing her again. She smiled, called to him and went and fetched him, determined to regain her composure.

"You recall our agreement?" Albert Wilson asked her.

"I recall your *sick* order, yes," she rejoined. Another kind of coldness had taken over her body, similar to the one she had felt the night she had received his stern pronouncement. Olivia fought to gain control of her physical being. She allowed her thoughts to wander back to the beach, to Karl, and to the moon and the sound of the waves. She looked at Blackjack, went over to him, and took his head in her hands and roughed his fur. The quivering in her neck waned and a new calmness settled over her, one truly the product of her own will: controlled, firm, resolute. She thought of hours in the library, and of the stoicism of Turner's black slave, clinging to his spar after having been thrown overboard.

"I am ready then." Her face had become a mask, frozen and unbending. Alex Wilson's eyes narrowed. She knew he had been expecting great protestations and an emotional collapse, and that, in the end, he himself would have to shoot Blackjack. Olivia had no doubt that he would.

"You said I had to shoot the dog," Olivia said calmly.

"That was the agreement." Albert Wilson said, emphasizing the last word.

"And you mother, you agree with this?"

"Your Mother agrees with...."

"Let her speak!" yelled Olivia, breaking Alex Wilson off in mid-sentence, and starting him backwards. He was stunned, but quickly recovered and moved to strike her across the face, but Blackjack was by Olivia's side and as she moved back from his raised hand, the dog sank his teeth briefly into Alex Wilson's ankle, and then withdrew, a pensive growl remaining in his throat as a warning.

"Bastard!... Hound of hell!...I should....." He was on one knee, rubbing his ankle firmly. Alex Wilson quickly regained his composure.

"I asked mother a question," Olivia said more firmly. There was a momentary silence as the petrified woman looked at her husband, then at the dog, then at Olivia, then at the ground.

"Your father... your father...your fa, fa, father... has...has... has...."

"Very well then, you agree." Olivia looked longingly at her, allowing her own mask to slip off ever so slightly for just a few seconds. It was the last disappointment.

"Where shall we do it? Right here in our own yard?"

"Yes," said Alex Wilson.

"Alright - but I need a few moments to be by myself. I'm going to walk down the street a bit, and then I will be back." Olivia did not wait for any confirmation of this plan. She just turned and walked down the driveway and onto the street. Halfway down the block, she withdrew the letter that had been lodged in her jacket for over three days, a letter addressed to Kirsti Kallela. When she reached the mailbox at the end of the block, Olivia slowly ran her hands over it a number of times, blew on it, whispered a few words to it, kissed it, and pushed it through the slot. In the darkness, the metal flap slammed shut like a door closed in anger.

Olivia turned around to take the measure of the street in order to see if her calculations were going to hold. There had to be witnesses. She had planned on the regular behaviour of the neighbours. All was still, but a block and a half away further down the street, Olivia was able to pick out a couple strolling slowly in her direction. So intimate are shapes that even in the low filtered light of the street lamps playing through the pines she was able to tell that it was the couple from two lots past their house, returning as usual from their late night stroll. Olivia turned abruptly and walked briskly towards home. She walked as does one who is going with the wind at thirty below. When she reached the driveway Blackjack strained against his tether, trying to reach her, but did not bark. She had been trained not to bark.

"Stay Blackjack, stay." Olivia turned to her father. "You have the pistol loaded," she asked.

"Yes, here, take it. We will try not to disturb the neighbours."

"Or let them know we are breaking the law," Olivia said. She faced the street and held the gun up towards the light, more to gauge the progress of the couple advancing along the sidewalk on the opposite side.

"The gun is alright," Olivia observed. Alex Wilson nodded in agreement. Olivia handed it back to him and then led Blackjack down to the end of the yard where she tied him to the dog house. "Stay Blackjack, stay." She walked back and took the pistol from her father and checked the action once more.

"Are you a happy man, father?"

"Life has its unpleasant tasks, girl. Always bin that way."

"Will you and mother be happy tomorrow?"

"I shall be resolved in my duty tomorrow, that is all. Nothing more." He had turned and was now standing next to Jean Wilson, all of them facing the dog.

Olivia then levelled the pistol at Blackjack's head from seven yards, straight-arm fashion. The dog was sitting upright, its large face warmed by the porch light, its eyes fixed on those of its master, with no sign of unease. Jean Wilson's face was downcast as usual, but Alex allowed his eyes to move along the imaginary line from gun to dog. All held their stance, like midnight sculptures in a park. Olivia could hear the footsteps directly across the street, the pace complicated by soft and happy chatter. A great stillness settled over the yard as the couple passed.

The tension in the yard was now severe and Alex Wilson turned his head slowly towards Olivia in order to prod her to the task, once and for all. His mouth froze with the words still on his tongue. In the brief moment of aiming the gun, Olivia had taken out a tube of lipstick and smeared it carelessly around her mouth and cheeks. Her head was cocked back in order to better reflect the porch light off her face. She had become an instant caricature of a woman of the street. A contorted and contemptuous smile played back and forth over her face. The barrel rested against her temple.

"Will you be happy tomorrow father?" On the far side of the street, the strolling couple heard what sounded like the sharp crack of a branch breaking in the aftermath of an ice storm.

ii

The afternoon suited the occasion in Mashkisibi Town. Great thick clouds rolled down, monsoon-like, from Hudson Bay. It was not raining but it was uniformly drear, a proper day for a funeral. Burl Manion sat alone in the Cypress Restaurant contemplating one more time the strange circumstances which had made the funeral necessary. He recalled his meetings with Olivia Wilson, particularly the one at the local library. He had thought much about that occasion over the last few days. Through the front window of the Cypress Restaurant he could see a series of cars moving out from the churchyard across the road. Left behind was a small group of chiaroscuro mourners, huddled on the steps of the white, functional, aluminum-clad church. The people milled about together for a minute or so before sloping off in several directions, as if seeking escape from some lurking predator. A few others then emerged from the church, filling the vacuum created by those who just moved along into the street.

"Where does pity begin, and for whom?" asked the man behind the counter. He had also been watching events unfold while hand-drying some mugs. He wiped the counter clean and Burl got up to pour himself another cup of Ardo's specially brewed Turkish coffee. "Do you know what they will be calling it soon?" he asked.

"What's that Ardo?" Burl replied.

"They'll be calling it *the night of the dog*. After all, I have already started to *call* it that." Ardo paused over the sink and then went over to the front window. "Yes sir...*the night of the dog*," he repeated a little more slowly and softly. Ardo Kulduhn was the only Egyptian in town, and he could always be counted upon to play the role of desert philosopher. He was a man who had been born into rural society along the Nile and he had lived in small towns most of his life, "as a matter of preference" he would say to those who enquired. "I look over there and I remember what my father would say to me back in Egypt. We lived south of Cairo you know. Yes, my father - as I have told you many times - was always quoting the Prophet. I think he quoted all kinds of people, now that I think about it. Anyway, my father would say - 'there are three things which cannot be retrieved: the arrow, once sped from the bow; the word spoken in haste; and the missed opportunity.' I look over there my young friend, and I fear that all three irretrievables are in evidence." As a social commentator, Ardo played his role well. From his little neon-encased, civic-observatory window, he was able to learn all about Mashkisibi and its goings-on. To his select customers he would sometimes outline the town's strengths and weaknesses, occasionally revealing an intimate knowledge of those privately zoned districts of heaven and hell which did not appear on any municipal planning map. To the discreet, he parcelled out tid-bits of information concerning who was on the take, and who was not; who gave to charities and who did not; who was bitter and who was content.

Burl picked up on what Ardo had said, and he slipped off into private reflection. Opportunities - civility - pity - towns - cities - Egypt. Words from an old radio news broadcast landed out of nowhere, bringing recollections of the Arab-Israeli War of 1967. In the aftermath of that event, there had been a remarkable encounter on the floor of the United Nations General Assembly. It was a joust between the American and Saudi-Arabian Ambassadors. The latter had found it necessary to firmly reply to remarks made by the former. The American had left himself open by citing favourably a speech made a few years before by John F. Kennedy. The late and lamented President had contended that the American-Israeli alliance had done much to bring civilization to the Middle East. The Saudi Ambassador quickly seized upon this historical blooper and took it to the races. He held forth at great length on the great antiquity of culture, learning, religion and science in the Islamic parts of the world. He concluded by rhetorically asking the American Ambassador: "Did the whiskey merchant's son presume to tell *us* about civilization?" The recollection faded into something Ardo was saying.

"What was that Ardo?"

"It's a bad thing to kill off one's young poets," he said with his eyes lowered. Ardo himself might have been a diplomat, thought Burl. He looked over towards the church again, but Kirsti had still not appeared.

Two of the office staff from Black Pebble Lake, Josie Linklater and Shelagh Dubcek, came out onto the steps of the church and stood with their hands in their pockets. Josie shifted and bundled herself up slightly against the increasing whip in the moist wind.

"I've heard about ten different stories at this point Josie - and none of them were repeated in there, that's for sure." Shelagh opened her purse and started fumbling for her cigarettes.

"I'm not sure we're ever going to get this one straight. All I know is, there are a lot of people talking in whispered tones around here. Lots of people mad as hell." Josie cupped her hands, flicked her lighter for Shelagh, and then lit one of her own. "So - did you know her very well?"

"Not really. Not so much until this past summer when she came out to the office to work. She kept to herself, but she was nice enough. I liked her. I baby sat for her a few times when she was little. Really bright. Those parents of hers though - straaange!"

"Wanna go over to the Cypress for a coffee?" asked Josie.

"No, I don't think so. I told my mom I would come over for dinner and do some cleaning up for her. Why don't you come with me?"

"Sure. Haven't see your mom for ages. Did she not want to come to the funeral?"

"I asked her about that. She just looked out her kitchen window with a stone face and didn't say anything for about a minute. Then she said to me: 'You go and give my condolences to her parents. I don't think I am capable of doing it.' That was it."

"Holy shit!" blurted Josie. "That's sure one more for the list." The two women walked down the steps and headed off down the darkening main street of Mashkisibi.

Burl watched them as they grew smaller and disappeared down a lane. He toyed with his coffee cup, doing justice to Olivia Wilson's memory in the only way he could. "What was it about Turner's *Slave Ship* that she had liked so much?" he said in a very low voice, intending it more for himself than for Ardo.

"Come again?" Ardo asked, with a puzzled look.

"J.W. Turner - do you know his paintings?"

"Seen a few in books. Wonderful stuff. Fine use of light."

"I was just remembering how she was looking at this one at the library. It showed slaves drowning in the sea after having been tossed overboard from a ship. Said to me that she really liked it!"

"Who did?"

"Olivia Wilson."

"It that right now." Ardo looked out the window again at the renewing mix of people on the church steps.

"You know, according to Kirsti, friendship was pretty difficult for that girl. She always seemed to be holding back a bit, always withdrawing." Burl got up and moved to a counter stool and positioned himself, leaning on one elbow, so he could still look out the window.

199

"Seems healthy enough to me in that case," Ardo said wryly.

"You know how Kirsti is. She's so open to everything. In fact, last year I gave her a blouse for her birthday - one with hearts stitched on the sleeves."

Ardo looked at Burl and then grinned. "Ah yes. You have that expression don't you. Is she over there then?"

"Yes. Pastor Martin asked her to play a violin duet with the organist. I think she played the *Meditation* from *Thaïs*. Burl paused for a moment while Ardo went into his kitchen. When he returned Burl said, "I think Kirsti may have been Olivia's one close friend, or more of a *confidante* perhaps, as Kirsti puts it. There was an age difference of course, but Olivia was old beyond her years."

"Ah! Music from the opera she is playing for everyone there. That is nice - very nice." said Ardo. "Such a talent she is!"

The congregation had dispersed totally now except for two last figures who stood like soot-stained statues on the church steps. They had separated themselves from the others filing out of the church, and from Burl's view in the restaurant they even appeared to be divorced from each other.

It was Kirsti who had received the letter, and Kirsti's version was undoubtedly the only official one - the one which the rest of the town was unlikely to hear about, even though some might suspect that all the facts were not out. If they did hear something, it would not be from Kirsti. Pastor Martin did have instincts about this sort of thing - but he was not a religious ideologue. He preferred to believe in accidental shootings and that in times of death, a community was well advised to mourn its dead together.

Kirsti had been shaken to her roots by the contents of the letter, arriving as it did after the terrible event. Kirsti had not stopped crying for hours and could only keep repeating to Burl that if she had only come to her, she would have got her through it. Burl had compelled her to see her doctor and get some sleeping pills. Two days later she asked Burl to come to her apartment and go over the letter with her. In it, Olivia had begged Kirsti for forgiveness, but pleaded that she "did not want to die alone."

After yet another coffee and more casual talk with Ardo, Burl saw Kirsti step outside of the side entrance of the church with a tall young man. They stood together for a moment and then she turned to him, put her arms around him, and held him for a very long time. They broke apart and walked towards the sidewalk at the front of the church.They had a few more words and then Karl Zimmerman turned and walked off down the street towards the centre of town. Kirsti turned to go up the church steps again, but hesitated, and then froze, having found herself unexpectedly staring up at Olivia's parents who were still standing immobile at the top, just outside the church door. They had been fixed there unable to look at each other, waiting perhaps for Kirsti, or someone else, to come and say a kind word to them. Kirsti turned and bolted in the opposite direction towards the Cypress Restaurant. She pressed her hands against the revolving door and her eyes met Burl's. The door refused to budge at first, and Burl saw her as a pinned and faded butterfly under glass, appealing to a higher order for release. Then she was across from him in the booth, her eyes tired and red. Burl took her hands in his and smoothed them. Neither spoke for several moments.

"And how's Karl handling it?" Burl asked.

"Pretty well, I think. He's strong. He just told me that until this all happened, he had been tossing around the idea of staying around here. But now he thinks he should go back to sea. Poor guy. He really is nice. He hasn't been able to figure any of it out. I see no point in binging him into it. It could only hurt him more."

Ardo came over with a coffee for Kirsti, extended his condolences, and then withdrew to his kitchen.

"Burl, did you ever encounter the living dead?"

"Yes, I think so - but not as directly as you have perhaps."

"I looked into their eyes for just a split second. Could you see me over there?"

"Yes, I was watching."

"They were ... dead...DEAD!.... I wouldn't give them two months."

"I've been sitting here thinking about that letter. It's important for us to both understand something. We do not really know if things happened as the letter stated. We can't because she wrote it all out in advance - she wrote what she wished would happen. All of that incredible detail, hoping she could carry it off and explain herself at the same time. But how do we know any of it happened that way? We can't really. We just know how unhappy she was."

"What do we know for sure?" Kirsti asked. She was looking into her coffee cup.

"Only that she probably did kill herself."

"There is something else."

"What's that?" Burl asked.

"You know when you saw me with Karl there."

"Yes."

"He told me that Albert Wilson had demanded she kill the dog. He was ready to go to the cops, but she wouldn't let him. He blames himself for not following his instincts as he had wanted to weeks ago. That's why he's leaving so fast - 'before there's more blood' - he said." Burl looked at Kirsti and tightened his hands around hers and said nothing.

"That thing about the dog is in the letter, isn't it."

"Yes. Do you think I should go to the police with this?"

"You don't have to decide right now. It was her last will and testament in a way. It may be nothing would be served."

"Burl - you know what?"

"Yes?

"I wish my parents were still alive right now." She closed her eyes and lowered her head.

"Kirsti...would it be good for you to leave Mashkisibi for awhile? The job here is over for now anyway. What do you think?"

"Why do you suggest that?"

"Because I know you so well. I know that this thing will not let you alone for a long time, and being around here will only make it worse. You have your friends and relatives over at Thunder Bay where you could stay. I would come and see you there. And you could think about Music School in Winnipeg."

"Yes...I guess I should think about it...you would come and see me?"

"Try and stop me."

Kirsti nodded. "I'm so tired... so very tired."

Burl reached his hand across the table and put the tips of his second and third fingers at the corners of her mouth and gently pushed upwards. She closed her eyes and with one hand flattened out, held his firmly on her cheek. Burl slowly raised his eyes over Kirsti's head and looked out the window behind her, just in time to see a raven circle by the front door of the church and disappear over the roof line. Its motion was like a black boomerang whirring past the church door where Alex and Jean Wilson had been standing just moments before.

14

Bawating

i

Burl Manion and Victor Simpson picked their way across the scum-covered cobbles and through the thick undergrowth which disguised the sites of the old fishing camps of the Saulteur.

"These rapids are a mighty pale reflection of what they used to be, wouldn't you say Vic?" Burl threw a flat stone, skipping-style, across a small pool. It was both of their hopes that these inconspicuous little islets, long lying abandoned in the shadow of the canals and assorted industrial buildings, might yet be persuaded to yield up some of their secrets. "Think you will have much luck down here?"

"Hard to tell," said Victor. "Been so much coming and going here since 1900 that the stuff may all have been reduced to rat-shit. We've done a lot better up river further around Point Aux Pins."

"Angus told me quite a bit about this place one evening," said Burl. "His people seem to have a pretty strong connection with it. Said he was related to some of the last group that worked the fishery here in 1905 before the last of them moved away." Burl sat down on some rocks and broke open a thermos of coffee.

"Well, the snow will be flying for good before too long, so I probably won't get to do a good survey until next summer. Perhaps you and I can get together then and you could even join me and the crew for a few days down here."

"That would be good," said Burl, who was rummaging around in his knapsack looking for a folder of documents. "Got something here you might be interested in. An account that I found in an old travel book over at the library the other day. It's by one Charles Penny." Victor took the sheet from Burl, adjusted his trademark glasses, and began to peruse it.

Thursday May 28, 1840. Sault. Ste. Marie.
It is very broad - perhaps averaging five miles and filled with islands - so thick that for most of the way we could see the mainland on neither side. The river at the falls runs a little to the south of east - is about half a mile in width, and the rapids extend up and down about one quarter of a mile - where the water dashes and foams and roars and almost equals Niagara in noise.

"Like you said, not much connection with what's here now is there."

"I'll be spending the winter and spring in the Sault, and I'll make some time to get as much material together on it as I can. Perhaps, if it looks good, we can put together a funding proposal for the boys and girls down at the puzzle-palace." Burl stuck the document back in his knapsack. Victor was busy puttering with a few plastic bags which contained various artifacts members of his crew had found along the river in recent years.

"Few things I want to show you here. Even at this stage, I think I can tell you that we can demonstrate uninterrupted Saulteur occupation here at the rapids since about 500 A.D. I expect we could take it back much further with some systematic work. The guys on the American side have been doing some good stuff lately. I'll be interested to hear about what you come up with on the documentary side of things." On a wide flat rock, Victor had laid out an assortment of arrowheads, hooks, stone sinkers, potsherds and other diverse fruits of the archaeological trade. Burl picked over them, grilling Victor on their import. The arcane language of classification never failed to amaze Burl, who kept simple page summaries on terms such as "Blackduck" and "Oxbow" and "Laurel" in order that he might keep up with discussions.

"Angus gave me a few names to check out down here, which I'll do for sure. By the way, there will be a few people down from Black Pebble arriving at the Algoma House tonight. Perhaps you can join us for a brew."

"Yeah - I'll try and make it. I head for Peru next week and I have some chores to do still. They're finding some pretty wild things in South America, especially in the high Andes. We may eventually have to change a lot of our thinking up here about Native origins as a result."

Victor got to his feet and put the bags of artifacts back into his knapsack and then the two men started the short trek back towards the north shore of the river. The low islets acted as sun catches, trapping the October light, giving a late season boost to the plants and sedges. Thickets of large trunked trees,their roots long sunk into the moist river bottom, gave an almost jungle-like feel to the islands, and they shielded out any hint of the nearby bustling city. Burl and Victor split off along different paths among the braided streams until they came out together again at the edge of the canal. At the parking lot they leaned on the railing, watching a large freighter as it worked its patient way through the locks.

"You could just hop on Vic. That ship has South American registry." They shook hands and went their separate ways.

Victor arrived at the Algoma House that evening, but stayed only a short while. Burl left the pub early as well, feeling sick to his stomach. It was unexpected, for he had eaten regularly enough and had only consumed a couple of draft. Outside, the nausea was suddenly overwhelming and he bolted for an alley, sure he was going to throw up. He propped himself against the wall of the side alley, head upon his forearm. He gulped in and expelled large breaths of air for close to a minute. Gradually the feeling of nausea passed, replaced by the chilling aftereffects of sweat all over his body. He managed to get home in one piece by moving slowly from one large willow to another, leaning against them until the gaps between the dizziness lengthened and finally disappeared. The next day he thought about a doctor. He remembered Kirsti went to a Dr. James Piper and he was able to get an appointment for the afternoon. The following morning he went back to the medical clinic to go over the results.

"You're strong as a horse, but I want you to take this to the druggist and follow this diet here for a few weeks." Jim Piper stuck two slips of paper into Burl's hand. "If you develop any new symptoms, come and see me again. Otherwise, I want to see you before six months is up. This is your present address and phone is it?"

"Yes. I'll be here over the winter and I'll probably go back to Black Pebble next summer."

Burl shook hands with the Doctor and left. Jim Piper went back into his office and spent some time going over the blood lab results. He sat back in his swivel chair, toyed with his pen and then flipped through his phone book and placed two calls, one to New York and one to Toronto.

By March, Burl had accumulated much information on the ancient fishery at the rapids and had carefully organized the results in a large cardboard file-box. He had been able to develop a documentary time line starting with the testimony of some of the old Jesuits, the venerable "Black Robes." In 1669 for example, Father Dablon had recorded the following:

> It is at the foot of these rapids, and even amid these boiling waters, that extensive fishing is carried on from Spring until Winter, of a kind of fish found usually only in Lake Superior and Lake Huron. It is called in the native language Atticameg, and in ours "white-fish" because in truth it is very white; and it is most excellent, so that it furnishes food, almost by itself, to the greater part of all these people.

Two years later, René de Brehant de Galinée, a Sulpician associate of the Sieur de La Salle, included news of the fishery in his *Narrative*. There he had written: "The Indians could easily catch enough to feed 10,000 men." Then there was the Joint Intendent of Canada, Antoine Raudot, who, writing around 1705 from second hand reports, had noted not just the good fishing but the ceremonial aspects of the activities at the "Bawating." The place is "inhabited during the summer by a number of wandering tribes, which come there to live. That is where they practise their witchcraft to excess."

And so unfolded the documentary record. There were many reports from down the years, each with differences in detail and emphasis, but always with a common theme: the fishery and its bountiful nature. Well before General Cass arrived at the American Sault in 1820, treaty in hand, a former Belfast Waterworks manager, John Johnston, had recorded his impressions of the fishery. A practical man, he had studied the mechanics of the fishery carefully, and of how the fishing canoes moved about the rapids. In 1809 he wrote:

> The eddies formed around the rocks are the best places for taking the white fish; that is done with a scoop net, fixed to a pole and bent so that the circle to which the net is attached can be brought to lie flat on the bottom. The man in the bow of the canoe lets the net drop right over the fish and the steersman gently lets the canoe descend, then the fisher gives his net a sudden turn, and hauls it up close to the canoe, and proceed to push up against the stream to the same pool, if he sees any have escaped, or else pushes off to another.

Then there was George Catlin, the well-travelled painter of Indians, who thought little of the daily activities of his frontier-conquering compatriots, and had the temerity to say so.

> Sault Ste. Marie. 1832
> It has been found by money-making men to be too valuable a spot for the exclusive occupancy of the savages, like hundreds of others, and has at last been filled up with adventurers who have dipped their nets till the poor Indian is styled an intruder; and his timid bark is seen dodging about in the coves for a scanty subsistence while he scans and envies insatiable white man filling his barrels and boats, sending them to market to be converted into money.

An observation worthy of Karl Marx himself, Burl thought. It was not quite so bad as Catlin had it. The fur companies needed the Indians to work the fishery for them, and they employed them to good effect, as Anna Jameson noted to her astonishment in 1837.

I used to admire the fishermen of the Arno and those on the Laguna, and above all the Neapolitan fishermen, hauling in their nets or diving like ducks, but I never saw anything like these Indians. The manner in which they keep their position upon a footing of a few inches, is to me as incomprehensible as the beauty of their forms and attitudes, swayed by every movement and turn of their dancing barks is admirable.

Burl considered once again what Angus had told him about a "binge" long ago at Gros Cap, the traditional Ojibwa settlement some distance to the west along the river. It had happened in his grandfather's day, the time of Chief Nebenaigoojing. Much "fire-water" had been consumed, and at the end of the night many were without their land.

iii

Kakayosha Maywins had spent the fall and winter terms at the Sault. She was late for this her final class of the year, but she slipped into the back row and listened intently to the last half of Simon Russell's lecture. She had developed a deep respect for this professor of history, for she could tell that he had thought carefully about his subject, and in this, he reminded her of her uncle Angus. Drawing upon their chance encounter on the shores of Lake Superior the previous summer, she had approached him a few times after class, and he had always made her comfortable, interested in what she had to say . He was summarizing his thoughts for the year.

History teaches little. In the cumulative international record there is sparse evidence that the dispensation of justice, natural or otherwise, has been anything more than a rare and fortuitous development in the habits of certain cultures and nations. These traditions have been difficult to sustain, but occasionally they have persisted and demonstrated a capacity for export. Even then however, the performance has been uneven and often selective with respect to its beneficiaries. Hence, Roman justice has had a long and well regarded history, and yet those who study its application in the actual days of the Roman Empire, are all too aware that its luminescence was much like that of the moon: there was a perpetual dark side as well as a bright side. Inspection of history can all too easily lead one towards a consideration of cycles of atrocities: person against person, group against group, nation against nation, and each person against himself. The violence at large is, it seems to me, traceable to the violence in our hearts. What tempers this? The stumbling accumulation of positive law, the slow perfection of skills transmitted between the generations, the occasional flowering of art, science and poetry. And perhaps that highest and most indestructible of all achievements - music - the qualities of which have been the possession of even the simplest peoples and the rudest times. These hard kernels of accomplishment have helped to ward off the all too regular advances of those many anarchies of the spirit which seek only to destroy, foisting their self-hatreds and resentments onto those who have actually managed to achieve an economic foothold, a sense of tranquility, self-worth, or a promotion of the public good. But there is the hook: who is to define the public good ?

He took off his glasses, and folded his notes, and then withdrew another sheet from his inside coat pocket. "I am reminded now that recently a very great man died in England. He was well known only among a few but commanded great respect. He was a philosopher and historian, and more recently he chose to live his learning in a small house of stone overlooking the Dorset Coast. Even such a person as this had his moments of despair about

212

the things I have just mentioned. He was a poet in such moments, and I would like to read you a very short piece of his, by way of remembrance. It is called The Historian Vulcan and here is how it goes:"

> I cannot
> beat history into shape.
> It will not fit.
> It has no shape.

Simon Russell then folded the sheet and put it back in his pocket, nodded to the assembled, and started to walk out of the room. He turned briefly and said, "I look forward to reading your examination papers. You will all do well I am sure. But I expect your answers to be a little longer than that." The class laughed, but after he walked out, many remained in silence, not having expected these reflections and poetry at the close. The students gradually trickled out of the lecture hall. Kakayosha Maywins sat for a long time thinking about the words of the final poem, wishing she might be able to hear them again. This item was not to be found in the readings.

iv

Spring returned again to Lake Superior with characteristic swiftness. Because many of the rivers in the north are large, they may discharge the winter ice in the course of a few days after break-up. With the proper combination of sun and rain, the land sometimes bursts from a soiled white to luxuriant green in the space of two weeks. The smell of rebirth was in the warming afternoon air.

Kakayosha walked out from the old college building, a former Indian residential school of mixed repute, moved on through a well-to-do neighbourhood and then down to the river bank path which she followed all the way to the rapids. Before winter she had regularly sought out this place for its seclusion. She was looking forward to seeing her friends again in Mashkisibi. There would be much to talk over with The Little Sturgeon. Jonas Beardy was anxious that Joanna go to the college at the Sault as well, but so far she had resisted. Kakayosha had been privy to a conversation between father and daughter. Joanna was "afraid of the city" she had said. "But you must learn to master it, just like a trap-line," Jonas Beardy had replied. "I think it might be me who will be in a trap," she countered. Last fall Kakayosha had suggested to her that they take a place together if she was worried, but so far Joanna wanted only to go back to the bush with her father. "If you're not afraid of Rory O'Flanigan, you shouldn't be afraid of the city," Kakayosha remembered saying to her. "But they are two different things," Joanna had responded."One of them you can see, and the other you cannot."

Kakayosha arrived at her favourite riverside roost and looked out at the rapids which were quickly defining a proper river through the shrinking winter ice. She stretched back, closed her eyes and the welcome sun carried her off into nothingness. Fifteen minutes later she lifted her head up and started feeling around for a soft-drink in her shoulder pack. She saw two men break out of the undergrowth about a hundred yards away. She recognized Victor Simpson and Burl Manion and called to them but held her place as the two men picked their slippery way towards her.

"Hello Kaka. Good to see you. Is this one of your favourite haunts as well?" asked Burl, dumping his bag onto the ground.

"Hi guys. Yeah - I love coming down here. Uncle Angus would bring me down here when I was small and tell me about what the old people used to do. This winter I have been across the river a few times talking to an elder about it. He's in a nursing home. Want a sip?"

"Thanks. We worked up a good sweat today," said Victor.

"And so what did you learn from this elder?" asked Burl.

"He's not very well, and he's very old, but his memory is still good and he's really alive to what used to go on around here. His father was a fisherman, and he knew my grandfather when they were both young. I can hardly believe what things used to be like here, according to him."

"Believe it, Kaka. I'll show you a few interesting photos sometime." replied Burl.

"Super! And just what have you two been up to down here?"

"Well I'll tell you, last fall Burl and I agreed to come down here again after we had walked the area. We've been doing quite a lot of surface archaeology around here and I've been working up a preliminary report on the findings. You might be interested in seeing it when it's finished. Hope to get some funding for more thorough work."

"Oh, Rims! I would really like to read it,. Will you need people to help with the work? I would love to get involved in that. I've even done some anthrop and history course work at school this year. Maybe I'll even get a degree sometime."

"Then we'll talk for sure. I think it might be arranged. Are you going back up to Mashkisibi?" he asked.

"Yes, quite soon. But I could come back for something that good."

The three sat and caught up on a winter's gossip. Finally, when nobody spoke, they all just looked out on the newly reborn rapids of spring, seeming to slip into a shared past, one in which they might have all been sitting together at this same place in some earlier time, each with different tasks and loyalties.

v

Two mornings later, Burl packed up his few possessions in preparation for the move back to Black Pebble Lake. Over the past few weeks he could not avoid noting that he had a persistent cough which refused to disappear, and so he had booked an appointment with Dr. Piper for mid-morning.

"Still strong as a horse, I see," said the Doctor. "I'll just

215

take some new blood samples and send you on your way. You can get this filled and take one a day for the next week. If it doesn't clear up over the next couple of weeks, give me a call from Black Pebble and we'll talk."

Burl returned to his apartment, finished cleaning up, loaded the car, dropped the keys off to the landlord, and then headed north along the lake shore route. The afternoon was clear and bright, one of the warmest days of May. The weather had turned around quickly from the previous day when the Lake Superior country was marked by wild thunderstorms. At four o'clock Burl turned on the radio of his car to catch the regional news.

"Mashkisibi. Sixty-five year old Joseph Perrault has been reported missing on Lake Superior. Mr Perrault is well known in Northern Ontario for his many important prospecting discoveries made since World War II. Mr. Perrault comes from a long established family in the Sault area, and he was reported last seen in the channel north of Mashkisibi Island. No further information is presently available."

Burl turned the radio off. He knew that Angus and Joe were friends and he assumed that Angus was probably up in Mashkisibi engaged in the search. He would call him from the Beaver Lodge Hotel and see if there was any other news, and perhaps take a room there for the night. The Beaver Lodge Hotel was a favourite half-way house on the east shore. When Burl walked in he found the proprietor, Fred Thomas, bent over the main desk doing some paper work. Fred had no further news about Joe Perrault. Burl looked into the lounge where he could see a familiar figure. Fred's brother Austin was sitting at the bar, well into his weekend cups. Austin was known to hole up here at the Beaver Lodge for days on end, something Fred tolerated, not just because he was his brother, but because he knew things about Austin which others did not. Burl went over and sat down next to Austin whose face immediately lit up. He instinctively suggested they have a drink.

"Perhaps a little later Austin. Thanks. Say - have you

heard anything about Joe Perrault?"

"Not a thing Burl, not a thing. Poor bugger. Knew the lake too. Not a thing - no Burl."

"Well - perhaps it's not all over for him. I just drove in, so I'll catch you later. I'm going to take a shower and get a bite to eat.

"Yeah, okay Burl. I'll be here. I'll be here for sure. Good to see you Burl."

An hour later Burl walked into the lounge for a drink. Austin was still at the bar. It had obviously been another of those two-day rounds of booze mixed with episodes of self-imposed exile in his room. Earlier when Burl had seen him his eyes still had a little sparkle but now they were defined by mere slits, his cheeks puffy with rye. Leaning on the bar, Austin looked somewhat like a chimpanzee, but too far gone to undertake one of his regular stunts, that of hanging by his heels from the great horizontal log roof beam which ran the width of the lounge. For those who had witnessed the "hangin' Austin" it was considered a remarkable feat. When it happened anymore, it happened early in the weekend. Fred Thomas was behind the bar keeping his customary eye on him.

Burl spotted some of the office staff from Black Pebble Lake sitting on the far side of the lounge, along with a few people from Mashkisibi and went over to join them.

"Long time since we've seen you," said Shelagh Dubcek. " Heading back up to Black Pebble?"

"That's right. Had enough of city life for awhile." Burl passed some small talk with the assembled and caught up on local lies and gossip.

"Anybody heard anything about Joe Perrault that's not on the news?" asked Burl.

"Not much," said Jan Polyanski, "except that Murdo called me about ten minutes ago. He said he and Angus were going to organize a search party tomorrow if it's decent weather."

The next morning, Burl called the park office to talk with Murdo, who suggested that if he wanted to help, he could organize an expedition in the south end around Flat Island, since it was not totally clear where Joe Perrault had last been seen. According to the travel plan filed with the mining company, he had planned to work south towards the end of the day. Burl then called Kirsti, now back in Mashkisibi, to see if she would go with him on the search.

"I'll meet you at Victor's camp," she said. "I'll see if we can take one of his boats. I know he and his crew are going to work the area up north of the Devil's Chair."

15

The Devil's Chair

i

The cobble beaches rose in great grey galleries along this stretch of Lake Superior. Approaching the coast by boat in this quarter was much more difficult than along the extended stretches of sand beach which, here and there, soften the line of crags and bluffs of the eastern shore. The storm had blown itself out, and on this morning the sky was clear and the winds low. Neenaby ("The Person who Hitches on his Pants") jumped into the cold shallows first, followed by Misconometos. Together they hauled the nose of the boat up a few feet while the others tossed out the gear and then leapt out themselves. Mongazid ("The Loon's Foot") and Dugah Beshue ("The Spotted Lynx") knew the area well, having accompanied Angus on many fishing runs. Over the years, Angus had kept a special eye on Mongazid and Dugah, two orphans he had helped place with a good woman from the reserve. They and their two companions had gladly responded to his call for volunteers to go and search the shorelines for any signs of Joe Perrault. Neenaby and Misco were both from the upper Mashkisibi country and were friends of Joanna Beardy. These four had become something of a collective at the school, known for their love of pranks, but also for their emerging talent. Their rock music group *Pictographia*, was gaining a certain notoriety at local school dances on the north shore.

Dugah and Mongy started setting up a hearth for cooking supper. They all agreed they would stay the night here and return to Mashkisibi in the morning if by eight in the evening they had not met up with any other members of the search party.

"I doubt we gonna find anything of that man," said Mongy.

"I agree. That lake swallows people up fast and turns them into ice that doesn't float." Neenaby reached for a six pack in the bow of the boat and hauled it out.

"Dugah, I see you got a bottle-opener on your belt," said Neenaby, who always grinned.

"That's no bottle-opener - that's a life-saver." The young men all laughed and sat down around the struggling fire and cracked open four bottles.

"So - did you two guys ever meet Olivia, the girl who died in town last year?" Mongy was looking at Neenaby and Misco.

"Not really," said Misco, "although Joanna knew her a bit."

"You savages know what some of the folks are whisperin' around some of the reserves about her?"

"Yeah, I heard a bit of whispering. What you hear?"

"Some say she been *bearwalked*," said Mongy.

"Yeah, that's what I hear a few say too." Dugah took a pull on his beer.

"You guy's want a cigarette?" asked Misco.

"*Bearwalked*?" asked Neenaby, with puzzlement.

"Bit like *Windigo*," said Mongy. "Least that's what Angus says. He's our godfather, so he careful to always tell us about these things."

"*Windigo?*" countered Neenaby again.

"Don't you guys have any storytellers up the Mashkisibi?" asked Dugah Beshue.

"Sure we do. Lots on television all the time. Reruns of the *Twilight Zone* and *The Shadow*. Lotsa good stories." Dugah pulled a cigarette out from the pack being offered by Misco.

"Think you guys gotta get together with Farmer Jones a bit more, see what he can tell you about old things." Mongy was looking moderately frustrated. "Anyway, its kinda complicated, this *bearwalking*. It's mostly shaman stuff, and bad medicine, and putting hexes on people, and getting someone killed who is bothering you. Angus says someone got tried in court for it down on Manitoulin years ago, just after the war I think. Angus was across the ocean fighting in that big war. Said he remembered reading about it in a newspaper when he got back. What's that you guys smokin' anyway?"

"Nuthin' special. Just tobacco. You want some?" asked Misco.

"No, no, just wondering, that's all."

"So Mongy, you believe in this *bearwalking* stuff or not?" queried Dugah Beshue.

"Do you?"

"Asked you first."

Mongy swilled his beer for a moment and tossed some more wood on the fire. "Not too sure. Lots of the older folks do. One even said to me it was the dog."

"The dog?" Dugah thought about it for a moment. "None of that makes too much sense, does it? I mean, even if *bearwalking* is possible, not supposed to apply to white-folks, only to us savages. Whites got their own way of driving themselves crazy - like school." They all laughed. Dugah was rolling some tobacco in a cigarette paper and then licked the edges. Mongy looked at Dugah and offered him a match.

"What's that you're smoking?" Mongy asked.

"You sure are fixated on this subject tonight," Dugah said in a low slow tone. "Just rollin' tobacco, that's all. You lookin' for something stronger perhaps?"

"We could fix you up with all sorts of shit up the Mashkisibi," said Neenaby. "Smokin'- sniffin' - you name it - we can get it."

"Did some hash last year," said Mongy. "Made me feel funny. I asked Angus about it."

"What did he have to say?" asked Misco.

"He says 'what you want to fool with that stuff for? Just cloud your mind. Humans have enough clouds in their minds already. Soon you'll be sniffin' gasoline or lysol. If I ever catch you sniffin' I'll cut you up into fish bait, cause that's all your body will be good for. Your mind will be gone, so you won't be *needing* your body anyway. Might as well give you to the fish, make some good use of you. You want to have a smoke and feel good, get some *kinnikinic* - its free. Hash maybe okay, but expensive as hell. Nobody gonna charge you for *kinnikinic*. Use your head and save your money for school or buy a boat. Learn a trade.' That's what he said."

"Your godfather sound like our teacher in Mashkisibi," said Neenaby.

"About this *bearwalking*," interjected Dugah. "What about this dog thing?"

"Well, it's not as if the dog is actually the *bearwalker*, only that the *bearwalker* has taken over the dog's body and makes use of it to get to the person who he's chasing." Mongy paused to see if his explanation had sunk in.

"So - that would mean you gotta kill the dog if you wanna get the *bearwalker* - is that it?" asked Neenaby.

"I think that's it," said Mongy. "That's what this old lady on the reserve say at any rate."

"Sounds a bit familiar alright," said Dugah. "My people originally from the American side over near Fond du Lac. They come here a long time ago when bad times over in that part. American army trying to move people further west. My people come over here when a priest set up a church at our reserve. He was European but study our language a lot. Anyway, some of my people still over around L'Arbre Croche and they talk about something like this - called 'getting the fire.' Johnny Roussain knows about this too. Over there they call it '*Sko-da-Manitou-Ka-win*.' I think what happens is this. They say an evil person takes on the form of some animal and when it runs at night, it goes so fast you can't see it, except only now and then, when you can see a patch of light. When you see this kind of thing you're supposed to know that its a *bearwalker* with mischief on its mind."

"Holy shit!" said Misco.

"Yeah - that's *exactly* right. You got it." There was a long silence.

"So what you guys think about Olivia's dog?" Mongy probed again.

"Can't see why anyone would bother, if they was Indian," said Neenaby. "Whites got to sort out their own problems. Have ways to do that. You ever ask Angus about this?"

"No, not yet," said Mongy, "but maybe I will. Why would a girl who loves her dog and got a boy friend want to shoot herself like that? Specially right in front of the dog?" Mongy looked into the fire and took another pull on his beer.

"Yeah, that is pretty strange isn't it? Maybe the *bearwalker* was in the dog," said Dugah.

"Where is the dog anyway?" asked Misco.

"That's the scary part. Kakayosha Maywins taking care of it now. She got it from Kirsti Kallela, who went away to Winnipeg or Thunder Bay or somewhere, so she asked Kakayosha if she would take it. She looks after it real good, but what if that dog really is a *bearwalker*?" Dugah looked from one to the other.

"Glad we're all out here together," said Mongy. "This stretch of beach gives me the creeps at the best of times, just like goin' around the Chair."

On the same day, Burl and Kirsti Kallela had driven south from Black Pebble Lake to Tawab's Cove and on to Victor's camp. From there they had set out to inspect the beaches of some of the nearby islands. Their landing on Flat Island had not been well executed. The blade of the propeller was slightly mangled from its collision with a submerged rock which both agreed they should have seen.

"Kind of ironic isn't it," said Burl. "We come in here to avoid going around the island with all those shoals and we prang ourselves on a rock near the beach." They decided to carry out their search first and worry about the boat later.

Kirsti walked up the northwest tending beach to a point where the shoreline turned abruptly southward. This she followed until the firm sand turned into a series of rough, low promontories jutting into the lake. Kirsti bushwhacked inland trying to get around the difficulties, but found the dense brush hard going and returned an hour later to the boat. Burl was just starting to kindle a fire, having carried out a similar reconnaissance on the eastern shore of the island.

"It doesn't look too good does it," said Kirsti. It was a statement more than a question.

"After we do a bit of food I'll make a pine-bough beach advertisement which anyone from a plane will be able to see if they are at least half awake."

"Make sure the lettering is really big - and don't say anything rude!" After tea Kirsti helped Burl gather up boughs and they spelled out "HELP" in twelve-foot letters on the beach.

"I fear this will probably work. I had been thinking about spelling out 'GET LOST.' Then the two of us would be free to start a new master-race right here on the island. We have spruce hens, which I can hunt, *Felix-style* , and then you can play the violin for me in the evenings, on the one I will make for you from local wood. Not quite the stuff for a

Strad, but what the hell."

"Now *that* I would like to see. I think the tone colour might be a bit wanting."

"We build a lean-to, do a little fishing - we would have it made. And no forms to fill out. No more taxes."

"Just do a real Robinson Crusoe, eh? What a romantic. Aren't you forgetting why we are out here? Have you forgotten how many people have starved or frozen to death around this lake?"

"Sure - but then it's relative isn't it? Compare with the numbers who have died slow and lonely deaths in some slum or forgotten apartment. Or right in Mashkisibi for that matter. Down the mines. Some of those men are dead already from despair. Look - the way I see it is this - it's lack of imagination that kills people in the bush - that, plus panic. The Indians must have come to terms with this long ago. When it's forty below you hunker down and relax, save your energy. I would say the greatest error is *not* to have lots of matches with you. With matches you can burn half the forest down if you really have to. If you get caught in the dead of winter, and you spend hours flailing around trying to get back out, you have lost the main chance, you've wasted your time and the light. No - you have to recognize the situation early, and then relax with it, using your energy to just hunker down with lots of fire." Burl cracked open a juice. "Want a hit?"

"I think I could use a screwdriver," Kirsti said, as she took the bottle from Burl.

"Fire will always get attention." Burl continued his ramble. "The forest boys will come and check a fire out, even in winter, cause that would be unusual, and it would give them something to do besides prepare forest cutting plans. Lands and Forests can do *some* things right after all. The politicians are the real problem, of course. They set the rules of the game. Having given the forest away for most of the century to anybody with an axe or a chainsaw, the bureaucracy at least knows enough to keep it from burning up. Lots of local votes in keeping it green, unless of course there is a lot of unemployment, in which case it helps to have some party hack go out and start a fire and generate some more government work for temporary fire crews. They usually wipe out that budget real fast so it can be requested again next year. Everybody knows about it, everybody likes this system underneath, long as it doesn't get too far out of hand. Good local politics."

Kirsti walked over to Burl and with her fingers started exploring around his right forearm.

"What are you looking for? Is there a bee on me or something?"

"No, no - it's not that - I'm just looking for something else here. Oh - you're ticklish, aren't you. I won't forget that." She winked at him. "Wait - roll up your sleeve. Here - let me do it."

"What is this?" Burl was starting to laugh as she backed him towards the water.

"Stop, silly, I'm not going to bite. Let me get this sleeve up - there - that's better. Now just take a look there, will you - stretch your neck a bit so you can see."

"Yeah - so - I can't see anything unusual there."

"Burl, you just haven't noticed before."

"Noticed what?" Burl was looking puzzled. Kirsti closed her fist around his upper arm and pinched up some flesh.

"You see - if you look really really close my sweet, you can just make it out. You see - it's quite clear by the marks - very early in life - it's quite clear - you were vaccinated with a phonograph needle."

"With a phonograph needle?...with a phonograph ...why you... you are *such* an extraordinary little nordic troll... you really are!"

Kirsti broke away from him and kicked some sand at him, laughing. "Got you that time. She came back towards him, weaving as she did, and then put her arms around him and Burl tightened his around her. "You're just filling up the air with all that talk to make me feel better aren't you," she whispered softly into his ear.

"You don't miss too much do you?."

"No - it's just my musician's mind. Never miss a beat."

"I was talking about fire, wasn't I?"

"Yes." Kirsti leaned back and smoothed Burl's hair back. They leaned into a kiss which was tentative at first, but which became long and lingering. Kirsti finally broke it and slipped her head next to his, but kept her arms firmly around him. "You know, I think underneath all of that analysis, you are really very gentle. I like that." They stood clinging together for a long time, neither moving, neither speaking, neither thinking, lost in the sound of the lapping of the waves and the goodness of the sun. Kirsti finally opened her eyes and tensed slightly.

"Burl," she whispered, "don't make any sudden movements. Be very still. There's a cow and her calf about a hundred yards down the beach. They just walked out of the bush where that little stream comes out. We're downwind I think. They haven't seen us, and they probably won't if we stay like this."

"Sounds good to me," said Burl. "Tell me all about it and I'll just keep holding you."

"I'll ease you around very slowly so you can see what I see. They're just beautiful. She's so brown and healthy looking, and the young one is all legs." Kirsti and Burl did a very slow pirouette until, still in each other's arms, they had revolved a hundred and eighty degrees.

"I feel like we're the feature dancers in Swan Lake," said Burl. "Oh yes, I see what you mean - aren't they a pretty pair. And no cars or trucks to worry about." Burl squeezed Kirsti a little harder as he watched the two animals take some water at the edge of the Lake. The cow raised her head and held it aloft for a moment sniffing. She turned her head towards Burl and Kirsti and then looked in the opposite direction. Slowly she backed up the beach again, and then turning, loped swiftly and smoothly with the calf up the stream bed and disappeared into the thick canopy.

"She probably didn't see us," said Burl, "but she must have caught the smell of fire drifting about."

"That was so neat Burl, so wonderful."

"The moose weren't so bad either," he said.

They broke apart and walked hand in hand down the beach towards the stream bed.

"So - what were you saying again about survival, before I so rudely interrupted?"

"We should be mellow, do a bit of hiking around this island, and find a nice strip of forest that we can burn down if we have to. If worse comes to worse, we torch it and soon enough we'll have fire crews overhead. I expect we won't have to go that far. Murdo knows roughly where we are and he'll send somebody looking for us anyway." They took a look on the sand where the cow and calf had so recently stood and bent down to inspect the perfection of the tracks in the firm moist sand.

After walking casually back to their landing site, Kirsti started to take an inventory of what they had in the boat. "There's a pretty good box of tools here - maybe we can fix it."

"Yeah - I'm going to get a few logs so we can haul this sucker further up the beach. Maybe something can be done. Jack Gifford showed me a few tricks about propellers. Poor Joe. They may never find him. Wish you had your violin here."

iii

At seven o'clock on that morning, with the wind at their backs, Angus Ashabish and Kakayosha Maywins had pulled out of Mashkisibi Harbour, intent upon probing the north eastern shore. The distress signals had been uncertain as to Joe Perrault's whereabouts owing to severe electrical interference in the air which had caused his voice to break up. He would have had an inflatable life raft and he might have made it to the north shore or onto Mashkisibi Island.

Angus had selected the largest of his three boats, the *Wabisi II*, which was covered in and had a small cabin. He had asked Kakayosha to come with him on this search, particularly for the sake of Joe's wife, who had always been good to Kakayosha during her visits to the Sault.

Kakayosha trained her uncle's powerful binoculars on the shore line. She had herself become skilled at lake navigation, Angus having taken her out many times onto what he referred to as "Kitchi-Gami." Angus leaned over the side and dropped a sizeable wad of tobacco into the water. They were entering one of the most unpredictable stretches of Superior's north shore, one Angus gave his closest attention to, even in good weather.

An hour passed before Angus turned the *Wabisi II* south and headed straight for the great Island of the Ghosts. On clear mornings like this it rose out of the lake like a pyramid in the Egyptian desert. He commenced circling the great mass of the island, pushing into any of the coves and inlets which might shelter a survivor, places he knew intimately. Angus thought a little more positively of the island than did one Isaac Hope. A century ago Hope had described it as "an exceedingly dreary and desolate place, entirely destitute of any accommodation whatsoever." Angus chuckled to himself. It was a quotation Joe Perrault had read to him in the course of a trip to the island, a venture which had paid off handsomely for Perrault, if only briefly.

No traces of Perrault were found that morning. At noon the *Wabisi II* headed further west along the inner channel, a stretch which in fur trade days had taken a regular toll of the paddlers of the great north canoe brigades. The coastline was inhospitable, broken only by the occasional bluff pushing out into the lake or by a river mouth. At three o'clock Angus wheeled the craft around and headed back towards Mashkisibi. By six the *Wabisi II* rested at the wharf in Mashkisibi Harbour, close by where the old fur trade depot once stood, and above which on an ancient beach ridge, lay the old cemetery, its weathered headstones now sheltered by large trees. Angus took on gasoline, and then, with only a short delay to allow Kakayosha to run Blackjack, they pulled out again and headed south. At eight o'clock, Kakayosha who was steering, said: "there are the rocks of Nanibojou, the old devil himself." Angus told her to turn in towards the shore on the southern side of the great outreach of shoals.

"I think we should stay over here tonight since it's getting dark fast, and I am feeling a bit tired. What do you think?" Angus looked at his niece.

"Good idea. I'm starving and I want to stretch."

In ten minutes they were on the shore in a sheltered cove which defined the beginning of a promontory which terminated at the rocks of Nanibojou . Only this low point of land, with its fine but narrow beach, separated them from a clear view of the great trickster's hide-away. Kakayosha set about building a fire and Angus plumped down on a rock.

"Tell me a bit more about Joe Perrault," Kakayosha said.

"Saw him about three months ago - in the Sault. There was a dinner there for him, and I happened to be going down, and he said he wanted me to come - that he probably wouldn't have found most of that stuff on the coast without my help."

"And was it a nice dinner?"

"Dinner was good. Company not all so good. Joe apologized to me later about some of the rude people there. Tell me he wished he sitting next to me instead of the'big-wigs' as he called them. Too many rich 'suit' people, he said. I felt better when he said that, and we went out after for a beer, down to the Algoma House."

"Hope we find him alive, uncle." The two remained silent and Kakayosha busied herself with some herbs for the meal. Then she said, "You remember that night when Burl came over and we looked at the scrolls?"

"Yes."

"You remember I said I wasn't sure if I was really cut

out for *Midéwiwin* stuff?"

"Yes."

"You didn't mind did you? I mean I really enjoy learning about plants and herbs and good medicine. Just not sure I can really get into the rest of it. I'm interested in the old ways. But my mind is not right for the real training part. I think anyway."

"That's okay. I don't believe in it much myself. Just the discipline, that's all. One has to feel right about it. You are now very far into the whiteman's world of learning. You can't do everything. Learning about plants and animals - that's what I really wanted for you all these years."

"And I will always have that, uncle. There is always more to learn."

"There is always more to learn. One can always go further. Back or forward."

"Why don't you lie down for awhile for a little sleep and I will call you when I have something cooked up. You've had a long day."

"Don't think I'll refuse that offer," said Angus. "Don't cook too much. I don't eat big any more." Angus went to gather up some pine bows and then spread them out in a sheltered area above the beach line, threw down his roll, stretched out, and fell asleep quickly. Kakayosha decided not to hurry supper, but to let him rest. She sat and watched him, thinking about how lucky she was. She remembered how as a small child she had first been taken out to gather plants and mosses by her mother and how Angus had named each of them for her in the old language. She remembered sitting in the bush sorting fish while her uncle took a picture of her.

A round roseate moon peeked through the pines which crested the low height of land ringing the cove. Kakayosha and Blackjack skipped down to the shore to get a better view of the moon as it came up over the south east coast, looking large enough to reach out and pick like a peach from a tree. A fish leapt and broke the water, creating ripples which radiated all the way to the shore. In the gathering twilight the lake had become as smooth and silver as mercury. She gazed out towards the rocks of the Devil's Chair which protruded out into the lake about a quarter-mile to the south. She thought of the Nanabojou trickster stories Angus had told her over the years. Kakayosha sat very still and cradled Blackjack's head between her knees, paying attention to all the small signs of life which gave the hour of dusk its own magic. The faint smell of smoke reached her from the fire, calling her back to her duties. Kakayosha gathered a few condiments at the forest edge on her way back and then started preparing fish and vegetables together in a pan along with a pot of strong tea. Kakayosha walked up the slope and gently awakened Angus.

"Any good dreams, uncle?" She asked.

"No - only sleep, thank goodness. Whenever I have vivid dreams, I feel like *Kitchi-Manitou* making me work unpaid overtime." They both laughed and then rolled up a large smooth driftwood log towards the fire to sit on. Angus had rediscovered his appetite and wolfed down the food with gusto.

"Don't eat big anymore, eh? Perhaps I should do some more for you."

"Maybe, maybe. Let me take some tea first, and I will see then." Angus rubbed his belly and smiled.

Blackjack snuck up to Kakayosha and licked her hand. She took his head in her hands and rubbed his nose with hers. "Oh, my sweet, I have not forgotten you either." Kakayosha scraped some fish scraps into a tin-foil pan, mixed it with some kibble, and put it before the dog. Blackjack lapped it up eagerly. She poured tea for herself and spread her blanket roll on the log for a softer seat. The two stayed silent for awhile, looking out over the lake until Angus finally spoke.

"You know, its a funny thing - Alex Wilson stopped me in the street about a month ago and thanked me for coming to Olivia's funeral last fall - and you - for looking after the dog. He also said that he would like to go out fishing with me some time - if I would take him." Angus was stroking Blackjack's neck.

"So are you going to do that?" asked Kakayosha.

"Said I would - if he really wants to."

"That would be good for him. I don't think there are many people who speak to either of them now."

"Yes - I've heard that. Not too surprising I guess. Whites have their own way of shunning." Angus got up and stretched and walked down to the shoreline and looked out towards the Devil's Chair. The moonlight was now strong and bright and it played upon the rocks so that they looked like miniature snow-capped peaks. "You old bugger you!" he yelled. "This is just when he's the most dangerous - when everything is calm and safe-looking." He put his hands on his hips and then walked back towards the fire. "I do thank you for coming out today. I am sure you have other things you might be doing."

"There is nothing I would rather be doing than being out here with you," said Kakayosha. "Especially when its something important like this."

"Nothing?"

"Well - almost nothing," she qualified.

"You know, I look forward to the time when you have children, not so that I can pamper them, but so they can pamper me. Even an old wizard has to think about his old age." Angus looked at his niece, waiting for her to laugh.

"Well, you may have to wait awhile, the way things are going," Kakayosha smiled hesitantly.

"That's not so much of a problem. No great hurry to get matched up. Not the way there was in the old days. Not so important now. Besides, you can choose better if you take your time."

"Do you think its okay for Indians to marry whites?" asked Kakayosha.

"You joking? Half of the country of Canada have to be returned to the Creator if I say no to that question. We're all cross-bloods now - if not in fact, then in our minds. All the young people streamin' back to nature, everybody doin' dope, governments settin' up departments of environment - that's all old Indian stuff. Not many people know what they mean by nature or environment, but they got an idea something's outa whack. Everything European and Indian all mixed up together now in a mish-mash. Even the Prime Minister's part breed. No - don't matter a damn."

"What about all this bringing back of adopted kids to the reserves?"

"That's crazy too. Hard on everybody. Lot of the young radicals pushing that. I tell them to always look at specific situation, not the general one. If a kid ends up with people who don't love him enough, nothing can be done. Don't matter if they be in the city or on a reserve. Whites and Indians been doing things in this country together for a long time. Doing everything together if you know what I mean." He paused for a moment. "There's something else though."

"What's that uncle?"

"No point in crossing lines if both people can't live with it. Not going to be easy in all situations. Relatives and friends on both sides can make more trouble for a couple than the couple itself. And I don't have to tell you that a couple always make plenty of trouble for themselves. So if two young people going to cross they gotta think about how to handle all that worry that may come at them from all directions. Not so bad in the old days when in the camps marriages often made by committee, and everybody, white and red, have to work together to get along and survive. But even then there were some problems - among the whites especially. More 'specially the rich ones. They couldn't always live with their actions those fur traders. They go back to Montreal or some place south to retire and sometimes leave their families back in the bush. I used to judge them harshly for that - but now - I'm not so sure. Maybe they thought they were being kind. Maybe they knew their own kind too well. Still - leaving your folks behind don't seem proper. That's part of what got the radicals all upset these days about adoptions. They think a kid bound to be lonely and ruined in the city no matter what. But, I'm not so sure. Things different in a whole lot of ways now." Angus reached for the tea pot and filled their cups again. "So - you got someone on your mind? - not that it's any of my business."

"Well - no. Not exactly. Been out with some of the Indian guys, and they're okay. Just not sure about what some of them have in mind. I like that Burl a lot. For a white, he's real quiet and gentle. But he's older and I think he's more interested in Kirsti. He's nice to talk to and I give him encouragement some times - but he holds back - although he wrote me a nice letter once."

"I think Burl more than just interested in Kirsti, don't you?"

"Yes. I know. You're right."

"I been out with Burl a good deal over the last couple of years. He like you, I know that. He also tell me a good number of things about his people. He's up in this country for a reason."

"What's that?"

"He's not sure himself. But I think it's not primarily a wife he's lookin' for. Men like Burl are restless in their minds. I saw all kinds of people like Burl in the war. They come to the war for a different reason than war - you get what I mean? - some kind of adventure - something they could never find where they been raised. Only thing is, when they get there, then they wish they was somewhere else. Sometime, when you go down to the Sault, go take a read of that stone they set up for the war dead - written up by a famous writer - Rudyard Kipling. It will give you a feel for what I am saying - but Burl - he likes you - he tell me that."

"Is it because I'm not white?" Kakayosha had her eyes lowered.

"You remember what I say a moment ago about crossing the lines?"

"Yes. You mean about relatives and friends and so on?"

"Yeah, that's right. Burl tell me he come from stock that's just like those old fur traders. So you see, I don't believe he ever even begin to think about you in that sort of way."

Kakayosha looked into her cup and swished the remnants around. "Looks like I'm having my tea leaves read for me."

"Could be. And maybe it's not what you want to hear. But how can I play role of tribal wise man if I don't tell you what I see?"

Kakayosha looked at him hard for a moment, and then started to laugh. "Do you suppose uncle, that the trick to being a wise man is to be able to tell people horrible things about themselves and make them laugh at the same time?"

"Now you please me niece. Why do you think old Nanibojou known as a trickster? Angus chuckled and leaned over and gave her a kiss on the cheek and then got up and stretched. "There's something else."

"Yes?"

"Knowing someone actually likes you, in my experience anyway, is worth a lot more than having a lot of fancy lovers. Lovers cause too much pain. Too much mess in the morning."

"I wouldn't know about that yet, uncle. Wish I did."

"I wouldn't know much about it either anymore, myself." Angus looked out over the lake. A solitary string of lights was moving across the lake in the eastern channel about three miles out. "There goes one of those deep-draught ore boats heading up to Mashkisibi," Angus observed. "Fast moving, those ships." He walked back to the fire. "I've had one snooze already, and now I'm ready for a really good one. If you don't mind, I think I'll just continue that sleep."

"Good night uncle - have sweet visions. I'm going to walk a little and stare at the moon."

"Good night Kaka - but there is one more thing."

"Yes?"

"Remember what every fisherman knows."

"What's that uncle?"

"There are a lot of fish in the lake."

"That's not really very profound uncle."

"No - but at this time of the night, wisdom is hard to come by."

Angus flicked his hand slightly as though blowing a kiss at Kakayosha and shuffled up to his pine bough lean-to and stretched out, content that he had told his niece some of what she needed to know.

The fire had burned low, down to silent red coals. A profound stillness had settled over Lake Superior, over everything. The moon shone intensely through a sky which was as clear as black ice, and through which every star was a shimmering refraction. Kakayosha was becoming more comfortable with what Angus had said to her. He was telling her to go slowly, she thought, and wait for the seasons to change. Kakayosha looked out toward the rocks, their crag-like surfaces still and tranquil in the light. No waves crashed on them. No danger was posed by the lake, so totally free of swells. No clouds had formed over the moon. She thought about his reaction to her words when she explained she was just not shaman potential. It was a relief. She had moved too far away from such things. She was like her classmates and Burl and Kirsti and Alf. She just did not believe very much. Least of all did she believe in devils in the depths of Lake Superior.

Kakayosha built up the fire again to give it strength and then walked over to the cove where the launch was moored. She waded hurriedly through the cold water and climbed on board. Blackjack splashed along behind and Kakayosha helped lift him into the boat. The canoe was suspended at the rear and she quickly released the mechanism and lowered it into the water.

"Come Blackjack. Let's go for a paddle. Nothing can happen on a night like this. Nanibojou will be asleep, along with Uncle Angus."

Kakayosha pushed off quietly from the stern of the launch and paddled slowly out onto the bosom of Lake Superior. Blackjack was in the bow facing her, sniffing the air. She had taken him out many times and trained him to be still when in the canoe. She paddled up the moon light allowing it to lead her towards *the rocks of Nanibojou* - the name she preferred for this place rather than *Devil's Chair*. She rested her paddle across the gunwales, allowing the lake to take the canoe where it would. It moved imperceptibly towards the rocks. Kakayosha looked back towards the camp where she could see the fire glowing low. Far to the south she could see Flat Island, lying like a pancake on the water, shimmering in the clear white light. In the other direction the line of lights from the passing ore ship had all but faded from view. She put her head down, closed her eyes and let her mind slip into a reverie.

The first warning swell from the ore freighter came upon them and raised the boat a foot up and lowered it again. Kakayosha jolted up with a start and looked to her right. The large after-wave was just about on them. She grabbed the paddle and tried desperately to turn the canoe's nose into the wave, but it was too late. The wave had been piling up over the shallows and shoals of the Devil's Chair for at least half a minute - the first barrier the crest had encountered - and now it pushed the canoe over onto the rocks like a matchstick. Kakayosha yelled to Blackjack as she was flipped out of the canoe towards a rock where she smashed her head and slipped unconscious below the canoe, down into the icy water. Blackjack scrambled onto the rocks and started to paw the water and then jumped back in near the canoe and then clawed his way back onto the rocks, looking in vein for a sign of his master. The canoe was sucked back off the rocks in the backwash and slowly began to sink from the great gash punched in the bottom. The dog barked and then whimpered and paced frantically up and down the rocks, jumping alternatively in and out of the water and splashing along the slippery weed-covered shoals.

Kakayosha did not surface. The dog went into alternate spasms of barking and whimpering. For twenty seconds the dog paced along the rocks and watched. Its nose finally picked up a scent and it jumped and swam towards the shore. Blackjack caught up with the body of Kakayosha and the dog sunk its teeth into the fabric of her plaid shirt and kept moving towards the shore. There was no movement as she lay still and face down in the water. The dog stood in the shallows and licked at her neck, pushing at her face, exposing it, as if it somehow understood the magic of the air passage. It stood silent for a moment and then broke into a furious run down the beach towards the camp.

Angus was startled awake by Blackjack's barking and by his prancing around his lean-to. The dog stopped, then barked, ran out, and then returned and barked again. Angus sat up and shook the cobwebs from his mind, and looked towards Kakayosha's lean-to. He walked over and saw it was empty. Blackjack ran towards him and then ran down the beach again. Angus pulled on his boots and ran after the dog, not yet concerned that there could be much amiss. The dog went far ahead and then stopped until Angus caught up. The pair came out on the far side of the cove in full sight of the rocks and then Angus started to run harder. The dog was again far ahead and standing guard over Kakayosha in the shallow water and pulling at her shirt. Angus ran up and hauled her further up to the beach and started to apply every artificial respiration move he had ever learned. He knew it was too late but he worked frantically for over a half hour. He finally stopped, fists clenched in the sand, exhausted. Turning his head slowly, he looked out towards the moonlit rocks and cursed them in language he had first learned during the war.

Angus gathered Kakayosha up in his arms and held her close to his chest for a long time weeping and giving out an ancient cry which he had not uttered since the death of his mother. He laid her on her back and began to clean the great wound on her head where the sand had mixed with blood, and then he began to prepare himself for one more ceremony. Blackjack was stretched out beside Kakayosha, his body flat on the ground, his head straight out on the sand, whimpering, knowing but uncomprehending. Angus reached over to the dog and smoothed its neck fur and head and tried to soothe it.

v

Three evenings later the drums had beat long into the night at Fireweed Reserve. The next afternoon, some seventy cars and pick-up trucks were pulled up along the side of the road leading to the small white frame Catholic Church which served all functions at Fireweed. The members of *Pictographia* were dressed in full traditional dress, and they played what they called their *Anishinabe Requiem*, a mixture of Bach, traditional drumming and Pink Floyd. Little Sturgeon, who had a beautiful voice, joined them as the lead solo and Kirsti played violin. The smell of sweet grass permeated the church.

Father Crebassa, who was both a Roman Catholic Priest and a traditional *Anishinabe* spiritual leader, presided. He stood at the front of the church greeting people as they filed past the closed casket, over which had been draped a coat of many colours given by Professor Simon Russell. Ben Bigsky had come down from Smoky Lake with Josie Fisherwoman, who then worked in the basement with the local women of Fireweed to prepare the funeral feast. Angus Ashabish sat in the front row with Minnie Maywins and other relatives. In the back row sat Albert Wilson along with his wife Jean. Angus was unable to speak and so Father Crebassa and Alf Anderson spoke words for him. Burl, Dugah Beshue, Jonas Beardy and Angus acted as the pall bearers and at five o'clock, they laid Kakayosha to rest on a little rise in the old Indian cemetery, a site with a clear view out over Lake Superior.

16

Forgiving

i

A week after Kakayosha's funeral, Albert Wilson drove down in the early evening to Tawab's Cove to meet Angus Ashabish at his wharf in order to pass on his further condolences. The two men talked in front of Angus's boat and before taking his leave, Albert asked Angus if he would still be prepared to take him out fishing some time. Angus agreed and suggested he come back in a couple of weeks, in order to give him a bit of time to test the early summer waters. Albert agreed and before getting into his car he left a fresh baked apple pie with Angus.

Summer eased into the north country accompanied by its usual social trappings. Traffic increased, tourists flooded in, family camps filled up with parents and children, artists painted, trinkets and amethysts were sold at road-side stops, and roadkill numbers rose. At Black Pebble Lake, Boisant Bollard continued to complain to the bull cooks about "too much par-tee" and Victor Simpson turned out new varieties of boomerangs for the weekend crowd. The seasonal Native workers at Black Pebble Lake were again subjected to Wolfie Wisdom's irreverence.

Three weeks after his meeting with Angus at the wharf, Albert Wilson placed a call to see if Angus was available to go fishing. Angus told him to drop by his cabin in the morning, provided the weather was good.

"It looks like this will be a good one," Angus said to Albert the next day. "We can certainly go out. We'll take the smaller of my fishing boats." He pointed at the *Wabisi I* which was standing at the wharf, freshly painted. Undertaking the steady tasks of maintenance was the way Angus had got himself through the last few weeks. He took Albert south to some of his favourite coves and estuaries. Over the day they dropped anchor, still-fished, and then trolled out before heading to some other special haunt. The day's catch accumulated on a line in a bucket, and at about five o'clock in the afternoon Angus decided it was time to make for shore and cook dinner. A slight breeze had come up, a sign to Angus that he did not wish to wait any longer if he was going to go past the Devil's Chair. As he raised the speed, the boat came thumping down on the large swells, sending showers up and over the men, landing well behind them.

"This is a good boat you have Angus. It puts the water away from us rather than on us."

"Oh yes. When you're out fishing for your living, you want some comforts. When I want to go swimming I prefer going to the pool at the High School." Albert attempted a modest laugh which came out more in the form of a self-conscious grin. Angus noted it. This was not a man accustomed to laughing.

"This point of land we're coming up to is one where you want a good boat. There is not much breeze on the bay behind us but when you get out there to go around the Devil's Chair the wind seems to get three times as strong. You have to get far enough out before you attempt to turn it or else you can have big trouble."

Angus had made the approach countless times. He veered the boat southwest of the series of the rocks for which he no longer had any reverence. They loomed off the shore to the left of the *Wabisi I*. Large waves were crashing off the jagged peaks which rose up out of the dark water like miniature stone volcanoes. Angus did not toss anything in their direction during the approach.

"We're passing the Devil's Chair now Albert. My people have a lot to say about this place, most of it none too good. I certainly don't." Angus gave the point of land a wide berth and then bore in on the shore.

"When we get to the beach, I'll show you an old book I have which you might find interesting - it's all about this stretch along here."

"I can see why they are not too fussy about it," said Albert Wilson. "I'm glad you're doing the driving right now."

Angus worked the boat hard and at an angle towards the shore, aiming for a sheltered spot south of the rocks, and well south of the place where he had camped for the last time with Kakayosha. Within fifteen minutes they were in Lighthouse Cove and Angus tucked the boat neatly up by the old dock, an abandoned landing which had hosted many a fishing vessel and many a campfire in earlier days. When the boat was secured the two men walked along the beach to stretch their legs before setting about gathering drift wood for a fire. These chores did not require many words. With the fire blazing and the coffee perking, Angus sat down on a large log and began to sift through his grip bag.

"Do you like to read now and then, Albert?" he asked. Albert Wilson looked uneasy.

"Never was much for reading - except for the good book, of course. Never had the time." He paused to take some coffee. "S'pose that's one of the problems I had with Olivia. She always had her nose in a book - thought maybe it was just one of her ways of getting at me. We didn't keep much in the way of reading in the house, and what we did, didn't interest her much."

"You mean the Bible, do you?" asked Angus.

"Mostly the Bible and such, yes. - that's what I and the wife were brought up on, and it seemed good enough to me. 'Course the teachers at the school had a lot of different ideas."

"Let me tell you what I have here Albert. It's an old book by a fur trader, Alexander Henry. He was up and down this coast quite a bit about two hundred years ago. He knew more about my people than my people did." Angus chuckled, enjoying the irony of his own words. "And since we've just come around those rocks, I thought you might like to read about what he had to say about them."

"Two hundred years ago you say? Sure - let me have a look."

Angus passed him the dog-eared volume which he had marked at an entry for the year 1768:

In the month of October, all the Indians being supplied, and at the chase, I resolved on indulging myself in a voyage to the Sault de Sainte-Marie, and took with me three Canadians, and a young Indian woman, who wished to see her relations there. As the distance was short, and we were to fish by the way, we took no other provision than a quart of maize for each person. On the first night, we encamped on the island of Naniboujou and set our net. We certainly neglected the customary offerings, and an Indian would not fail to attribute it to this cause, that in the night there arose a violent storm, which continued for three days, in which it was impossible for us to visit our net. In consequence, we subsisted ourselves on our maize, the whole of which we nearly finished. On the evening of the third day, the storm abated, and we hastened to examine the net. It was gone.

Albert paused to take some more coffee.

"This *Island of Nanibojou* - where would that be again Angus?"

"You were just lookin' at it right back there, all that

stuff around the Devil's Chair, as some of us prefer to call it. Albert raised his head and looked up the cove for a moment, and then resumed his reading.

> To return to Michipicoten was impossible, the wind being ahead; and we steered therefore for the Sault. But in the evening, the wind came round, and blew a gale all that night, and for the nine following days. During all this time, the waves were so high, and broke so violently on the beach, that a canoe could not be put into the water. When we first disembarked, we had not enough maize to afford a single day's provision for our party, consisting as it did of five persons. What there was, we consumed on the first evening, reckoning upon a prosperous voyage the next morning. On the first and second days I went out to hunt; but after ranging for many miles among the mountains, I returned, both instances, without success. On the third day, I found myself too weak to walk many yards without stopping to rest myself; and I returned in the evening with no more than two snow-birds.

"This is some story this man is telling Angus. But as I sit here remembering the waves breaking out there, I can believe it I think."

"There's no lie in what he is writing there, believe me. I've come too close, too often, myself." By now Angus had cleaned two good-sized whitefish, and was busy spreading some butter in the pan, along with a few carrots and onions.

"Looks like we'll be eating a little better than poor old Henry did," said Albert. He put the book down for a moment, adjusted himself on the log, and then turned to it one more time.

> On my arrival, one of my men informed me that the other two had proposed to kill and feed upon the young woman: and on my examining them as to the truth of this accusation, they freely avowed it, and seemed to be much dissatisfied at my opposition to their scheme.

"Good Lord Angus. Do you remember what some of these fellas wanted to do?"

"Oh yes, yes. And its not so strange you know. The wilderness can make people desperate before they know it. My people even have a word for it -*Windigo* - yes -*Windigo*. Its something that stalks the land when people are starving and which makes you feel that you might be able to eat anything - *absolutely anything* - perhaps even your own flesh and blood. I can remember such stories being told to us during the days of old Tawab when there were too many *Windigos* on the loose." Angus was stirring the fish around the pan now, and a pleasing smell started to play about the fire. Albert stared at the pan for some time, but did not reply, and then lowered his eyes to the book:

> The next morning, I ascended a lofty mountain, on the top of which I found a very high rock, and this covered with a lichen which the Chipeways call *waac*, and the Canadians *tripe de roche*. I had previously been informed, that on occasions of famine, this vegetable has often been resorted to for food. No sooner, therefore, had I discovered it, than I began to descend the mountain, to fetch the men and the Indian woman. The woman was well acquainted with the mode of preparing the lichen for the stomach, which is done by boiling it down into a mucilage, as thick as the white of an egg. In a short time we obtained a hearty meal; for though our food was of a bitter and disagreeable taste, we felt too much joy in finding it, and too much relief in eating it, not to partake of it with appetite and pleasure. As to the rest, it saved the life of the poor woman; for the men, who had projected to kill her, would unquestionably have accomplished their purpose. One of them gave me to understand, that he was not absolutely a novice in such an affair; that he had wintered in the northwest, and had been obliged to eat human flesh.

Albert Wilson closed the book, and looked into the fire. The fish were now sizzling amidst the vegetables. Angus had his eyes on Albert. There was just a hint of a suppressed smile at the corners of Angus's mouth as he began to serve up the meal. Albert looked at his plate and asked Angus if it would be all right for him to say a blessing.

"Of course it would," said Angus.

Albert mouthed a brief and traditional thanks for food, quite sure now that it was, in fact, whitefish in the pan.

ii

Wolfie Wisdom was sitting alone in the Snake Pit Lounge, his thin, dissipated frame draped like a net over the chair and table. His posture and expression reinforced the image of something tattered and full of holes. He hung on the table like a rusty anchor which had lost its points, having been dragged through the sea, continuously raised and lowered to no purpose. He was a mime of his own dilemma, his right arm moving up and down in an irregular rhythm, glass to table to mouth to table. His eyes clouded over periodically, but almost as quickly the mist would disappear, then descend again, as with those who dream, but do not remember. Wolfie's persona was that of one perpetually scratching at the surface of a great wall where there was reputed to be some secret entrance way.

The lounge was not crowded yet and the few clients there were relatively sober. It was mid-afternoon, a good time, if there was any good time, to be at the Snake Pit. Burl watched Wolfie from the doorway. It was true then. Wolfie had not been seen since two days before Kakayosha's funeral. At Black Pebble Lake, rumour had it that he was holed up here at the hotel. Wolfie shifted his position and recrossed his legs. Then he slowly looked around the room, but his gaze still did not fall upon Burl who, even at a distance, could see a look of black despair in the deep set eyes, eyes old long before their time. Defeat hung like a veil over Wolfie's face. Burl walked over to his table.

"Burl - howarya man? Have a beer?" The offer was tossed out like a lifeline.

"Sure Wolfie. Be glad to join you."

"Burl, can you spot me for a few ciggies? I'm getting real low."

"Sure thing. Here - here's something for the machine."

"Helluva guy Burl. Helluva guy. Thanks man."

Burl bought a round from the waiter while Wolfie shuffled over to the machine and back cracking open the new pack of cigarettes.

"Hell Burl, you're a good shit for an historian. Heuheuhuhooo! Hey Burl, do historians screw? Sure they do. I know a woman you should meet then - she's a lady with a *past*. Heuheuhooo!" Wolfie was off and running. The starting gate for Wolfie was always any audience of any size.

"Cigarette man? No?... That's right - you don't put this crap in your body, you smart son-uv-a-bitch - yeah - you're right man - its all a lot of bullshit. Just like my trip down to Duluth last week was a lota bullshit. Yeah, I had to leave man. I just couldn't hack it around here. Too damn heavy lately. You see, I had a few engagements at the Muskrat and the Monsoon in Duluth. Heuhuhooo! - the Monsoon - what a joke. The only wind that comes out of there is from the can. Yeah, and out of a few other holes which I won't mention cause you're so full of couth and etiquette and all - heuheuhoohoo! What a lot of bullshit man! So I had this two-bit room - cockroach city I'll tell you - and you know me Burl, I'm so fuckin' choosey, right? - Heuheuhooo! Anyway - I'm down there - no woman - no friends - shit. Really the pits man. Anyway - and oh ya! - on the third night, to make matters worse, I get into this fight with this real dink from the south. I was a bit lit myself, as you can guess, but he told me my singing stunk.

Well - I know that Burl - everybody in this town *here*

knows that - right? But who the hell cares? Right? I sing and if people don't like it they can leave or put a bag over my head or something - right?" Wolfie paused to take a gulp of beer and then looked down towards the floor for a moment. He raised his head and looked hard at Burl with something approaching concentration. "Good fuckin' people in this town here Burl, good fuckin' people - anyway - what was I saying? Oh yeah - so anyway - this prick-wick from Carolina starts getting real vulgar and alien and he really starts juicing me in a way I don't take from anybody. So there I am, right in the middle of my song - room full of people - and this guy yells out that I sing like a deaf nigger - and that in South Carolina they would string me up. You believe that Burl? Well shit, I ain't no angel, I know that, and I tell lots of jokes on the Indians around here - but I at least make sure they're funny - and I always tell them to their face - right? But this guy - this was real bullshit man. And that son-uv-a-bitch - he knew there was some black folks in the room that night. Anyway - I figure that did it. There was going to be some trouble. But I wanted to get my licks in first. I stop playing and there is this real deathly silence, kinda like Grant's Tomb - say Burl? - did you ever have it in a graveyard? - me and Anna got it on one night - right up against the tombstone of one of those old horny-bastard fur traders. Heuhuhuhooo! Those guys - they weren't called beaver-traders for nothing Burl - Heuhuhuhooo!" Burl was holding his sides now and almost spilled his beer as he caved in to Wolfie's spontaneous non-stop performance.

"Wolfie - I hope you can tell me which tombstone that was." Burl could barely get the words out.

"Yeah Burl, sure I can. It was Fraser Haggis McFucken-something. We figured that old boy down in the ground would appreciate it." Wolfie now broke into a longer than usual stream of laughter. Colour came back into his face and life was good again.

"Burl - Jeezus Christ - you're a hell of a guy for a wildlife technician. Shee-it." A beer glass toppled and Burl grabbed it just before it rolled off the table.

"Anyway - where the hell was I?- oh yeah - so in this bar - it's starting to feel like the calm before the Battle of Britain - all real quiet and strange - and so I finally yell back to this guy - 'Hey, who do you think you are? The Cornhole King of Carolina?' - well Burl - that just brought the bloody house down. No shit! The blacks were up on their feet yelling 'Hallelujah Brother!' - and that fucker was mad as hell and left. But he waited for me. 'Course, by the end of the night, I was pissed to the eyeballs and wouldn't have been able to win a fight against a sleeping toad. My ribs still hurt man. Just glad there were a few folks around from the pub to chase the bastard away. I kept an eye out for a Carolina licence plate for a couple of days and finally saw it down the street from the hotel one night. Hope the bugger likes all the sugar I put in his gas tank. Bastard!' Wolfie stopped to light up another cigarette.

"Do you want a couple more Wolfie?" asked Burl.

"Hell of an idea, man. Sure. Thanks Burl. Shit - what a man for a Torontonian - Heuhuooo! Hey - I gotta take a piss man - be right back."

Burl ordered up four more and, without looking around the room too obviously or making any firm eye contact, undertook a survey of the Snake Pit population. It was a good unofficial name for the Open Pit Lounge, for there were vipers of many kinds waiting to strike the unwary. Rory O'Flanigan was at the far end playing shuffle board with a couple of mine workers. It was only a matter of time, according to local report, before he would single out some person whom he would goad into a fight. That normally came much later in the evening, unless some particularly inviting prey presented itself. Burl hoped that the few favours he had done for Rory still passed as current credit on account. When it came to fist-fights, Burl regarded himself as both incompetent and a first-rate coward. Wolfie returned looking much more alive than he had a half-hour earlier.

"Shit Burl, it's really good to see you man. I've been feeling like the bottom of the Black Pebble septic tank lately. Guess you know why, eh man? Anna and Kakayosha been together since they were kids on the reserve. Anna's real broken up, even though they've gone their separate ways."

"Some of us are going down to the cemetery at the reserve tomorrow, Wolfie. You and Anna can certainly join us if you like."

"That's real good of you, man. I'll tell Anna. She will be real grateful for that offer, man. But me and Anna are real spooked by those places - except for you now what - Heuhuhooo! - maybe... maybe sometime we will go down there...hope you understand, man. We don't mean no disrespect." Wolfie took a long pull on his glass and looked down to the floor. The eyes misted over.

"Sure, I understand that Wolfie. If you and Anna ever want to go there, just let me know and I'll tell you where to find her."

"That's real good of you, man. I'll tell Anna for sure. She really likes you, man. She thinks you're okay."

"For a wildlife technician?" Burl replied, raising his eyebrows slightly.

"Oh shit man, you break me up." Wolfie nudged Burl's arm with his elbow.

"Have to get back to Black Pebble Wolfie. You better watch out for the *Ku Klux Klan*. They're going to be after you."

"Oh shit man, the *Klan* - the fuckin' *Klan!* Heuhuhuhooo. Jeezus you break me up. Take it easy man. Helluva guy, heuheuhuhooo!"

Burl drove back to Black Pebble at a slow rate of speed, keeping an eye out for moose. It might be, he thought, that the story Wolfie had told him was true. Or it might be that some version of the events took place right in Mashkisibi. One thing Burl knew was that Wolfie had never been to Duluth. Wolfie had never been further away than the Sault in his entire life.

All was darkness at Black Pebble and Burl went to bed without delay. There were only a few people checked in at the staff house so far. In the morning he picked up a few messages at the office, including one to call Dr. Piper in Sault Ste. Marie.

iii

On the same evening that Angus and Albert were out on the lake, Minnie Maywins and Joanna Beardy walked into the Legion Hall Annex for Wednesday Night Bingo. Smoke already swirled about the place like a morning mist dissipating before the sun. There were many regulars and they usually sat in the same place, week after week. Most were from Fireweed or from Fisher River. Mixed in with them were retired miners and loggers, their wives, and an assortment of transients or stranded hitchhikers with time on their hands. Plaid shirts and large shifts were the main orders of dress. Joanna Beardy was the youngest person in the place. She told Kaka once that she wasn't very interested in Bingo but didn't want Minnie to have to go alone.

"You not gonna do more than one card Joanna?" Minnie asked. "I usually do three or four. Know some people who can do ten or twelve. But I'm not that bright. Maybe you are."

"I'll just do one, Aunt Minnie. I like watching people too much." Joanna looked around the room and noticed the crowd was smaller than the other times she had come. "Don't you think there are a lot fewer people here tonight?" she said. Minnie looked around the hall and did a quick review of the faces.

"Maybe. Usually those two over there sit over here on this side. Maybe they wanted a change of pace. Then there is a bunch of Fisher Creek people over there who usually sit over this way more too. Who knows. Maybe they gonna try and get lucky on that side tonight."

"Do you want a coke or anything Aunt Minnie?"

"No. But you get yourself one. Here, take this." Joanna got up, looked around and then walked over to the canteen arriving just as Anna Bluesky came through the nearby main entrance.

"Hi Joanna," she said. "I remember you from the Bear Pit Lounge. I'm Anna."

"Hi. I remember you too. Just getting a coke. I'm here with my aunt."

"I'm going to get something a bit stronger. Come and sit with us if you like. I'll introduce you to some of the Fisher Creek folks. They're all really crazy. Just like me."

"Okay - thanks. Maybe for a little while." Joanna hadn't noticed before the scar above Anna's left eye.

Anna led Joanna back to a row of tables and introduced her as "Farmer Jones' daughter." Some of the women looked at her sharply. One said: "Oh yeah - you're the swimming kid aren't you?" and then turned back to her fist full of Bingo cards. Anna moved Joanna over to her own table and sat her down next to her.

"I can hardly see these damn cards let alone play them. Never win a damn thing. Just come for the booze and the laughs. Then I go over and listen to Wolfie play at the Pool Side. If he's still on his feet that is. I love the little shit though. You stayin' with Minnie then?"

"Yeah. She's real nice. I'm going to school."

"That's good kid. Real good. Minnie was always real good to me."

Joanna sensed a distant look in Anna's eyes, as though she was suddenly far away. Anna reached into her purse for a pack of cigarettes.

"Want one?"

"No thanks. Don't smoke. So do you guys come here pretty regular?"

"Yeah -we hardly ever miss. All those old girls at the next table hope to meet some men. What a joke. Do you see many men here? The ones that are will be in the grave soon. Can't figure out the sisters sometimes. But what the hell. It's a night out I guess." The Bingo caller started his regular banter mixed in with numbers.

"Well, my card is over at my aunt's table. Guess I better get back. Nice seeing you again." Joanna got up and walked over towards the little corridor which led down to the woman's washroom. She went in and into one of the stalls with a copy of the Mashkibisi Prospect and flipped to the entertainment section to see what films were playing in town. Two of the Fisher Creek women came into the washroom, talking bingo. They went into two nearby stalls but kept talking.

"I'm doin' pretty good tonight. Lot of folks not here tonight. Gives the rest of us a better chance."

"I guess that's the good side of that woman being here," said the other. "Keeps the numbers down. Can't understand why she's here. Doesn't she know the word's out on her?"

"Probably Angus put stuff on her so she don't even know," said the first woman.

"How can you even know when there's a *bearwalker* in the family. That's too much to even think about. After all, relative or not, he was with her and the dog when she died. Calm night on Lake Superior. You tell me."

"Why would he want to do her any harm?" asked the other.

"Got something to do with that white girl. She died strange and now that girl's dog live with Minnie. Old Winston says it has something to do with Angus not liking that girl's father. He's a man of strong belief too. Angus don't like other people with strong views around. He doing everybody in. Look how for years he's never been afraid even of the Devil's Chair. You tell me. Anyway, maybe she'll get the message. Not many folks sitting around her tonight. Only a few from Fireweed, and what the hell do they know about anything. Bunch of apples." The two women then started talking about their men and their shortcomings. The air was suddenly filled with the sound of flushing and Joanna heard them leave. She waited a few moments and then slipped out the washroom, bought another coke and went back to join Minnie.

"Where you been? You're missin' quite a bit of the calling. I been playin' your card though."

"Needed some fresh air, auntie."

17

Departing

i

Angus Ashabish sat fixed like a sculpture at the end of the pier in Tawab's Cove, silhouetted against the late June afternoon water, outlined by a warm, shimmering glow. He was waiting for the evening calm before going out to fish, and also for Burl Manion. After parking on the ridge overlooking the cove, Burl started to walk down the familiar winding dirt road which lead to the wharf below. When still a good fifty yards from the ramp, Burl stopped and fixed his eyes on the back of the man who had become so close to him. The pause turned into a minute. Neither of them moved. It was as though the universe had temporarily ceased all motion. Tears almost overwhelmed Burl, but he regained control, set the image before him in memory, and resumed walking towards the pier. He walked up behind Angus with a certain self-conscious scrapping of his feet so as not to startle him, and then sat down, legs over the edge of the dock. He looked down into the dark water but remained silent. Angus did not say anything, but finally pulled out a roll of lifesavers and offered one to Burl. Angus resumed repairing his net and then got up and tossed it into the motor boat.

"I'm going out for awhile - will you come along?"

"Sure - I would like that," said Burl.

They threw the rest of the gear into the bow along with a small cooler. There was already a bucket of fresh fish at the back of the boat. Angus gave one pull on the rope of his small engine and it kicked into action. Burl thought how much this engine was like Angus: totally unobtrusive. At half a mile out Angus stopped and set some nets and then steered for a beach south of Tawab's Cove where they built a fire and cooked up some of the fish Angus had in the bucket.

"Angus, I'm very reluctant to open up this topic with you. You've had too much sorrow this summer. Kakayosha was so very special to you, I know...as she was for many of us. I am really wondering how you are doing in all of this?" Angus puttered with the utensils for a moment and then looked at Burl, moisture at the corners of his eyes. He looked down again and cleared his throat.

"Something snapped in me that night. I'm not sure what...but it's been broken ever since. The sun is not so bright, the rainbow not so colourful, the taste of the fish not so good. I felt that same thing snap in the war once - the first time I killed a man - but it mended - life was eventually good again. But this time...not so sure. Not sure it will ever mend...her name - you know its meaning?"

"Yes - she told me once - its a beautiful name. Just right for her."

"Yes - *A Bird in Everlasting Flight* - and yet, she ends up in the bottom of the lake. Something out of whack there... too young." Angus's voice trailed off for a moment as he stirred the contents of the pan. Burl got up and walked over to Angus who was still kneeling, and he put a hand on his shoulder.

"I know Angus, I know. There are a lot of people who feel the same way." The men remained quiet and both looked out at the lake which was working towards a dead calm. A pure white gull sailed out past them and settled on the water, its reflection making a perfect match.

"Victor and I have been working on a little project to help restore her name to her. Perhaps the ceremony will happen in the fall if we get the right wind."

"Yes," said Burl. "He's told me about it. It's a wonderful idea." Angus served up the plates and the men ate slowly without speaking.

"I see you have a bottle opener on your belt," said Angus, looking at Burl, who then reached into the cooler and opened a couple of beers.

"So - you went to see him again?" queried Angus.

"Yes - yes I did. Last week... I sensed that he had something he did not want to tell me. I have something terrible alright. It's some kind of very rare leukaemia. Almost nothing known about it, except that it moves steadily - sometimes quickly. One in about ten million."

"I see. This is not what I wanted to hear." Angus reached out his strong right hand and placed it firmly on Burl's shoulder." You have become more and more like the son I never had."

"That means a great deal to me Angus. I was never very comfortable with the parents given to me. Nobody's fault. Just the way it was."

"Yes - I know that. There is never any choice in these things. I have often thought there is a deep well of loneliness in you on that point. You never talk about them."

"And there is nothing I can do for them in this situation. If I did, they would never condone what I have planned. It would fly in the face of everything they believe. And I do respect their commitment to their beliefs. I just do not share them and was never comfortable with them."

Angus looked down into his plate for a moment and then looked at Burl. "Yes - that is alright. Respect is good. But there are things one must do alone in some situations. Now my friend - tell me - does Kirsti know anything about this? Where is she anyhow? Haven't seen her around for a long time."

"No, I haven't' told her anything. She's been mostly in

Winnipeg since September, going to music school. She went to the Bay for awhile and stayed with her uncle after Olivia's death. Then her uncle decided she should get proper music training at Winnipeg. I totally agreed. She's a real talent and that should not be wasted, even though she is a very good biologist. I was glad about it, although I have missed her like hell. But now, it's really much better this way. I might ask you to do something for me later, so that she will understand." Burl's eyes were on the ground. Angus picked up his plate and walked down to the water's edge and stood facing the lake, came back, put his plate down and then fumbled in his blue overalls for his pipe.

"You remember the conversation we had about three months ago?" Angus asked.

"Yes - it's been much on my mind."

"You still feel the same way?"

"Yes - even more so."

"Good. Good. It is best not to flip-flop about in the mind like a fish on a dock. One either has air, or one does not. Sometimes our way can be a better way to finish than that of the European. There is much good in the ways of your people, but there are some bad things too, and I am afraid many among you do not know how to end things properly. Except in war of course. They are very good at that through long practice." Angus looked at Burl for a moment, and then they both broke into restrained laughter. "Oh yes, I remember some things from my days in the War. There were many of yours who I helped to die. They wanted to know about the secret to my great calmness in the middle of all that was going on around us, and so I would tell them about my Grandmother, and how she had raised me, and how she chose to die when the time came. Men talk about death a good deal in war, as you might expect, but not with any depth. More like jokes. It was all very comforting to some of them when I talked seriously about this matter and I think it helped them."

"I am sure it was Angus. I can hardly imagine what it

260

must have been like on the ground over there."

"Not so different from most other days in other places, except if you were not ready for the high moments, and for what might come, you could be in trouble. Those were the ones who were always in trouble - the ones who were too bloody confident."

"Sounds kind of like everyday in the workplace."

"Yes, yes - just so. Work is war." Angus chugged some beer. "So then - you must start to prepare yourself. That is an important part of the journey. One needs to start early and plot the course for such a difficult route. But this is also its own reward, for it becomes a form of work too. And like all work that is well done, it gives much satisfaction, like a well-made canoe. To make all the proper arrangements, to - as your people say - *put your affairs in order*. Do you understand?"

"Yes - and I have chosen the place. I want it to be at Last Lake - if that would be alright with your people."

"Last Lake? Yes - Last Lake - Mashkisibi Island - to the great *Island of Ghosts*. I see. Yes - our people would be honoured. You have many friends among us you know. Now, the real question. How long do you have - did he say? - and what do you think yourself?"

"Perhaps a year. But I prefer to go early before it makes inroads on me. If I become weak, my mind might also weaken. I might lose my resolve to do this."

"Well said. You tell me when, and the place shall be prepared. Remember now - there was usually a choice with the ancients. You could go and prepare a place where you wished, or others could intercede on your behalf. They would come and prepare a place with some comforts and some of our medical aids. Just like a hospital, but closer to home. They would then take you there and then leave when you told them to go - or they would stay with you if you wished. It was more a sign of solidarity and co-operation than anything else. But everybody felt better about it. Some of your people think we just abandoned people, but it was not quite like that. There were some times when people were out of their minds and other measures had to be taken - that is quite true. It may have seemed brutal - but everybody understood these things might happen. It was part of the way of survival in times past. They were raised to understand this."

"I am thinking about mid-September. That gives some time. It's the time I love best here."

"A good choice. Close to the moon of the falling leaves. You tell me when and we will make the arrangements you wish. Meanwhile, I will prepare you a good map into the island and some of the other things you will need. I could go in with you if you want. Or perhaps there is somebody else?"

"That is generous," said Burl, "but I think I should do it alone. There is something though. It's about Kirsti." He paused.

"Yes?"

"I have thought about writing to her, but I feel that would just create the worst sort of situation for her. She has had one too many letters from the dead already. I would be very grateful if you would wait for the proper moment to talk to her and explain why things had to be this way. Explain my great love for her and that there was nothing for it but a speedy departure. I fear that if I tried to do this now, I would weaken, and if she came back we would try to cling to each other and resist the inevitable."

Angus's face grew dark and grim and he puffed heavily on his pipe and did not speak. He walked back down to the lake and then backed away from it towards the fire once again.

"I will gladly do anything for you. But we must talk about this further now. I want to advise you strongly against this approach where Kirsti is concerned, and if you ask me now, I will tell you why."

"Yes, please tell me what you are thinking. I want to hear it."

"Do you remember what we said about the quest for

the final vision? About how it must be sought from a base of calmness and tranquility?"

"Yes."

"This is, after all, the one great chance to reconsider one's name. The first vision comes when we are young and full of hope, when we are still foolish and know nothing. But this last vision - it is a chance to sum things up before going out the eastern door. There is so much that can go into this vision. But it requires great energy and discipline to bring it on. I know you understand discipline. You work hard and you write and you understand art. Just as the canoemaker understands discipline and art. The slightest error in the birchbark assembly or the framing will make for a bad trip on the water. So here - the mind must be clear of obligations. That was what many of the old ones said in their teaching scrolls for the departure ceremony. They said it in different ways. I never did figure out what my Father's teaching scroll said on this. I was hoping for more scrolls to be found out by the dams. But so far, nothing. Perhaps there are no more scrolls. Anyway, where was I? - back to the point. You must deal with obligations. Yes. Do you remember quite some time ago, how we talked about economics?"

"Yes. It was late at night and we were on the beach at Mindemoy Bay. I remember it fondly."

"We talked about community. About communal things. We talked about Indian economics mostly. You were interested in that word. We do not talk much about economics at Fireweed. I never got to study it as you did. I only understand when the fish are there and when they are not there. And then I try and look and see if I can understand why they are not there. But I think I understood your argument. I think we agreed that a person does not ever really act alone... in anything."

"Yes. It's something some economists and businessmen love to go on and on about in error, the drive of the mighty individual and his power in the marketplace. If we all work harder as individuals, everything will automatically get better, that seems to be the argument. And if we just get rid of most taxes, keeping just enough for the military and prisons, everything will be ideal. And you might even get rich." Burl grinned and slid down and stretched out on the ground, leaning back against the log with his hands behind his head.

"I think it's a strange thing that. As though I would have ever become a good fisherman if there had been nobody to teach me, or if I had not been born into a life where fishing was done by many others or at a place where there was also an opportunity to fish."

"I think you want to go somewhere with this Angus."

"I do. What we're are talking about here is another part of economics. I know why you wish to do things this way, the old way, and you have already agreed that you are not acting alone, do you agree?"

"Yes, absolutely."

"Even though you are to be the main actor in this, there are many others behind you, sharing in this with you, helping you along, you understand that?"

"Yes, I hope so."

"When one person moves through the eastern door, part of the rest of us go with you, just as when we have children part of us goes ahead into the future. It is a comforting feeling, is it not?"

"Yes, very. Especially when you put it that way. I know too, Angus, that nothing can be said about this to outsiders. There could be serious difficulties for you and for others."

"I am glad you understand that. Our people are familiar with the European law and its iron ways. We have learned over the years to be careful about this and other matters as a result. But I am glad that you understand our position. Events such as this I discuss with a few members of the *Midéwiwin*, and then we each take on certain duties with a minimum of conversation. Things will just happen. Things will be done quietly. But there may be people you want me to look after on the outside, if I may put it that way?"

"I will give you letters which I would ask you to mail out when you think the time is right."

"Very well. And personal contacts perhaps?"

"I will try and deal with those myself, as well as I can."

"Good - that is best I think. But there is something else."

"Yes?... Tell me then."

" I think you must go and see Kirsti. Spend time with her. Have a good time together, even if a short time. And then, you must tell her what you plan, and· stay with her until she understands. You need her permission to divorce in this way. Then you will both be at peace when the time comes. If you do not, your energy will be wasted at the end. You will fret and fidget about unfulfilled obligations, and it will be too late for you to make things right. You have to take care of all these obligations to your satisfaction, in advance. This is how it was with us. The departure ceremony, as we have talked about it, was not an individual thing. It was a communal thing. One was asking for the support of the community to ease oneself out the eastern door. And so in your case, you must get the support of not just us Indians, but of those close to you. And Kirsti is the one who is close to you. Am I right?"

"You are right. So very right. It is just that...."

"It's just what?"

"It's just that...what with the mess with Olivia...this will be just one more horrible thing for her. I am not sure she is strong enough."

"You are wrong. She *is* strong enough. It will be sad for her at first. But not horrible. It will be horrible if you leave her without conversation. I will look after the others for you, and help make your farewells for you. But you must deal with this one person on your own. If you do not, your final vision will be a damnation more than a salvation. You need to go and spend time with her. Enjoy each other. Pick your time to tell her - just like spearing fish - and then you can wait for her to come to terms. Don't leave her until she has. It will be time well spent. Do it soon. Go to Winnipeg."

"Yes - yes, you are right. I should have seen that."

"You would have seen it eventually. But your time may be short. You want to be healthy together now. There is no point in dilly-dallying."

The sky over Lake Superior was darkening and the wind was up slightly. "I think we should head back before it gets too risky. Even in my boat, we might both disappear without ritual." Angus started to pack things up. When it was all thrown into the boat, he turned to face Burl and looked hard into his eyes and put his hand firmly on his shoulder: "It's summer. It's warm. The waters of Lake Winnipeg are always warm. Go soon. Swim. Eat. You are young. What better things do two young people have to do than to make love in the sand? Most people don't have to be told. Don't wait. Go soon. You must trust her."

Burl thought about his connections at Victoria Beach on Lake Winnipeg and the next day he started to arrange for a rental cottage for the month of July. He called Kirsti from Black Pebble Lake with an invitation to spend the best part of summer at the beach. She hesitated because of her summer job but then accepted when he told her he was feeling poorly. Burl arranged things at Black Pebble and within two days was on the road to Manitoba. They spent long days on the warm sand beaches, frolicking in the great breakers, watching the white pelicans circle in formation in the sharp blue above, and playing tennis. The days slipped into evenings spent sitting by the fire or stretched out on the soft couch in the screened-in porch, lullabied by the string of soft yellow lantern lights which snaked around the roofline and cast a cave-like warmth over them. They watched movies they had never seen before on the television and they talked endlessly of music, of her teachers and fellow students, of Kirsti's future and of animals. On the twentieth day, Burl felt poorly, and he knew the moment of conversation had to come soon. How to do it? In stages perhaps. She watched over him that night and occasionally he could sense her anxiety. In the morning he was improved and they went for a long walk up the north beach where they waded across the shallow channel to Elk Island. The small islet was a nature reserve and usually devoid of people. As they lay stretched out half in the water and half on sand, Burl told her what she had to learn. Kirsti drew her knees up under her chin and buried her face on her legs, holding out her hand in Burl's.

The evening meal had been sombre, filled with long silences. From behind the porch door Burl looked long and hard out towards the tranquil stillness of Lake Winnipeg. He turned and walked over to where a despondent Kirsti was curled up on the couch in the semi-darkness.

"I can see the moon coming up over the trees. There are some wonderful sitting rocks just off the shore near the children's beach. Let's go and watch this *claire de lune* shall we?" He put his hand under her chin and raised it slightly. In the low light he could see her eyes were red from sobbing. He put his hand on hers and gently drew her up and pulled her close to him. She was like jelly. "Things will look better from the lake."

Burl led her out of the cabin and down through the corridors of tall protecting pines and spruce which had grown up around the lots. They waded together out into the warm water and onto the large flat rocks and perched there together like two cormorants waiting for something to break the surface. The large orange ball of the moon was rising swiftly out of the east. Burl slipped his arm firmly around Kirsti's waist and sought her eyes.

"Listen to me now. I need you to understand, not just in your mind, but deep down inside where it counts. Will you try?" She nodded her passive assent.

"You know how it is when you have your violin in your hand and you are practising intensely."

"Yes."

"Tell me how it is then."

"Its...solitary...alone...intense...peaceful in a way...and...and exhilarating. Its...kinda like sex...but longer. I mean...its different from sex...but similar in a strange way. Is that crazy?'

"No...absolutely not...I agree. Anything creative is like that I think...but that's just it. Its why I found it so easy to spend so much of my youth trying to compose...it was all heat and ecstasy...even if it all failed in the end. Its an attempt at birthing. Tell me, when you're practising for a performance...how is that best done?

"The same way. For much of it you have to be alone, until there is a need to coordinate."

"Yes - or writing, or anything that takes concentration. You wouldn't want me or anybody else around would you? I mean not right up there by your elbow, right?"

"No. That would be very distracting."

"That's why there are all those neat little isolation-chamber-type practise rooms at the music school right?"

"Yes. True. And so what are you trying to tell me?"

"Just that I want to leave in the full bloom of creation, not in a wash of tears. I want to see clearly at the end and in colour. I need to bring all those things together that are incomplete. If you were with me we would just get in each other's way. We would try and reverse what cannot be reversed. And in the end, that would be much more worse for you. You would have to clean up the mess out there in the middle of nowhere. That is not what I want for you. Other arrangements have been made which will be easier on everyone. I know that for many people, they want someone there at the end. But for me that is a great strain, and I could not bear the idea of it all taking place in some hospital ward, people waiting for the end, for the relatives to leave so they can turn off the machines. No - it will never do. Not when there is open air and sky to be had. I want to be composing at the end, and you will be there at the centre, smiling at me. You will be part of the great vision. You will be front and centre. I will not be yearning for you. You will be there. Think now...it will be like this. It would be just like you finally doing the Sibelius at Massey Hall. You would want me there in the audience. But you wouldn't want me up on the stage next to you, looking at you from close range, getting in the way of you and the orchestra and the audience, right? It would be a massive embarrassment for everybody. And don't you see? Whenever you are practising alone, whenever you are playing, I will be there, sharing it with you. Dearest comrade, do you see? I will be your violin bow. The one who believes in you." Kirsti was looking at Burl as he got carried further and further away with his analogy and she slowly started to radiate a great smile. Burl saw it and stopped and fixed his eyes on hers... hopeful.

"I've never quite known why I love you so much, but now I finally do." Kirsti leaned up and put her lips softly on his, and held him for a long time. She pulled back and put a finger on his lips. "That's why that first night you heard me playing in the basement, you didn't come down isn't it?"

"Yes. There are many ways to violate people. But violating their communion with God is one of the most unforgivable."

"I've never heard you talk about God very often."

"No. We haven't been on very good terms."

"If we do it your way, you must promise me something. If you change your mind, you will call me?"

"Yes."

"And you will allow me to talk with Angus - later - sometime."

"He has already agreed to that. In fact, he insists."

"I have no choice then," said Kirsti.

"You always have a choice in things where I am concerned." Burl looked at her, seeking agreement. Kirsti remained silent, her eyes fixed on the calm waters around them. Burl put his hand under her chin and raised it towards his face. "There is something that Casals once said. It is quite perfect and I believe it. Shall I tell you?"

"Tell me."

"He once said that 'when we die, we become music.' Is that not perfect?"

"Yes...that... that is... it is..." Kirsti could not go further.

"One time Angus and I were sitting on a beach taking in the northern lights. It was a most wonderful show. He told me once how he had gone all the way to Churchill once, with some of the Cree brothers, and how he had achieved a wonderful peace by sitting out on the rocks night after night. It was not so long after the war. The aurora totally captured him. He asked some of the locals what they thought about it, and one said to him that around that part of the cournty they called the lights "the dancing of the spirits." So you see, I think Casals was probably right. And always when you see the lights in the future, that is when we can be together again."

"Come into the water with me." Kirsti pulled Burl into the shallow waters.

"Kneel with me here." Hip-deep in the water, they faced the moon together, hand in hand.

"Call me 'wife'."

"I call you 'wife'. Call me 'husband'."

"I call you 'husband'."

ii

By mid-September the landscape had turned into patches of fire and gold. According to plan, Burl had Angus cast off in the *Wabisi II* for Mashkisibi Island. The day was fine and the crossing cheerful. The men talked of many things as they would have on any other day. There was no disguised sense of regret coating their words. At Dusty's Cove, Burl unloaded his gear and then gave Angus his last letter, addressed to his parents. Standing on the shore, they embraced for a long, tranquil moment, and then Angus waded back out the ten yards to the *Wabisi II* and climbed aboard. With hands in his pockets, Burl watched as Angus prepared to start the boat. He was standing at the helm, the motor still silent.

"One last thing," Angus said.

"What's that?"

"Do you like your name?"

"Never thought too much about it. It has served me well enough, and it's short, which can be a virtue," replied Burl.

"Yes - good. That's good. You know how some of my people make quite a bit of noise about naming. They think it's good to get it right. I am reminded now that there are several ways to consider the great circle. When one is young one comes into the circle and is named. But when leaving the circle, one may perhaps think of it as another time for a vision quest. So how do you do that? Well - the same way as when we are young. It will be easy for you. You do not want to stop eating altogether, as we already discussed, but eat smaller amounts each day. That way your body will not fight your mind too hard. And then towards the end, when you withdraw from food altogether, like the youthful faster, you will bring on your greatest vision. And you will know your proper name. And who knows? It may still be Burl."

"That's good advice Angus. I will do as you suggest." Burl smiled at Angus and Angus smiled back in a way which he rarely did. His face shone like the moon.

"By the way Angus?"

"Yes?"

"What about *your* name? Are you content?"

"Yes. Not only am I Angus - the first born son - but I am also a fisherman."

"What does *Ashabish* actually mean?"

"It means *a useless old net*. But you know how my people like laughter and jokes."

"Then the choice was a good one."

Angus took out a paddle and slowly backed the *Wabisi II* far out into the bay, unwilling to break the mood by the sound of the engine. He sat a few moments about a hundred yards out, and then finally pressed the engine button. Angus described a long, detouring arc to the northwest of the cove and then swung back in a large loop towards the shore, slowed the boat, stood up, and waved long and slowly to Burl who was standing on a large rock on the beach. Burl waved back long and gracefully. Angus then turned the craft a last time and moved off slowly into the vastness of Lake Superior.

"And so," whispered Burl to himself, "the last journey home has started." He watched until Angus was just a speck in the distance. He placed the backpack on and took out the map Angus had prepared for him. The walking was difficult at first, taking him through thick and swampy lowland coniferous growth; but soon the way became easier as the land started to rise. The map was excellent, executed in a fine *Anishinabe* style on new birchbark. The oddities of the topography on the map entitled here as *Island of Ghosts* were all laid out in a simple and straightforward way.

The autumn had so far been one long, brilliant splendour. In the valleys, gold birch leaves flickered through the closely knit groves of black spruce. On the slopes, choirs of poplars stood in radiant masses shimmering in the low autumn light, resembling the faithful bearing candles in some vast, roofless cathedral. Burl moved along lightly, but steadily, as if approaching some longsought shrine. He walked arm and arm with the poplars, listening to the soft peddle-notes of nature which had completely taken over his senses, dissolving his memory of things past. The regular sounds of his footsteps became the beats of the *Sibelius Fifth* which now rushed through his mind as though a full orchestra was walking with him. He strode over newly fallen leaves, still moist and coloured, and it was as though he was walking through childhood forests along the Humber River. Every sweet memory of his youth started to appear before him, first from behind this tree, and then from behind that. They smiled at him as he walked by.

Late in the afternoon Burl reached the shore of Second

Lake. This had been well named for the benefit of the hiker. The island at the centre of Second Lake was his destination, the one so accurately described by Angus during their medical sessions. Angus had told him of small canoes concealed under overhanging cedar bows on the south shore. The sheltering grove he sought was marked by a great protruding tongue of rock into the lake. It was not difficult to spot. By looking into the water from the toe of this arm of rock, he could see the accumulated offerings of many who had passed this way before. His knapsack contained a sealed box into which he had placed a few mementos of his past. He took it out and threw it into the water and watched it sink rapidly to the bottom where it nestled among the many others.

After locating the hidden canoes indicated on his map, Burl set out the short distance to Middle Island. The canoe provided, packed with a few additional provisions, was no ordinary one; the bark was richly inscribed, inside and out. Nor was it an old canoe. It had the appearance of having been crafted recently, and Burl suspected he knew the source. He had seen some of these symbols before, although not often. They were reminiscent of figures he had seen in the old books and reports which had attempted to fathom the ways of the *Midéwiwin Rights* of the Ojibwa, so familiar to Angus. One panel defined islands within lakes, within other islands, within other lakes. How much these drawing resembled this island itself, he thought. In the canoe there had also been placed a sealed rifle with ammunition, in case he was bothered by animals or more troublesome spirits.

Once ashore, Burl decided to walk around the periphery of Last Lake. He searched out the contours of the island and, after consulting Angus's map, headed for the height of land indicated as his final destination. A steady rise brought him to a promontory where he was offered two views. The first was of Lake Superior, which he could see from a cliff of moss covered rocks garnished with ancient pines and spruce. The second was in the opposite direction and offered a view of Last Lake. It lay below him, a small, perfectly round body of water which in the Autumn sun, shone like a diamond set in jade. Burl climbed the short distance to the cliff lookout which showed him all the great expanse of *Kitchi-Gami*. He rested and looked, no longer concerned with time as a measurable unit. He was feeling drowsy and got up to seek out his place of shelter. The map showed the way once again. Finding his well prepared nest of pine bows beneath a lean-to, he spread out his sleeping bag, lay back in the late afternoon warmth, and fell into a deep sleep.

Dreams rather than visions came. He dreamed his old age, the one which might have accrued to him some forty years later. In the dream he was bent over a wooden table in the last of what had been a long series of shoddy, ill-smelling, rooming houses. He was fussing over papers. Noises of a desperate sort floated in above the transom, indicating he was surrounded by alcoholics and others of the less-eligible, and by wheezing, sick old men, all of whose numbers he had long ago joined. Burl seemed to be looking down upon himself, as if from the centre of the bare light bulb above the table in the spare confining room. He could see himself sorting out sheets of music into piles and then slipping them into clear plastic bags which were marked "Beethoven", "Bach", "Brahms" and so forth. On the wall was a large map with pins marking spots where the bags were to be buried. Across the top of the map was written: "Salvation of Music Project - Easter - A.D. 2023".

Burl woke with a start, conscious of the fading cry of a loon which had roused him. How good to have loons near at hand. Burl smiled at the memory of how his mysterious "wolf-loons" had startled him three years ago. The first stars were faintly showing themselves through the funnel-like canopy of dark blue directly above. He had slept for several hours, slept deeply - perhaps for the first time in months. Not to be a burden on others right now, he thought, and more important, not to be a burden on oneself. To die young is but a momentary tragedy surely, with no known effect upon the universe - Mozart, Schubert, Mendelssohn, Chopin, the possible exceptions. But to know this - to accept it gently - to re-enter with good feelings for what has come before, and for what has been learned during this mysterious interlude....

Burl could feel his body releasing itself from the desire for food. "It's an act of will now," he spoke firmly. He smiled at the comforting idea that he was cheating the disease of its longevity. Ideas of death floated back to him, fresh from his dream. "How wonderful to have disarmed that depressing scene of its reality," he said to the trees above, and then laughed out loud. "Here I am now, *really* talking to the trees," he said. Kirsti would enjoy this, he thought. It would be her final triumph over my rational ways. Burl started to think of the many Ojibwa and Cree who had resorted to this place to undertake some variation of what he was now doing. He thought of how they too had left special ones behind, forbidden hopes perhaps, such as his lingering love for Kakayosha; or loves full of promise for the future, such as his love for Kirsti. He closed his eyes and it was as if Kirsti and Kakayosha were both there, stretched out next to him. He greeted them both and then they vanished and he was back in his youth, whiling away hours at night, face up on the back lawn, gazing up at the milky way or charting the moon's monthly cycle. He opened his eyes again and looked up through the hole in the canopy of the trees above him. The stars seemed much sharper and more urgent than they had ever been. Thoughts of the evening with Simon Russell on the shore brought the words of Mary Boyle flooding back to him.

Over the next forty-eight hours Burl took sleep during the hours of light in order to save his energy for watching the heavens. He ate more than he should, for the drive to live was still strong, but even while eating he thought of Angus's injunction to him. On the second day it had rained heavily, but the lean-to worked well. A third day passed during which some sleep was taken. The fear of sleeping overcame him. Was he never to awaken again perhaps? He wished to slip into the universe fully awake, but under the cover of night. Two more days passed. Dusk descended once again. Was he in his fifth day now or his sixth? His vision was wobbly. He had managed not to eat for at least two days. He reached for a small bag in which there were a few books and some notepaper and plastic bags he had brought along in which to seal any last thoughts. He shakily lit his small candle lantern and placed it in the network of roots near his head and then tried to write by the low light, but the poetry would not come. Words would not gel, ideas would not connect. Fragments of his life seemed to be rushing through his mind, uncoordinated. He dropped the empty paper at his side, shut his eyes and let himself be carried off into the realm of the senses.

The clear September night was warm and perfumed with the odour of newly fallen leaves. They became faces at his feet and sides, memories of shoulders briefly rubbed against, but never seized in an embrace. The vision came upon him. It was in the form of voices calling him, the familiar voices of the women who had eased him gently into their bodies and convinced him that his need was good, and that they too, needed. Behind this first chorus of voices, standing in dark robes and without faces, were his failures; they spoke as one, asking him to forgive himself. And behind these was a third chorus, composed of those he had hated. In unison they asked him to cry, not for them, but in regret for the errors made. The density of stars straight above him, which had been so sharp, rapidly faded in brilliance. He closed his eyes again and tried to summon up his remaining energy yet again. He slept and then jerked awake, his eyes open wide. Through his chimney to the sky, star faces took on sharp forms in brilliant colours - faces - which then elongated themselves into coherent bodies - each reaching out to him to meet him, and greet him, and guide him into their company - and joining hands, they all crossed Last Lake together.

18

Kakayosha's Flight

On the same morning that Angus put Burl ashore on Mashkisibi Island, Mongazid walked out of the staff house at Black Pebble Lake and pranced across the lawn to the workshop. He stuck his head in the door and saw Victor Simpson bent over the lathe. Mongazid waited for a pause in the high-pitched whining of the machine.

"Hey Rims - we gonna test it again soon, man?" he asked.

"Give me about fifteen minutes and we'll do it," Victor replied.

Since Kakayosha's funeral Victor Simpson had spent many hours in the shop modifying the large new boomerang and meeting with Angus, who was taking care of the artistic side of things. On two windy days of the previous week, Victor and Mongazid had ventured out to Mindemoy Bay and tested a pair of demonstration models, identical to the large elaborate item now being modified by the lathe.

"Hot-dang," said Mongazid on the day of the second test, "I think that sucker almost went to heaven - or at least to the Pool Side Bar in Mashkisibi. Of course, there's not much difference anyway, eh Rims?" Mongazid guffawed and went into a quick circle dance, part of the new routine which *Pictographia* was working up for an upcoming school sports weekend.

The boomerang had stayed up for about half an hour on the second attempt. It was of unusual proportions, measuring a full two metres from corner to corner and was extremely wide and thin, but with a slightly heavier and thicker front edge, which gave it maximum lift, much like the V-shaped fixed wing of a modern aircraft. By a judicious choice of wood, Victor managed to give it a weight and balance which would allow it to maintain an upward trajectory.

In the dead of night during a full moon, when the whitefish were running, Angus had come into the shop and applied luminescent colours of the rainbow to the boomerang, along with various obscure symbols which he engraved along its length. These were patterned on his own father's Sky Scroll, the one he had never been able to interpret. After he had shown the scroll to Victor, he explained to him the aspects he understood, but about the rest he only said: "These figures will go into the sky with Kakayosha. They will be her secret as well." At the point where the boomerang started to bend, the name *Kakayosha* was written in blue.

September turned into October. Because of the unusually long and warm autumn, the hills around Mashkisibi remained ablaze with reds and yellows. Another week passed. Victor and Angus monitored the weather carefully now, watching the nature of the cloud formations moving out over Lake Superior. There was a special wind Angus was waiting for: the one which blew down the Mashkisibi from Hudson Bay and then picked up speed over the lake in a strong easterly, piling up clouds and tempting the Thunder Bird out of his supreme nest. Angus had risen early that morning, for he sensed it, he smelled it, that unusual, moist, uncharacteristic, powerful wind. For just a moment he was back with the Yugoslav partisans in the Julian Alps.

Angus got up, dressed quickly, and drove down to Black Pebble Lake where he walked into the dining room. Victor and the others were still at table, finishing breakfast. Angus exchanged pleasantries with them all in the briefest manner and then spoke with some urgency.

"We must go now, those who wish to come. Please finish up eating and I will meet you all at the cliff over Mindemoy Bay. Victor will explain everything, I am sure." Angus did not wait for a reply, but merely smiled broadly and waved a thick hand in a parting gesture to the groggy assembly.

Victor had dropped a few hints about an upcoming event, but nobody was sure exactly what was going on, or when, or why. He hauled himself up from the table and asked them for their attention.

"You all know that there was a funeral for Kakayosha some time ago at the Fire Weed Reserve, but today is the day that her uncle - our good friend Angus - wants to send Kakayosha off in style. It is a special day for us all - and for her, since it is hoped that we restore her proper name to her. Please come along and tell any others who might wish to come. Many of her friends and relatives will be there at the Mindemoy Bay lookout." Victor paused to gulp down the remainder of his coffee. "I'll be heading down there shortly, so I hope to see you there." Victor took his dishes to the sink and then walked out the door and headed for the shop. Mongazid, who was already standing, was out the door in a flash.

There was a buzz at the table as the assembled collectively pondered the mystery of this break with routine. Even Boisant Bollard had a restive look and seemed tempted to break his customary silence and talk. Years of discipline quickly rose up and seized his tongue however, and he merely finished his coffee. The others started clearing off their dishes. June and Will Bender scraped the plates and said they would load the dishwasher and leave the rest till later.

"Lunch will be late, you people," announced June. "Or

maybe not at all."

"Guess we better get down there and see what the hell this is all about,"Jan Polyanski said to Porky Schiller.

A few fast phone calls were made into Mashkisibi in order to spread the word. The people at Fireweed had been told that morning by Angus. When Victor and Mongazid turned into Mindemoy Bay they found an assortment of mainly older cars and pick-ups parked along the road out to the cliff. They could see a number of people talking with Angus over near the edge of the 400-foot sheer drop into Lake Superior. Victor parked and lifted the great boomerang out from the rear of his pick-up. Angus had made a great circle of rocks near the edge of the cliff and he was standing at its centre.

The wind was strong without being erratic. A red banner, attached to a radio antenna on a black 1958 Ford convertible, was stretched out in a steady horizontal position, like an airport weather sock. It pointed straight out towards the edge of the cliff. Victor placed the boomerang on a table at the centre of the circle where people quickly gathered around to admire it and stroke it. Mongazid was making sure nobody walked off with it. Victor then walked over to meet Angus who introduced him around to Farmer Jones and some others. Over by the edge of the precipice a woman was sitting on a boulder and facing the lake. Victor asked Angus if that was Kakayosha's mother.

"Yes, that's my sister, Minnie Maywins - the Berry-Gatherer - and she would like to meet you again. She could not say much at the funeral. Shall we go over now?"

Minnie Maywins talked with Victor for a few minutes and thanked him for his help at the funeral, and then asked him about the whereabouts of Burl Manion.

"I'm not sure. I thought he would be here. He has not been feeling so well lately, and I haven't seen him for some time. Yesterday, none of us knew that today would be the day. He may be in the Sault."

"Oh, that does make me sad. Those two were close you

know - in their own way. But I guess we can't wait anymore. This is the right day isn't it."

"Yes, I think we should go ahead. Angus seems to think so too. Shall we walk over to the circle?" Victor took her by the arm and led her to some large logs which had been brought up around the stones.

Misconometos and The Little Sturgeon were passing out tea to the Elders while the youngsters ran off to the edge to look down at Superior. Anna Bluesky ran after them to make sure none were looking too closely. Neenaby was curled up under a tree with Wolfie Wisdom and Anthony Hole-in-the-Wind. Wolfie was doing his utmost to show some reverence for the occasion, and appeared to be sober. Misconometos was setting out some food on a make-shift table set up by the women from Fireweed, and Dugah Beshue was almost as quickly consuming it. Murdo McFaddan walked over to the table.

"Well Dugah, I see you still have as good an appetite as when you worked for us in the bush and ate us out of house and home last year?"

"Even better," said Dugah, "except now I have to steal it since I not get paid anymore."

"Well, you come and see me in a month. Think we're going to cut out some dead wood in west of Cowie this winter."

"Sure, I'll do that. Thanks Murdo. Have some bannock?"

"Don't mind if I do." Murdo picked up a well-turned piece and started to look about the field to see who was there. "Well I'll be a son-uv-a-bitch. There's that little bugger Wolfie Wisdom, and he doesn't appear to be drunk. How did he do that?"

"Yeah - he's been here for awhile, sitting around looking sad. Not like him. He usually running up some tree to talk to the squirrels. You know, what you say about Wolfie and the booze, reminds me of my sixth great cousin, you know that Murdo?"

"How's that Dugah?"

"Well you see, I never knew he drank, until one day I saw him sober." Murdo and Dugah broke into a fit of chuckling, but then looked around self-consciously, and then stopped before drawing any disapproving glances.

"Dugah - you Lynxes are a bad lot you are. Just for that I'm going to have some more of this bannock."

A contingent from the "rear oven" was standing beneath a tree, attempting to impress upon Alf Anderson the virtues of a World War II German reflex action camera. Not far way from them, old Erkki was conversing with Boisant Bollard in a broken French. Boisant was smiling and nodding approvingly, adding a few observations of his own about his days during the war when he had served abroad. *"Tu parle bien, Tu parle bien."* he said to Erkki when the latter apologized for his lack of command of French. Ardo Kulduhn was setting out an assortment of middle-eastern dishes on the table and The Little Sturgeon was asking him about the fabric in his boldly coloured green shirt. Felix Smith and David Dawson were moving about the grounds feeling as though they should be in charge of public safety, but somewhat uncertain of their authority. Rory O'Flanigan and some of the miners had moved in on Josie Linklater and Shelagh Dubcek, but were not sure why they were here or what was going on, except that Wolfie had told them it was some kind of "farewell party."

Murdo McFadden picked up another piece of bannock and chewed upon it slowly as he fixed a stern eye on Rory O'Flanigan. He beckoned to Felix Smith who then walked over to talk to him.

"Morning Murdo, what's up?"

"Felix - you see that son-uv-a bitch over there?"

"You mean Dawson?"

"No - he's not a 'son-uv-a-bitch' - he's just an 'ass-hole' - I mean *that* 'sun-uv-a-bitch' over there - O'Flanigan. You and Jan and Dawson keep an eye on him. Any sign of trouble just chuck him over the edge."

"Gotcha Murdo."

Angus and Victor had now moved into the circle where they put their heads together for a moment. Angus raised his hand to get the attention of the people. He was dressed as he was always dressed, except for the small finely beaded medicine bag which hung around his neck.

"Friends, I thank you for coming out this morning to help us all say goodbye to Kakayosha this one last time. And I would like to thank all of the people at Black Pebble Lake who have come to join in with us. Kakayosha had many friends there you know, and we are glad that so many of you have come today. As some of you know, in the old days we paid a great deal of attention to how we named the children, and it was always hoped that their name would be accurate of how they lived. And on this day, when we know that *Mishepesiu** has had a temporary victory over Kakayosha, it is time to restore her name to her - *A Bird in Everlasting Flight*. And our good friend Victor here, has worked very hard to assist us in this. If you would all walk by now and look at the great boomerang he has fashioned for her use, then we will send her on her way."

The crowd started to walk by in single file and many touched and stroked the wooden arc, giving approving comments on its elaborate rainbow hues and upon the excellent nature of the midé figures which had been engraved on it. The children were led by and encouraged to touch it.

Austin Thomas finally descended from a tree about sixty yards from the circle where he had been doing the "hangin' Austin" to amuse some of the boys and girls. He led them back over to the circle and then pulled a bottle from his jacket and said that he always needed something after hanging by his heels. Boisant Bolard came up behind Austin and made a sign of the cross on his behalf, and then whispered to the sky: "*Christa, Christa, Christa.*" Boisant was looking upward and it was as if he had not seen the true light for many years.

---

* A traditional Ojibwa term for an underwater monster

Victor walked over to the side of the cliff and faced the lake, putting his arm straight out to the side to feel the wind. "As far as I can tell," he said to Mongazid, "it's blowing even stronger than it was on the days we did our tests. But now is the moment of truth. Here we go." Victor returned to the circle where the children were still looking at the great arc of wood. He picked it up and trotted in a broad half-moon towards the cliff edge, eyeing the banner on the car aerial as he moved. The banner remained stretched out and steady. He circled one more time and as he approached the lip of the cliff, he released it with all his might. Kakayosha took off with what appeared, at first, to be hesitation. This was mere illusion brought on by its great size. The boomerang spun, reflecting the light like a prism, as it moved up in the wind. When it started to come round it banked ever so slightly so that it was pushed up even higher by the strong easterly, curtailing its natural tendency to cut back towards the ground. It whirled overhead and then went into another wider ellipse, tracing a longer path out over the lake. The boomerang rose in a spiral as though it was caught in reverse in some invisible whirlpool, and as it ascended, it caught up the sunlight, like a coloured twinkling star.

Kakayosha looked down and could see all of her receding friends waving farewell to her. She could see Angus and Minnie; she could see the children she meant to have, firmly in the hands of neighbouring mothers and aunts and sisters; she could see the Islands of Nanibojou, which had robbed her of her earthly presence; behind the great dam she could see the slowly filling-in outline of Lake Mashkisibi, consuming the past as it went; she could see the small cemetery overlooking the harbour; and she could see Mashkisibi Island, long, and beautiful, and green, stretched out on the horizon, like all the boundless hopes of the young.

About the Author

Alexander Binning was born in Toronto and has lived in many places in Canada. He has worked as a teacher, librarian, park planner, historian and as a heritage planning consultant. He currently lives in Calgary where he writes full time. Currently, he is working on two books of short stories: *Bureaucratic Tales* and *Bush Tales*.